# Praise for Broken

"Robin Ayele has penned a great suspenseful novel that will keep you on the edge of your seat and biting your nails until you turn that last page. With a taut storyline and believable characters this author delivers and doesn't disappoint at any turn! **DEFINITELY A MUST READ!!**"
  —D.L. Sparks, author of *All That Glitters*

"Broken will delight crime fiction enthusiasts everywhere. Robin Ayele has crafted **A COMPELLING PSYCHOLOGICAL THRILLER.**"
  —Quintin Peterson, author of *SIN*

"I couldn't put the book down. I was actually crying at the end. I know it's not real but I cried anyway...**IF YOUR NEXT BOOK IS ANYTHING LIKE *BROKEN* THEN I CAN'T WAIT!**"
  —Barbara McMullen, Real Sista Girls Book club
    Division of Personnel Security & Access Control, ORS

"**FROM THE PRELUDE I WAS HOOKED**...once I started reading it was hard to put it down. I read a portion in the bathtub so my copy of the book is water-logged! I am anxiously awaiting the sequel!"
  —Brenda Howell-Watts, Real Sista Girls Book Club

"*BROKEN* **IS GREAT**! It kept my interest from chapter one to the end. I wanted more! It reminded me so much of *Kiss The Girls* by James Patterson. Please write a sequel...I want more!"
  —Minnedore Green, Real Sista Girls Book Club

"I found *Broken* to be **VERY ENTERTAINING!** We would be honored to preview your next book as well!"
  —Melissa Green, Real Sista Girls Book Club

# Broken

*Robin "Robbie" Ayele*

# Broken

Robin "Robbie" Ayele

*Chocolate Angel Publications*
*Hebron, MD*

PUBLISHER'S NOTE:
This book is a work of fiction. Names, characters, businesses, orga-
nizations, places, events and incidents are the product of the author's
imagination or are used fictionally. Any resemblance of actual persons,
living or dead, events, or locales is entirely coincidental.

Published by
CHOCOLATE ANGEL PUBLICATIONS
    7871 Bitler Way, Hebron, MD 21830
    broken@robbieayele.org
    www.chocolateangelpublications.com
    *202. 615. 5257 (office)*
    702. 368.1298 (fax)

Robin Ayele, Publisher / Editorial Director
Danyell Sparks, Editor
Yvonne Rose/Quality Press, Project Coordinator
The Printed Page, Interior and Cover Layout
Cover Art by Iman Jordan

Copyright © Robin Ayele 2008
ISBN: 978-0-9815028-0-9
Library of Congress Control Number: 2008902361
First Printing March 2008
10 9 8 7 6 5 4 3 2 1
Printed in the United States of America

*In Loving Memory of*
*Tasco D. Thomas,*
*one of the first*
*African American barber shop*
*owners*
*on*
*Georgia Avenue.*

# Acknowledgments

First of all I have to thank God! He has given me this talent and I am trying to use it to the best of my abilities—to entertain and maybe inspire. God allowed me to be able to leave my job and write to my hearts content in another country with my husband by my side. It turned out to be a life changing adventure that I will never, ever forget and now I have a great writing place in my second home, Addis Ababa, Ethiopia.

I would like to thank my beloved husband, Yidnkachew Ayele for providing tremendous amounts of love, support, strength, protection, faith, and comfort every single step of the way during our wonderful life together. He has helped me stay focused and on the job, feeding me constant encouragement. I am grateful for having great loving parents, Diane T. and David B. Mitchell who have constantly reminded me of how wonderfully made I am. They never lost faith in me or my talent, no matter what. Even giving great advice on anything when I needed it and being there always. Much appreciation to my sweet sister Thea Mitchell-Anderson for giving me that first kernel of confidence and always being a good friend and supporter. Thanks to my brother David J. Mitchell, for being there with the laughs and love. He has always been a steady Rock of Gibraltar. I also have to express much appreciation for my gorgeous niece, Mia Anderson and loving nephews, Jamal Anderson and Asa Mitchell who are all my ultimate inspiration. I also am appreciative for my in-laws Dionne Mitchell and Calvin Anderson who have been like siblings to me and always have had my back. I want to thank my grandmothers, Frances B. Thomas and Maude D. Mitchell, who were both powerful black women with immense character and writers in their own right. I want to thank my grandfathers, Edward Mitchell and Tasco Thomas for the legacy they left behind. I want to thank my mother-in-law and father-in-law as well as my brother and sister-in-laws in Ethiopia who took such good care of me while I was in Addis Ababa and have loved me like one of their own. Thanks to Dianna Johnson-Atkins who gave tons and tons of encouragement. I want to give thanks for my god children, Alexis Blunt who is a budding writer and Wesley Blunt who is smart as a whip!

Shout out and much love to my running partners especially Janine Blunt who has always been like a big sister and has been there for me, no matter what; and Renee Jones who has stayed in my corner and been my clean eye. I have to thank Ravenna Chase, Renae Ross, Greta Sawyers, Vivian Guerra, Janel Dear and Leslie Belloso for being there through the ups and downs. I cried on their shoulders many a day and we could always be honest with each other and still give love and acceptance. I want to thank Judine Slaughter for her pearls of advice on writing. I thank others who have given me much sister love over the years including Etta Swift, Tracy Bryant, Gwen McCall, Sharon Morris, Dr. Lisa Godette, Patsy Fletcher, Debbie Crain, Anita Hairston, Beverly Harris, Cindy Petkac, and Clara Fenwick. Thanks to those that have given their own brand of help like Lori Carter. I must thank Fandreia Bowman for her encouraging words via email; she always came up with the right thing to forward. I want to thank Maria Broom, Shirley Bailey, Audrey Rivers and Jeanette Morgan-Chavous. I also want to express much appreciation for the Diva Writers Guild who has been plugging for me like I plug for each of them! I want to say thanks to the Real Sista Girls Book Club and Brenda Watts for their advice and support.

Much thanks to the PG Plaza (Marie) Starbucks for allowing me to spend hour after hour working on my book with plenty of yummy hot Java. Much thanks to the PG Office Depot for helping me get through especially John, Jenenia and Jeff. Thanks to Mount Calvary Baptist, which gave me the spiritual backing to go out and fulfill my dreams. God definitely speaks through Bishop Alfred Owens and Co-Pastor Suzie Owens. To the Write On! Competition that showed me that I actually had it.

I have to thank Melissa Freeman for working on the marketing! And I have to thank Quintin Peterson for giving solid advice on the District of Columbia Police Department's protocols and policies. I have to give much thanks to Iman Jordan, my talented illustrator who came up with a truly dynamic cover. I have to thank Ella Curry with EDC for helping me with marketing tips and other good old fashioned support. I would also like to thank Everett Webb with Top Cat Live for recognizing my talent! A special thanks to the Black Writers Guild of Maryland for giving me that confidence boast and advice when I needed it. It provided me with the tools and resources that I needed to get the job done. Thanks to Simba and the entire Karibu Bookstore crew for teaching me the ins and outs of bookselling! Also I would like to thank Danyell Sparks for doing an awesome job as my editor. And finally thanks to Memphis Vaughn with TimBooktu!

I am also glad for CSI, The New Detective, Forensic Files, City Confidential and even Unsolved Mysteries for feeding my hunger for the criminal element. Also much thanks to Temple University for teaching me a thing or two and more about criminal justice in the US and to Quality Press and Amber Communications Group, Inc. for the professional touch they applied to *Broken*.

## ROMANS 3:10

*"…there is no one righteous, not even one…"*

# Broken

# Prelude

Autumn was cornered.

There was nowhere to run because she had her back against the wall. She tried to make it past him but he grabbed her tiny body, lifting her into the air like a rag doll.

"Gotcha."

His large arms squeezed her petite frame as he wrapped them around her in a steel tight grip.

She knew there was no escape now or ever.

He threw her on top of the bed and she bounced across the stained mattress. He jumped on top of her, taking her breath away. She tried to hit him with her small fist but he punched her in the mouth and she immediately tasted blood.

She touched her fingers, piano fingers her teacher told her, to her lips. Once she had been told she had beautiful hands, made to play the piano, but now the tips came back bright red with her own blood. She whimpered, hot tears at the corners of her eyes as she tried to escape but he grabbed her roughly.

"Stop all that noise or I'll really give you something to cry about little girl," he hissed.

She tried to stop but something deep inside couldn't, so he back-handed Autumn causing her vision to black out for a second.

"*I said shut up!*" he growled. "You'll learn not to fight me girl. You just need to give me what I want and stop playin' with me. All you women like to play. Like to dangle that carrot then try to snatch it away."

"Please don't hurt me," she begged as he pulled up her plaid skirt decorated with yellow flowers.

"I'm not. I'm tryin' to help you!" He yanked down her pink panties, and let out his breath, which smelled like cigarettes and alcohol. Before she could cry out, he roughly entered her and she winced from the pain that almost paralyzed her.

He started groaning and moaning as he forced himself into her small frame. Then he picked up the pace and she shut her eyes, just wanting it to be over. Wanting him to stop hurting her. She tried to think about anything else other than the fact that he was crushing her, killing her. She tried to breathe as he tore into her, stealing her childhood.

"Please stop," she whispered breathlessly, tossing her head to the side to see the dim light coming from the green lamp with the torn shade. She looked out the window to catch the flicker of the neon pink sign of the motel indicating vacancies. She wished she could change that sign to "Help". Then maybe someone would come and save her.

"Naw girl can't stop now. You know you like it girl!" he said, moving above her with this crazed look on his face, beads of sweat tap-dancing down the sides of his blowfish like jaws.

He was no longer her uncle but the boogieman. After what seemed like forever, he stiffened and groaned and shuttered.

"Oh yeah that's what I'm talking about," he gasped.

She felt herself grow cold and numb as always.

*This is a time to give thanks for all that we have,* she remembered her lines so well.

He rolled off of her and got up to a sitting position. "All that beer ran right through me like water."

He lumbered toward the tiny bathroom as she scurried to the opposite side of the huge bed, and calculated the distance to the door. She knew she would never make it in time.

She listened as he peed in the toilet with a steady stream that lasted a long time. Finally she heard the toilet flush and he emerged not having washed his hands.

He rubbed his stomach with this strange grin. Rubbing his big belly like Autumn saw women do when they were pregnant. With that thought she prayed that she wouldn't get pregnant. Her friend Joy told her when a man stuck his thing in you it could happen. She said that her cousin had read it in a book.

Joy was the only one Autumn had told what was really going on because she didn't trust anyone else. She had no one to protect her anymore. Her Uncle Harry was supposed to look after her or at least that was what Nanny had told her before she had died too. But Uncle Harry had not protected her. He had violated her at every turn and made no apologies for it.

He climbed back on the bed and lay on his back with his arms folded underneath his head.

"Girl that was some kinda amazin'. I feel so good now, like I could fly. How 'bout you? Tell Uncle Harry how you feel? The love doctor is listenin'."

Her stomach lurched at his comments.

*"At least he didn't hurt me too bad this time,"* she thought. Last time she had ended up with a broken arm and had to be out of school for two weeks. And she didn't want to miss this coming week especially since she was in the school play on Tuesday. She was supposed to play an Indian girl and she had memorized every single line. Her teacher had told her she was a natural.

"Give me a big ole' kiss little girl." He turned his head toward her, smacking his pink lips. She squirmed on the covers, feeling a chill run through her. The last thing she wanted to do was kiss him, just the idea was gross. His lips were peeling with white flakes against the pink. She would have rather kissed Brandon at school than Uncle Harry.

"Did you hear me little girl?" He raised one bushy eyebrow and grinned, exposing his gold front tooth.

"Yes sir." She rose up on all four and crawled over to him. She leaned over and planted a quick peck on his parted lips. And before she could let out a breath of relief, he had his hand on the back of her head, pulling her back to his waiting mouth and forcing his retched tongue into her mouth. She knew this was how grown-ups kissed on soap operas and movies but she wasn't a grown up yet, she had just turned nine that day.

It was her birthday. But there was no cake, no candles or singing for her.

Uncle Harry laid back down, letting out a long fart. Within seconds, he was snoring loudly; his bulging eyes half-open and bloodshot from all the beer he had drunk. The cans still littered the stained carpeted floor. She stared up at the ceiling for a minute, watching a scary black spider scurry across the white surface. She put a fist in her mouth to stop from screaming. Gross or not, she didn't want to get slapped. Instead she kept one eye on the fast moving spider and another on getting off the bed to get Krissy.

When she was assured that the spider would not jump down on her and gobble her up, she put one toe on the cheap dingy carpet and then her entire foot, imagining it crawling with a gazillion bugs. But she had to get Krissy even at the risk of waking Uncle Harry.

After checking over her shoulder, she stood to her feet, feeling the familiar sticky stuff oozing out of her and clinging to the insides of her thighs. She glanced at the purple Barbie backpack that had her small collection of stuffed animals hanging out the front flap. They sat staring back at her with sympathy. They had witnessed everything but were powerless to help her. Still she needed them. She darted across the motel room, tripping on one of his shoes. She balanced herself, looking back one last time before grabbing her Raggedy Ann doll. She tiptoed across the floor and crawled back in bed, glad for the warmth as Uncle Harry continued to saw wood, as Mama J would say.

She brushed off her doll's face, staring into the one shiny black eye. She smoothed down the sides of the neatly braided red hair, which had been her own handiwork. She loved to comb and brush all her dolls' hair especially the Barbie dolls. She had gotten that from watching Mama J who had owned a small beauty shop. Autumn used to sit in one of the swivel chairs and study the way her mother used a sizzling hot comb to run through piles of thick, woolly heads, turning them into soft angels with flowing hair. They called it a press and curl.

She clutched Krissy to her flat naked chest, knowing that was the only friend she had. Feeling cold and exposed, she reached under the bed sheets groping for her clothes. She slid on her underwear, feeling somewhat protected even if she wasn't. At any time, he could come at her again and again and again like he had for so many years.

She imagined herself to be Superwoman, using her powers to get rid of Uncle Harry, making him disappear.

He turned his body to face her. His mouth was open and a bit of spittle flowed out from his bottom lip.

She held her breath against the horrible smell coming from between his lips.

She noticed that the spider had crawled to the other side of the room and was relieved. She pulled the covers up to her chin to try and get warm. As she slid further down, the bed creaked again except louder and Uncle Harry opened one sleepy eye, which was aimed at her. His lips curled back into a croaked grin, his gold tooth glistening. He reminded her of the big bad wolf. She squeezed her doll. Could Raggedy Ann protect her?

"You ain't tryin' to escape are ya?" He narrowed his eyes into slits.

Autumn shook her head with fear. *"N-n-no sir."*

"You better not!" he snapped. "And you better not tell anybody either or I told you what would go down right?"

She trembled at the thought. *"Yes sir, I'll be dead,"* she said in a small voice.

He smiled, satisfied with the answer. "Come 'ere girl. Oh and happy birthday to ya too girl. You ah Halloween baby, my, my. You gonna scare me?" He reached out, his fat fingers peeling back the edge of the sheet and grabbed her, yanking hard and tearing her shirt. Before he could pull again and really hurt her, she scrambled towards him as he loosened his grip. He took her in his arms and kissed the top of her head before forcing her to lie against his hairy chest. It felt like tiny needles stabbing her cheek as his chest heaved up and down. She could even feel his heart pounding. She closed her eyes and tried to sleep but she knew it wouldn't be easy because she was in pain down there. Uncle Harry let out an extra loud snore that scared Autumn. She sucked on her thumb, closed her eyes and tried to remember the song that Mama J used to sing to her at night. It was 'Go Tell It on the Mountain' and something about Jesus being born. Mama J used to say that Jesus would save everybody and how he loved the little children the best. Autumn wondered why he didn't love her though.

Was she a bad little girl? Is that why he took her mama and daddy away?

# Chapter One

"Hey is anyone out there? Holla if you hear me, this is Road Dog on the handle over." The guy barked on the CB. He was a southern brother telling from the accent. Probably some corn-fed country boy from Georgia or Tennessee, just the type she wanted to respond to.

"Road Dog this is Caramel on the dial. Sounds like you want some company. Maybe kick it after being on the road all morning, over," she said, her CB radio raised to her mouth, steering her red Beamer down 95 South.

"Um yeah, Caramel, girl whatsup'? I'm lovin' the name. Your mama named you right I'm sure, over," he said.

"Damn right, over," she replied.

"So sweet thing you wanna meet up with me?"

"Maybe."

"Oh trust me, you won't regret it. You give Road Dog a chance and he'll make aaalllllllll your fantasies come true girl. He'll give you a little sumthin' sumthin' to talk to your girlfriends about. And by the way you sound sexy as hell with that low raspy voice. It's makin' a brother quiver, damn," he purred. "I'm hard as a mug, over."

"Um all sounds tempting, over." She tapped her fingernails on the steering wheel, enjoying the play like always."You really want to make this happen? Over."

"Damn straight! Sweet thing I do want to make this thing a reality. Just when, where, and how? A brother just wants to get and give some love, over."

"Let's meet up at the Cracker Barn off Route 126? Then we can go from there, over." She had to be sure that he was her type first.

"That's a plan."

They made their other arrangements and she hung up smiling. It was done.

Caramel loved road trips. She always looked forward to getting in her wheels and going where she wanted, when she wanted. It was the only time she could feel completely free. Nothing could harm her, not anymore. She could just be herself, local traveler checking out all there was to see up and down the East Coast. She always found the coolest little places that no one would think to visit like the Luray Caverns or small bed and breakfast spots in West Virginia. This time she was headed to Virginia Beach. It would be good to be near the ocean. It would be peaceful and she wanted peace.

She cracked the passenger side window to let in the warm July air. She fell back against the leather seat chilling to the sounds of Rare Essence spewing Go-Go music. Yeah she felt pretty good and not at all sleepy, which was good given she had left DC early that morning and was only running on a few hours of sleep.

She ran a hand over her scalp, which was still tender from being corn rowed two days ago. Once she got them taken out she was going to get it twisted. What was ironic was that she had stopped putting those chemicals in her hair two years ago even though she owned a successful hair salon. It just seemed to fit her better and allow her to be who she was.

She popped the top on her sunroof and slipped in a new CD of an old favorite, a legend, Roberta Flack, a true diva that never got her due like Caramel. She turned up the volume on the song that told her own story: "Killing Me Softly." She was always comforted by the mournful voice and she sang along knowing it word-for-word even though she had been a kid, actually a baby girl when the song had first come out. Still it reminded her of sunnier days and warmer nights when her parents had been around, before their accident. She always wondered how she would have turned out if they had survived. Maybe she would have been the type to settle down with Mr. Right and produce a couple of rug rats. Maybe have dinner on the table every night for her man. But then she couldn't dwell on the shoulda, woulda and coulda's at this point. For what? Reality was life. Life was a rabid dog that had taken a huge bite out of her ass. She thought about the twentieth year anniversary. It had given her this lease and idea to start special projects. In honor of the children that she had lost…Her and Uncle Harry's children.

Just then a fly flitted in buzzing near her ear like it sensed she hated it. She swatted at it, imagining all the things it had landed on including shit, toilet seats, trash, and filth. Her hand chased it around until it decided not to hang a moment longer and flew out the window, probably thinking, she's crazy and there is a big world out there so why sweat it? She rolled the window back up and hit the button to the air conditioning. Then she stepped on the gas and floored it. Her stomach was growling and snarling, which was right on time because Cracker Barn was about another five miles up the road according to her GPS.

Suddenly she heard a horn beep angrily behind her. She looked in the rearview mirror and saw some red pick up riding her tail. She was pissed and held up the finger, which caused him to beep even more. She slowed down, which would either result in him ramming into the back of her car or letting up. He pulled back a few inches from the car and she smiled. He just needed to stay out of her way. He didn't know her and road rage was dangerous. Could get him in a lot of trouble. He got in the other lane and zoomed by her, giving her a look. She signaled for him to pull over but he just passed by her and got in front of her cutting her off. She thought about catching up with him but decided she had other things to focus on.

She smirked, grabbing one of three cancer sticks lined up side by side in her ashtray.

Yeah she knew it was supposed to kill you but everybody had to die of something right? No one lived forever.

And these laws banning smoking were outrageous because no one understood that it kept people like her stable, calm and in check. Without it, it was like unleashing a monster. She picked up the one closest to her, feeling calmed by the smooth whiteness between her fingers. She slipped it between her lips and flicked her gold lighter. The red flame cooked the butt of the cigarette and the aroma filled her nose. That first puff was always the most exhilarating. Made her feel like she could do anything.

She spotted the dark blue sign for the exit just as the GPS announced that she needed to get over. She crossed three lanes of traffic, nearly colliding with a white Navigator as she hopped on the exit ramp.

"Shit!" she mumbled, knowing that could have been a hot mess with metal on metal and mangled flesh. She decreased her speed as she went around the sharp bend in the road and followed the signs for restaurants and gas, knowing she needed to fill up while she was at it. She pulled in front of the restaurant's small parking lot, set the car brake and turned off the engine.

There were rows of family cars—vans, SUVs and Volvo station wagons.

"Taking the wife and kids on a vacation huh?" she muttered, taking a final satisfying drag before crushing the rest of the cigarette in the ashtray.

She reached for her black leather duffel, knowing it had everything *including* the kitchen sink. And yeah it could put a strain on her back, but she couldn't leave without her tools and other essentials no matter where she went.

Opening the door, she stepped out and slung the suitcase over her shoulder, drawing in the smells of exhaust, gas and straight up pollution, reminding her of the global warming thing and understanding why. The sound of her rubber-soled tennis shoes slapped against the blacktopped lot. It was going to end up being a blazing day for sure and she was grateful to be wearing a backless top.

As she approached the quaint country porch entrance, she noticed what looked like a family sitting in rocking chairs. It was a mommy, daddy, and two little boys. They were giggling and just enjoying each other, probably taking a rest before continuing their trip maybe to Busch Gardens or King's Dominion. She had a flashback of her, Mama J and Daddy D holding hands at the Black Family Reunion all those years ago…she stopped herself. She was thirty-three now and her parents were long gone. Sighing, she climbed the wooden steps averting her eyes, keeping her shades on just so no one could identify her. *Well first things first*, she thought. She had to use the john badly. All that OJ she had guzzled back at the Mickey D's on her first stop was now begging to be released.

She had ten minutes before Road Dog came on the scene so she moved toward the rest room, which was at the back of the store. She smelled pancakes and sausage along the way. Ummm…they had the best food and she could not wait to bite into some thick slab bacon, cheese grits and buttermilk pancakes. My lawdy yes ma'am, she could forget everything after she indulged at the Cracker Barn.

She made a beeline towards the sign marked "Ladies".

"That would be me," she mumbled going inside and finding it clean, which was wonderful opposed to the absolutely appalling and disgusting state that most public bathrooms were found in. The kind that made you want to shower by the time you left out. For a change, she didn't have to tap dance around soggy brown paper towels dotting the dingy white floor. She pushed through the first pink stall, pulling a can of Lysol from her bag.

After she handled her pressing business, she stepped over to the wash-bowls. For her, using public bathrooms was never an option unless there was an emergency. She used tissue to turn the hot water faucet handles to the on position. It was really hot but she needed that. She scrubbed her hands vigorously to get the dirt off, using her nails to make sure that all the germs were gone. She caught a glimpse of herself in the filmy mirror. Her face was still a photographer's dream even with flushed cheeks and round gray eyes that were drawn up at the corners from the pull of the tight cornrows. The cornrows accentuated her features though: an aquiline nose, high cheekbones, luscious lips and a smooth toasty brown complexion. Yeah her face was supposed to have launched her modeling career but Uncle Harry had ruined her chances years ago. She touched the deep scar that ran from her jawbone to the base of her neck.

Scar or no scar, her face had gotten her in a lot of trouble over the years. Sometimes she looked at it as a curse and wished she'd been born ugly. No such luck though because she had been born to Mama J, one of the finest women of her day. She hunted in her bag and found the blunt-cut wig. She slipped it on and it gave her a totally different look. Now she was a sexy blonde-mysterious and alluring. Yeah it was the alluring that she needed for her project…She made sure the hair covered the scar.

She pulled a paper towel from the dispenser, dried her hands and threw it away. She gave herself one last look-see before leaving out; almost running straight into a blue-haired lady wearing an oversized T-shirt that hung off her bony shoulders. But what caught Caramel's eye were the red words sprawled between the two lumps sticking out of the lady's chest, *Watch out for the Old Bag*. Caramel smiled at the lady, because she was as old as Mama J would have been.

"Excuse me dearie." The lady flashed kind blue eyes and smiled, lighting up what would have been a plain face.

"No problem." Caramel lowered her head and walked on as she overheard the lady mumbling something incoherent. "No problem at all ma'am."

She went to the area where they were supposed to meet but it was empty. Where was Road Dog? She decided to pick up some snacks for the rest of her three-hour trip while she waited for him. The candy counter was empty and a woman with a toothy grin stood there. She selected three pecan logs. She also got some jellybeans.

She suddenly felt someone behind her, riding in her personal space. She glanced over her shoulder to face a five-foot short, midnight black dude with a five o'clock shadow wearing a *North Carolina Panthers* baseball cap chewing on a huge wad of gum. A black T-shirt with the words *All muscles baby* was sprawled across his thick upper body and he had a small waist. He probably worked out and yeah it showed. The body wasn't bad but his grill was just below average. Was this Road Dog? Had to be.

"Road Dog right?" she asked, pointing down at him.

"In the flesh baby." He scratched his chest looking up at her. "You are all woman. Damn!"

She kept a straight face deciding to play this right. "Hold on please." She turned back to the counter and pointed at the gummy bears and the lady behind the counter added it to her growing pile of goodies.

"Loading up on snacks for the road?"

"Um hum sure am," she said in a sing song voice.

"Well you are like a Snickers bar for me girl. Sticky and sweet baby. Just like your name Caramel," he murmured, staring up at her from a far distance. She didn't like short men. They annoyed her and this one would be no different but she still had use for him. He would make a nice little project for her.

He flared his nostrils and looked like he wanted to do her right there, nearly climbing up her leg. "Those eyes are turning me on too girl. They're yours too. I can tell."

She raised her eyebrows slightly amused. She noticed his lips that were bright pink like Uncle Harry's had been. She imagined biting them clean off, blood spurting all over the place.

"Your mama blessed you baby," he continued popping on gum. "Yeah you're one hot lady sister. I mean on fire. I've had fantasies about a woman like you all my life." He rubbed his nose with his stubby fingers. All she could think was this man was making it way too hard for some action but she would continue to go along.

"Is that right Road dog?"

"Yeah, yeah," he said, pausing to flex his muscles. They jumped in his chest and he smiled like she was supposed to be impressed. "So am I even better looking than you expected Caramel?"

"You a'right," she said blinking.

"Damn, I guess I can take that." He nodded. "My body is tight though? Got it going on huh?"

"You work out I see."

"Ya know it." He held out his arms and flexed them. "A muscle head," he said, smirking. "Like to try a brother like me on for size?"

"You might be a good fit." She smiled. Yeah he might be perfect for her purposes. "I think you will do." She folded her arms over her chest watching his expression. His eyes told the story, hell yeah he was up for this! And he wanted to get it on quick and in a hurry and be back on the road in time to get to his destination. She was a skeezer and a ho to him, period. Yeah he wanted her at all cost. Just like Uncle Harry who got what he wanted no matter who he had hurt. He probably imagined her while he waxed his miniature pecker every night. Bastard. "It would be an adventure huh?"

He balled his fist into his palm. "Well yeah and I've been kinda hoping we could see how that could happen. Make it happen." His eyes landed on her tits. She made a mental note. Let the games begin. He would get no mercy from her now.

"We could do that Road Dog," she said laughing. She handed a twenty to the lady behind the counter lady.

"Thanks for your business and come again," the lady said passing Caramel the bag of candies. Caramel turned back to Road Dog.

"I can serve you. Give you a little somethin' somethin'." She got close to him and her hand brushed over his private part. It was small as she suspected but she had no plans on experiencing what he had to offer anyway. He had no idea what she wanted from him. No idea whatsoever.

"Oh suky suky, yeah that's what I'm talking about girl. Put it on me Caramel."

*Little girl, you better stop cryin'. Give me what I want and everythin' will be all right. You know you want it. You always want it.*

"So where're we gonna hook up?" he asked eyeing her from head to toe like she was a lollipop that he wanted to lick. "There is a motel down the street that I go to. I can get that for the afternoon, after we grab a quick bite to eat." He ran his finger along her arm making something in her click. It gripped her in a headlock. And once it became rage, she would be perfect to strike. "What do you think?"

*You gonna give it to me right girl. Open up! I've been waitin' for this all day.*

"We can do that."

He flashed a toothy grin. "When I woke up this morning I knew this would be a good day."

"You were right," she said smiling at him. He would be project number six.

# Chapter Two

*C*aramel stood in the middle of the room in a red silk kimono and satin heels. Road Dog was staring up at her with his mouth hanging open, his head eye level with her breasts. *Midget.*

"Damn you are like one of those Amazon women. Girl you have legs for days and nights. I hope that you wrap those doggies around me. Just get me in a headlock," he said salivating. That just made her stomach turn even more. How disgusting. Get a man down for some sex and he would do anything and say anything. *Bastard.*

She didn't respond to him puffing on her cancer stick, feeling that euphoria fill her up. She crossed the room that he had paid for. It was ridiculously pitiful with a working TV and two double beds. It had a little area to eat and a cheap couch shoved up against the wall. Normally she would never have stepped one foot in a broke down spot like this. She was a classy sister and always gave herself the best of everything. And yeah, she always pulled out the stops when it came to spending on herself. She never spared any expense, charging it all to her Amex including room services, massages, and facials. She *could* afford it though because her shop was bringing in the dough.

Stupid bastard couldn't do better than this for the privilege of being in her company? Just like the rest of them and that is what she had expected. She knew them so well. Black males between twenty and forty years old shared the same M.O. They were selfish, self-centered, horny little boys who expected women to serve their every need.

Just like Uncle Harry.

He came up behind her and wrapped his short arms around her waist. "We are wasting time baby."

"You want to get down to business don't you, little boy?" she asked.

"Little boy, oooh, I like that talk. I'll be whatever you want." He started rubbing her ass like it was a crystal ball. "Yeah baby got back. Junk in the trunk. Shelf butt—"

She whipped around and slapped him off, feeling the tigress come out from her den. She hated for them to touch her. "No free feels."

He licked his lips and grunted like it only excited him even more. "Um go head Caramel now. Put me in check. You're right, you're right just keepin' it real huh?"

"I always do but I'm in control of this little boy," she said, hitting him upside the head. "So back up."

"Um, you like it rough. I like it like that too," he said licking his pink lips together. Can you strip for me Caramel?" he asked, hopping his naked behind on top of one of the beds and rubbing his ashy ass feet together. She went over to the pack of cigarettes on the stained table and pulled another out, opened her gold lighter and lit up. She squinted.

"You're too fine to smoke," he said.

"Is that right," she said, letting out a steady stream of smoke.

*Girl when your parents died, they gave me a gift.*

"True dat." He nodded and she studied him, thinking about how unappealing he was especially without clothes.

"You ain't gonna handle this brother Caramel?" he said, spreading his little arms wide. "I'm all yours now. A brother like me don't come along everyday," he paused and she was appalled that he was blind to his obvious limitations.

"I mean you're a cool sister. We need to make some beautiful music together now." He eyed her and she sensed the arrogance in his voice. Another black man trying to tell her what to do. Like he owned her. Like she was beneath him literally and figuratively. She unbelted her robe, revealing the red peek a boo nightie underneath.

"Damn baddoowwww!" he shouted, his eyes bugged. "You are no joke Miss Caramel. I had a feeling about what you looked like underneath of all those clothes though and I was right as rain."

"Does your woman do this for you?" she asked sashaying over to where he was.

It was turning him on. "Uh, I don't have a woman anymore Caramel," he said reaching out and caressing her thigh.

"Is she a sister?" She stepped closer, wondering if he would lie. She saw the picture in his wallet earlier.

"Excuse me?" He raised an eyebrow, obviously caught off guard.

"Is she a black girl, Road Dog?"

"What does that have to do with anything? I want us to stay in the moment now. Ride this thing out."

"Answer me little boy!" She shoved him against the headboard like a doll. She could break his puny neck.

"Damn Caramel, you like to bring on pain huh?" He rubbed his little head.

"Answer me!" she shouted.

"Uh well, my ex-wife was white." He cleared his throat growing uncomfortable with the conversation.

"And did she take care of you, little boy?" Caramel cocked her head.

"Uh well yeah, she did actually. I messed up," he said, licking his lips nervously.

"Figures," she mumbled. "And now you're here with me."

He shrugged. "Thought we could kick it. You wanted it and I wanted it. We're adults here. No one gets hurt."

"I understand. You just need someone to keep you warm on those nights when you can't be with her. I understand," she said putting one foot on the edge of the bed as her robe fell to the side, giving him another peek.

He shook his head and closed his eyes.

"Are you thinking about her now?"

"I'm thinking about you," he said sitting back down. "Now where were we?" He put a hand on her knee.

"Wherever you want to go."

She let him rub his midget size fingers up and down the length of her leg. It was confirmed. He thought she was a prostitute just like Uncle Harry and his friends had. His hand slid underneath her robe, caressing her thigh.

"You are something," he said.

*You gonna be a dime piece when you grow up girl. You know what a dime piece is little girl? It's shinier than a penny or even a nickel. More valuable too.*

She disrobed, watching him take her in. "Let's handle this."

"Now that's what I'm talking about," he mumbled under his breath, licking his lips again and scrambling to the other side of the bed to let her lay down.

"Oh I'll be right back." She hopped up. "Don't go anywhere." She sang feeling good. She was ready to take things to the next level.

"Hey!" he called out.

She turned back.

He had a look of disappointment on his face. "Hurry back because the old boy is ready and waiting to hit that and make you scream baby."

"Uh-huh, I can't wait." She went to the window and snatched the drapes closed, causing total darkness in the room. "To set the mood."

"Yeah, yeah that's right baby," he said.

"Oh and let me get some protection too. You can never be too careful," she said reaching in her bag and pulling out what she had been looking for. She hid it behind her back, coming over to the bed, ready to use it any minute.

"Yeah come to big daddy," he groaned.

"Oh I am," she said smiling.

# Chapter Three

Damn, it had finally happened. He had gotten what he deserved. Karma had caught up with him. All the trifling, low-down, dirty things he had done in thirty-four years were all summed up in these final, terrible moments. The last ones of his life.

Henderson had lost a lot of blood. He struggled to breathe. He felt like a weight had been placed on his damn chest. He didn't have long. Maybe another five or ten minutes at the most. But funny enough, he felt no pain with the butcher knife stuck up in his chest cavity.

Now wasn't that a bitch. He couldn't take a paper cut without crying but he could take this? Go figure. If he really thought about it, it was funny as hell but with his current circumstances, there would be no laughter. Some female had straight up outwitted him. Had beat him like he stole something.

And what could he say? Nothing. Nada. Not now. Not ever. It was too late.

He sucked in air and tasted blood in his mouth. He was actually dying and couldn't do shit about it.

Sighing, he weakly moved his hands, which were in handcuffs and shackled to the bedposts. Even if he wanted to get up, he couldn't.

She had left him here to fucking die. And then they would find him naked and in an uncompromising position. Janet, his fiancée would hear that he had been found like that and it would break her heart. He hadn't meant to hurt her. He loved her, but in a moment of weakness, he had cheated.

*19*

He started to feel sleepy and, well, kinda peaceful. Was this what happened when a MFO was about to meet his maker? And where would he go, heaven or hell? Most likely he'd be conversing with that guy who holds a pitchfork. Yeah he wasn't one of those Christians. Even though he heard it was never too late to come to Christ, he had never thought about it until now. Maybe, just maybe he would be saved if he accepted Jesus now.

He blinked, staring at the corner of the room where the coffee table was. It looked like his Aunt Wadine was standing there in a flowing blue dress. And then his cousin Marius was standing behind his aunt. Oh damn, then it looked like his mama.

"Lord, I accept Jesus," he said before closing his eyes and going limp.

# Chapter Four

Caramel heard footsteps approaching the door on the other side. She swung her red wig and smacked her lips together. They were coated with Candy Apple Red lipstick. She was ready for her next project. She felt in total control and ready. She waited for the knock on the door of her luxurious hotel suite.

It was a strong knock, she smiled. She hadn't been satisfied with Road Dog. He had been like a teaser…yeah he just hadn't been enough. She had an unquenchable thirst for more. She met this one through the CB radio too. He told her he was passing through Virginia Beach and wanted to hang out for a while. She had been game of course.

He stood filling up the doorway. This one was wide and pudgy, reminding her of Cedric the Entertainer in jeans and a plain shirt. He wasn't quite as disgusting and repulsive as Road Dog had been but she couldn't help but wonder by the nervous way he held the bunch of roses in his hands if this was his first time.

"Caramel?" he asked nervously, biting his bottom lip.

"That's me," she said.

"You're so beautiful," he gushed.

She stepped aside and he pushed the bunch of limp red roses at her, which was problem one. Stupid bastard could not do better than that for the privilege of being in her company? He had probably picked them up from the Piggy convenience store down the street. All she was worth was $12.99? Damn!

She snatched the roses and smelled them. Of course there was no scent because they were not fresh. She shoved them back at him. He seemed embarrassed but gave a nervous smile.

"Wow. What a nice spot!" he said.

She turned toward him and noticed he had stretched his free hand toward her and she looked down at it imagining all the microscopic germs crawling on the surface. Not to mention it was probably wet and nasty and sweaty as hell. There was no way she would take that besides this was not some social event, this was a booty call. She left him hanging but not before she caught a glimpse of the platinum wedding band adorning his ring finger. She laughed to herself. He was macking, even though he had a wife somewhere. *Lock down brother trying to be a player*, she thought feeling a kernel of irritation settle in her stomach.

She read him like a book. He wanted something to shake up his dull existence of trucking and going home to Lawanna, Tonya, Angela or whatever the hell her name was and then facing those out of control kids of his bouncing off the walls and breaking everything in sight.

He dropped his hand and slipped them in his jean pockets, looking at the floor.

"I just don't shake hands Scott," she said point blank staring him straight in the eyes.

He nodded like he really got it. "Hey Caramel, I can respect that. Everyone has their own hang ups I guess."

"You can put those flowers over there." She gestured toward the glass coffee table. He rushed over putting them in a vase and turned to her for approval.

"You are just as I pictured," he said.

"Um." She turned away knowing his eyes were following her as she went to one end of the black leather sofa. She lowered herself onto it, sinking into the soft cushions while he studied her. She crossed her legs so he could get a full view of them laced in black fishnets. He cleared his throat and placed his folded hands in front of his private area making her stomach turn. This man had absolutely no mystery. Truckers were not deep men by any stretch of the imagination. Not great intellectuals either, their role was not to figure out life or ponder the wonders of the world. They were made to do one thing and that was to dominate the great open highway in their huge moving machines on wheels, transporting goods from one good old American town to another. As she watched him watching her she knew this was not the first time Scott had dipped his hand in the cookie jar. She knew she was just one of a string of women he met on his trucking route and if she did not stop him now, there would be more. Maybe on another trip down to Georgia or Tennessee or North Carolina. Mama J was from Winston-Salem, North Carolina. She had been more like a Georgia Peach though.

He came over to the couch, sitting on the other end and clasping his hands together. "So Caramel, that is your name right? Your real name."

"Yes." She puffed again, eyeing him. He had a better grill than Road Dog too.

"What line of work are you in?" he asked politely like they were at a cocktail party.

"Hair," she said, tilting her head and blowing smoke out her mouth. She studied the wedding band. When sex at home had become too routine, Scott had decided to holla at some new meat.

"Oh I'm sorry, what did you say?" he asked.

"Hair," she repeated, still tripping off the ring on his left hand.

He frowned in total confusion and she suddenly realized that this one wasn't too sharp. He might not even recognize when the end was coming.

"I own a beauty shop Scott," she said in a tight voice, blinking.

His eyes lit up. "Oh wow! Good business to be in," he said. It was obvious that he admired her; it was all in his eyes. She always enjoyed that look from them when they found out her status. Yeah she was accomplished and they had a right to be intimidated. She was miles above them in class, prestige and everything else. They were losers and she had made something of herself. Even Uncle Harry knew that, probably watching her every move from the gates of hell.

"I have no complaints," she said.

"So what made you take up my offer?" he asked timidly.

"What made you ask?" She blew smoke out in his face, making him grimace and cough.

*Girl, don't fight me. You'll never win*

"You sounded so, well, mysterious," he paused searching for words. "Alluring."

"I see," she said. He had a decent vocabulary too, using big words like 'alluring'.

"Uh, do you mind if I use the bathroom?" he asked softly, half rising from the seat.

It was an unexpected question but she nodded. "Long as you put the lid down baby doll." She laughed.

"Be right back." He flew off like he really had to go and she shook her head watching his big ass jiggle as he made it to the guest bathroom door and yanked it open and disappeared inside.

Like the others, he wanted her, with no thought to what happened next. Hadn't even considered that maybe she had a sexually transmitted disease like AIDS or some other STD that he could carry home to wifey? No, it had not even crossed his pea brain. So as far as she was concerned, he was no better than Uncle Harry. *You are mine. You ain't never goin' anywhere. You and me are meant to be together little girl. We were meant to share this thing we have goin' on.*

"Shut up," she whispered, tired of the voices in her head. She had to have peace to do what she needed to do. She reached for another cigarette just as he came out. She tried to hide her anger by smiling as he came over and stood in front of her.

"Now where were we?" She suddenly grabbed between his legs. He was rock hard. He groaned as she pulled down his zipper. She stroked him as he started squealing like a pig. She was his little girl. She was his sex slave. "Scott, take off your clothes," she ordered.

"I want to," he stammered. "It's just been a long time since I've been around anybody but Tonya." He looked at the floor. "I really want to though. Guess it won't hurt if she never finds out." He grinned at her suddenly. "And it's Saturday night. People have fun on Saturday night, don't they?"

This fool had completely put wifey out of sight, out of mind. That made him no different from all the rest and it disgusted her to the point where she was physically sick. A few videos and blow up dolls were never quite enough. No they wanted the real thing.

"Take off your clothes," Caramel demanded.

"All right," he said, slowly pulling off his shirt and standing there in a stained undershirt, belly swollen like he was due any day now. She didn't flinch but the corners of her mouth went up. He was so pathetic. He tossed his shirt to the carpeted floor and stood there half naked and bloated. She wondered if his show was really supposed to make her hot and ready.

She did not move an inch or give him any verbal encouragement but he took it upon himself to continue pushing down his jeans. He reminded her of Chunky Monkey, one of those stripper men at the Max Two spot she used to check out. Her stomach churned again and something was ticking inside her head like with Road Dog.

"Is this okay?" he asked, eager to please as he yanked off his tight boxers, which not only had yellow ducks on them but also a shit stain in them. Have mercy! She felt anger spreading like a cancer inside her.

"Do what you feel Scott," she said, staying where she was. She reached for her glass of red wine and kept her eyes on him as he dropped his eyes, humiliated as he stood there totally naked and exposed. Yeah he was a hot mess and the worst part was he had the skinniest legs she had ever seen with long black socks gripping his ashy calves, reminding her of granddaddy pop. The big toe on his left foot peeked through a hole in his sock.

"I-I-I know I'm not the sexiest man you've ever been with." He seemed self-conscious probably based on the look she continued to give him.

"You think?" she asked, smiling at his understatement. *Do you really think you bastard? You just don't know.* She knew she could not master her fury and she was going to allow it to be released. Her hand wanted to squeeze her wine glass until it disintegrated between her fingers. Or maybe smash his big head between her bare hands like a pumpkin. *That would be kind of cool,* she thought.

"I should have put on my bikinis to really turn you on. To make me irresistible."

She chuckled. Was he serious? Like that would make her want to come out of her robe.

"Stop, please," she said, blinking. "Moving kind of fast aren't we, Superstar? You're about to fly past the station Scott. Slow your roll a minute."

There was confusion in his eyes and he cocked his head to the side like he was listening for something. Maybe the crickets outside or the roar of the Atlantic possibly? "Should be your damn conscience!" Caramel wanted to shout but she kept a plastic smile on her grill.

"Come over here Scott," she demanded in a husky voice before draining her glass of wine. She was feeling kind of fuzzy but not enough to lose control. She had to keep the control. Being in control was what made her Caramel.

He made his way toward her, his little peter was standing straight at attention and pointed right at her. He stopped in front of her, not the least bit embarrassed with his underachiever or even the way he was carrying all this. What kind of women was he used to bedding she wondered?

Maybe they weren't women at all.

Maybe they were little eight-year old girls. Innocents who wanted to just play with their dolls and go to school and be safe.

"You are really ready," she said in a low tone. The cancer was spreading as he put hands on his hips and smiled at her like he actually had something to be proud of.

Something in his expression reminded her of Uncle Harry as she could still hear him tell her to get butt naked. *Strip girl, what you waitin' on?* What a dirty bastard. She was so repulsed but she would be compensated for that soon.

"Let's play a game Scott, make it kinda fun," she said.

"Yeah," he said rubbing his hands together in excitement. "I'm all ears."

"First, drink some wine and relax while I get everything set up." She rose, patting him on the shoulder. "In fact let me get you that glass of wine while you wait."

"Cool." He plopped his nasty ass on the couch. She hoped he wouldn't leave any butt chips on it."I'm glad I came over."

*It is on and popping,* she thought, going over to the wet bar.

Humming to herself, she grabbed a cut glass, opened the fridge and pulled out one of the bottles she had bought earlier. She filled the glass and glanced over her shoulder to check out what he was doing. Her stomach turned when she realized he was picking his nose.

"Ice?" she offered.

"No I have sensitive teeth," he said.

"Okay Scott," she said quickly, pulling the vial from her pocket. She twisted off the top and poured the contents into the juice and stirred it vigorously. Oh yeah, he was going to enjoy his last drink.

She handed him the glass and he guzzled the liquid in one head flip. "Ahhhhhhh! That hit the spot."

She went into the bedroom and came back with the handcuffs and a silk navy-blue scarf. He let her blindfold him and lead him back to the bedroom.

"I-I- feel kind of funny," he said slowly.

"Probably just tired." She instructed him to lie down on the bed and she handcuffed him to the bed.

"What are you going to do?" he asked, the first hint of uneasiness creeping up in his voice. Much like an animal, he had finally sensed danger. Everyone had that sixth sense, some used it and others ignored it, wishing they hadn't especially after it was too late.

"Just try to enjoy it big boy." She flitted off to get what she needed to finish her project.

"I didn't tell you this but I'm married. But my wife and I are separated. Have been for six months now." He fought against the handcuffs. "Man, these are tight."

"You have kids Scott?" She hummed to herself.

"Five," he said proudly.

"*Five*, oh wow you *are* a viral thing," she replied.

"Yeah guess so," he said proudly. "The men in my family have no problem in that department."

"I always wanted kids and a family Scott," she said.

"Ww-w-why didn't you?" he asked.

"I can't have any, my Uncle Harry took all that away from me Scott," she said quietly.

"Uh, you know," he paused, twisting his big head from side to side. "I am really sleepy and need to get up early in the morning so maybe, maybe we can play this game later Caramel."

"Oh no Scott now is the right time baby." She hummed even louder coming back over with the knife. "Just lay back and let Caramel work out all the kinks in your life Scott. I want to make you feel special right now."

*What a sweet thing you are. Better than candy girl. Like caramel, nice and sticky, sweet. Um um um.*

"Yeah, yeah I like that idea of making me feel good. I uh, want you to make me feel good Caramel. I knew you would," he said nervously as she traced the tip of the knife across his hairy leg causing him to jump.

"Oh shit, what you got there Caramel?" he asked in a shaky voice.

"Just something that I needed to help me finish my project," she said.

"I-I'm a project?" he asked.

"Uh huh you are," she answered.

"Please no Caramel," he said drowsily.

"Oh yes Scott," she said.

# Chapter Five

The endless squawking of sea gulls woke her up early the next morning and she squinted against the raw sunlight hurting her tired eyes. She sat up, feeling every muscle in her body scream for relief. She had a jar of Ben Gay and she would definitely use it. She scanned the bedroom of the hotel room that she had enjoyed last night. She noticed just how neat and clean things were. Just as they should be and just as she liked it. Her clothes had been arranged in the drawer and her three pair of sandals lined up in a straight row. She needed total order in her life. If things were even a little out of whack, she would get a bit crazy like she had lost her grip. No, she needed cleanliness and organization. That was the world that she needed to create for herself.

Satisfied, she realized she was hungry, which was typical after the kind of night she had. She was always ravenous after one of her projects. She leaned over and picked up the glossy seven-page menu from the nightstand. It outlined everything from breakfast to midnight snacks.

"I think I'll order me a great big southern style breakfast. I damn sure deserve it," she said before humming to herself. She chose option C, which included: grits, buttermilk biscuits, bacon, cheese eggs, fruit and coffee. After calling in her order she stood up and suddenly felt a bit dizzy.

She decided maybe she needed to lay off the spirits for a while. She had finished off two bottles after taking care of her business. But there was no reason to focus on that now.

She went over to the gold drape covered window and ran her finger along the edge. She couldn't understand why they would even have window treatments in a room like this. The room overlooked the ocean and was so far off the ground that no one could possibly see in anyway.

She pulled the plastic stick on the sides, opening the heavy drapes and revealing a breathtaking view that instantly gave her a lift. It was worth the extra money she had paid for the view of the ocean. The massive body of water was calm and as smooth as glass, sparkling like a trillion blue diamonds. The never-ending stretch of stark white sand resting against the blue of the water reminded her of a painting she had seen once. Sea gulls flew low, dipping every once in a while to check below the cool waters surface for their own breakfast. The whole scene made her feel somewhat tranquil for a change. For a few minutes, she was not broken in a million pieces. No, she felt whole.

She hugged herself and stared up at the stunning blue sky remembering when she was a kid and would go down south to see her grandmother and cousins. The sun had always seemed to be shining there no matter what time of year it was. At night the stars and moon always lit up the nighttime sky, sparkling like crystals against black velvet. She and her cousin Derrick would stretch out their worn cotton blanket and lounge while nibbling on Mama J's hot cornbread as they stared up at the wide universe. They would imagine what it would be like to be up there looking down on the earth, almost like God surveying his amazing handy work. Those were the times when she had been happiest…now she rarely had a joy filled day. She was living and striving to make it in DC. How could she get a sense of balance there? The only thing that was a constant were the memories that haunted her.

She noticed the row after row of naked pink backs sunbathing on beach towels, trying to deepen that summer tan. A lot of other folk were jumping around in the water with complete abandon. Personally, she would never consider even sticking a toe in that water, not with all the stories of shark attacks or was that on the West Coast? She was a land person who never even learned how to swim. She used to beg Mama J and she would always say that swimming was for fish and besides if God wanted man to swim, He would have given him fins. So she left it at that, content to do safe things at least until Uncle Harry came along. After that she'd never felt safe again.

There was a hard rap at her door. Room service. She picked up her robe from the floor and slid it on, belting it tight. She checked herself in the mirror and was satisfied. She was presentable or rather 'decent' as Mama J used to say. She went through the living room, making sure everything was as it should be. She took special care with the sofa, checking it twice even though the odds of the room service guy going over to inspect it were nil. Why would he? No one at the hotel would expect anything to be out of the ordinary with their guests. She was just someone else dropping in for a brief stay.

There was another knock but louder this time. "Coming!" she called out, darting to the door. She pulled off the double lock and stepped back as a breeze hit her face. She looked up at the really tall Asian dude who looked like he should be dunking a ball instead of standing in a crisp white shirt and dark suit that actually made him appear even thinner than he probably was. His sparse eyebrows were knitted together in a deep-set frown and she had the feeling that he walked around with a scowl all day. He sighed like he just didn't feel like being bothered and cocked his head, giving her an impatient look. He gripped the handles to a cart, which was draped in white linen. A covered silver tray was on top. She stepped aside as he wheeled the cart in without a word.

*What an asshole*, she thought, rolling her eyes. She watched with crossed arms as he set the tray on the coffee table in front of the sofa. Then he turned holding out a bill for her to sign. She snatched it from him, and scribbled her name quickly, crossed out the tip line and handed it back to him. She could get some satisfaction in the fact that he would not get a red cent from her. Shithead. She could easily make him another project even though there would be no motivation for her really.

He glanced down at the bill but did not show any emotion while closing it. "Have a good day ma'am," he mumbled, stepping out.

"Have a bad life bastard," she hissed, locking the door with a loud click. She had to say that as rude as he'd been, she could respect that. At least she knew he didn't like her. He was honest about it, not caring what she felt but then he wasn't trying to get anything from her either. Not like Scott and the countless other faces. They all blurred together into one, ugly monstrous one over the last few weeks.

She went over to the table and lifted the lid to her food. Everything seemed in order though. The eggs were a nice pale yellow with lots of melted cheese and flecks of black pepper. They were perfect so she moved on to the grits, which were creamy and not lumpy. Even the bacon was brown and crispy just like she wanted it. At least the grub was right because she needed a hearty meal to build her energy back up. She sat down and hit a button on the remote and the TV hummed to life with CNN. She sat listening to the weather lady promising a perfect summer day and then a newscaster giving an update on a nearby union strike.

All that was fine and dandy, but she was more interested in following the ongoing saga on the East Coast slasher.

She picked up her coffee cup and sipped. The taste of the robust coffee beans filled her soul, heart and mind, reminding her of Mama J's kitchen back all those years ago. She would sit at the table, swinging her legs and taking in the smell of French Roast percolating in the pot while Mama J set the good silverware and China for their Sunday breakfast.

Mama J would wear one of those half aprons to prevent anything from spilling on her good church clothes and Daddy D would sit at the head of the table perusing *The Washington Post*, grunting every once in a while as he pulled on his beard. Then Mama J would bring her a pink plastic teacup filled with hot milk and a few dashes of coffee in it just to give her a little taste. Then she would set a steaming cup of coffee for Daddy D and a plate of warm Danishes, fried potatoes, slab bacon and cheese grits. Daddy D would smile broadly and dig into his plate, chewing with his eyes closed. He would tell Mama J that she was thee best cook in the world and then slap her behind.

*"You are getting mighty big young lady. Before we know it you'll be feeding your own family,"* Mama J had said with her thick North Carolina accent, putting her hands on her wide hips and purring in pleasure.

Daddy D looked over his paper and winked at me. *"Yeah but don't rush it. She's still my baby girl."*

She missed both of them like crazy, opening her eyes and realizing she was still in the hotel room and not in that townhouse in Columbia Heights.

She turned her attention to the television.

"Now on to some other news. The body of a trucker was found in the Wright motel over in Fredericksburg yesterday. It is believed that he was killed by a stab wound through his heart. He had been stabbed numerous times leading police to believe that this vicious attack may be the latest work of the East Coast slasher," the dark-haired white female said with a thick southern accent and deadpan face as if she really cared. No one really cared. They just reported on the news.

"This is the third killing in the Tidewater area. There have been two other killings in New Jersey and one in Delaware."

They flashed to a round-faced black man in a gray suit with thick glasses. He reported on the connections to the murders of Edwin Brown, Dwight Hill and Chancey Billard who were all murdered last month. "If anyone remembers seeing any of these victims or witnessed any of these crimes, please contact us."

Her mind went back to Henderson. He had been such an ass. He deserved to die more than Scott or even Road Dog.

"Some people deserve it. Just like Uncle Harry," she mumbled, holding her fork up to the light to check and make sure that it was squeaky clean. Not satisfied, she wiped it off vigorously with her napkin and then arranged all her utensils side by side on the table. Everything had to be just so, from the fork lying next to the knife with the blade facing out. She slipped the linen napkin onto her lap and dug in as the reporter informed the viewers that the public would be posted on the latest developments in the case.

She poured mustard on the eggs before digging in. She slowly chewed the eggs letting them melt in her mouth. They were tasty but still not as good as Mama J's. She cut the bacon into small bites, popped a few in her mouth and crunched the salty meat. She wondered what Scott was nibbling on about now. Maybe some worms or maybe, just maybe they were nibbling on him. She laughed out loud. Poor Scott. He had been so damn gullible. He really had deserved what he had gotten. She had absolutely no sympathy.

"The name of the victim is not being released until next of kin has been notified. Back to you John."

*Girl you and I make a good pair.*

As she went to dip her fork back into the eggs, she noticed something out of the corner of her eye, causing her to pause. She turned and spotted a man's leather black shoe lying on its side near the TV stand. It wasn't just anyone's shoe though. It was Scott's shoe and though it appeared to be leather, it was more than likely pleather. But the real issue was that she had left it in plain view for anyone including the evil demon serving as a room deliveryman to see. She had somehow overlooked it while she had cleaned up last night. Was she getting sloppy in her work now?

"Oh no, no baby doll we can't have that," she whispered, dropping her fork and moving across the room so fast her pants whipped against her shapely legs. She grabbed the shoe and immediately was engulfed in good old-fashioned foot funk. She carried it out in front of her, holding it between two fingers as she went to the bedroom and tossed it in one of those plastic dry cleaning bags. She rolled it up tight and slipped it deep into the bottom of her overnight bag. She had never left any evidence behind before so this would have been a first. She couldn't afford any slip-ups. Everything had to have a place including her spoils of war.

Humming an old Michael Jackson tune, she sat back down to her food again and polished off the now cold, hard grits thinking about her fun last night.

No there was a place for everything and *everyone* including Scott who had found out sooner than later.

# Chapter Six

Joy stuffed the last of the dark clothes into the medium-size washing machine, filling it to the top. She slammed the door, hit heavy load, cold water, one rinse and permanent press all in one second flat. She stood back and watched through the glass as sudsy water drenched her sweat pants, jeans and several other articles that had sat in the bottom of her hamper for more than two weeks now. Truthfully, more than anything else, she absolutely hated doing laundry. In fact, she avoided it as much as possible like other undesirable tasks including cleaning the bathrooms and studying. She only broke down to do it when she was down to her last pair of undies. Her mother would be absolutely appalled by that and worried that her only daughter was not exhibiting her home training. All black mothers needed to know they had raised a child who could be perfect to a world that found them the opposite. And for Joy, she fought that every step of the way lately, doing the opposite of whatever her mother wanted. Even her hair, which she had chosen to wear in locs, was against her mother's will. Call it rebellion or just a belief that no matter what she did, she wouldn't be perfect anyway. The best she could do was be the best Joy she could be, period. And with all she had on her plate, that was a full time job. Just trying to pass her classes and take care of her man was enough to fill a day.

She stood listening to Tupac's *Dear Mama* and singing along to the lyrics. This song was definitely the black man's homage to his mother. God knows he had been such an amazing brother back in the day and even now several years after his supposed murder, he still had a major impact on her and millions of other fans. A small part of her wondered though if he had really died. It was still possible that he had run off somewhere to escape all the drama and strife from his troubled life. Maybe he had just up and gone to Paris, London or even the Bahamas to live out his days in peace and quiet. Hey, anything was possible especially since he had been seen all over the world. Every year somebody spotted him. It was like he was the black community's very own Elvis.

"Hey J, are you coming back in here anytime soon? I'm hungry as a mug baby girl!" Ricky shouted down to her from the top of the basement stairs.

"Yes in a few minutes sweetie," Joy yelled back, staring at the three gigantic and intimidating piles of clothes waiting for their turn in the steel suds filled contraption. Lord if she could wave a magic wand.

"And bring me some more of that cheese dip and a glass of Kool Aid on your way back too!"

"Sure baby!" she hollered back.

"And a ham sandwich too babe!" he called out again. "Make sure you slap plenty of meat and extra mayo on it now. Don't be stingy on a brother. Set me straight!"

"All right," she responded, shaking her head. She was absolutely crazy about her man, even if her mother absolutely hated him like he had killed somebody or stole something. Joy knew it was because he wasn't saved and sanctified and that was too much for Reverend Jocelyn Henderson to take; and she felt her little Joyful Lynn deserved much better.\The second thing was that he had not come up in a community like Woodland Hills in prestigious Bowie, Maryland like her family had. Instead he was a product of a disadvantaged and God forbidden broken home over in the Anacostia and that was something that her people most definitely looked down on.

Her parents were wrapped up in who so-and-so's parents were and they always had to be someone of some decency. But truthfully, Joy wasn't into all that elitist nonsense. Black folk had used it as a way to separate themselves from the other Black folk for years. She was of the opinion that everybody just needed to get along as Rodney King had put, or even better, couldn't everybody just kiss and make up?

But it was not meant to be. She had to just accept it and move on and when they made negative comments, she dug in her heels and defended him like a good woman should. She was proud of her man. He had pulled himself up by his bootstraps and became a chemical engineer and now he made great money. He had a solid future and she wanted to be a part of it. She planned to be his wife, in fact, and they would create that perfect life. Be a power couple…with the practice that she planned to start…her own psychology office once she graduated, which was only a year away.

When that happened she could put the past behind her and move into her future with a clean slate. Forget the secrets that had haunted her for longer than she wanted. Secrets that didn't need to be a part of her anymore.

"And throw some tomato on it while you're at it!" he yelled down again.

"No problem!" she said smiling to herself. She realized that Ricky was spoiled but she could never turn him down. She loved to take care of him. As far as she was concerned he was her life. He made her existence complete. She just wished he would have some love for her best friend.

She lifted the side lid to the washer again to dump in a bit more fabric softener and watched the pale blue liquid swirl through the dispenser. \She knew that Autumn didn't care for Ricky either, the one thing they disagreed on other than housekeeping methods.

Autumn was her girl though and they had been tight for a long time. They knew each other inside and out, things that other people didn't know about them. And when it came to loyalty, they would always have each other's back no matter what went down.

Joy would never forget when they first met all those years ago and quickly became fast friends. Funny, but it seemed like centuries since Harry bought Autumn to Shepherd Hill Baptist where Joy's father was the pastor. They had been no older than six or seven at that time. Autumn was this scared, timid kid in a pink coat with a fur collar. Joy had shyly taken Autumn's cold hand and led her to Sunday school class. After they both realized a mutual interest in paper dolls, roller-skating and hand-clapping games, they stuck together like peanut butter and jelly all through elementary, middle and high school.

Joy always worried about Autumn cracking one day, after all she had been through with her Uncle Harry and the violent deaths of her parents. Her studies had taught her that people acted out their childhood in one form or fashion. Joy figured it came out in Autumn's obsessive need to clean. Even after living together for ten years, that was one thing that Joy would never be able to reciprocate on.

She switched off the backlight and crossed to the steps leading upstairs. When she was a kid, she used to be afraid of basements. Afraid of what could pop up in one. She glanced over her shoulder, feeling kind of childish. She was a grown woman now and knew this basement like the back of her hand. She had considered getting her own place a few times but why? She didn't have to pay rent and it really was a nice place to live, fitting like a comfortable old shoe. And Autumn would not hear about her leaving anyway. She considered Joy family, and even her feline Boris was accepted.

As if reading her thoughts, Boris appeared out of the blue purring and rubbing against her leg. She knelt down and scratched his warm dingy blonde fur. He was old as dirt, having more than nine lives after being run over by a truck and poisoned but he hung in there, not ready to go.

"How's my sweetie today? Want a treat?" she asked.

Boris studied her with serious hazel eyes and meowed feebly. Homeboy never turned down food. That's why his gut was dragging the floor now but she always did as he asked just like she did with everyone else. He was like her child. She stood up and headed straight to the kitchen with Boris on her heels. She had to feed her big baby and her little baby. She pulled out his dry food, filled up the silver bowl with fish nuggets and set it down on the floor, watching him race over to it like it was the last meal. Then she went to the pan of chops she had been preparing for dinner. That was one thing she did better than Autumn. Joy could burn in the kitchen and she enjoyed it.

"Hurry the hell up J! Damn!" he shouted from the living room. "Game will be over before you get back in here!"

"I'm coming. Trying to finish dinner."

"Just drop a brother his food right quick."

She threw the pan of chops in the oven and hurriedly made him a sandwich to his specifications. She didn't go off like some sisters would; it wasn't part of her nature to contest. She enjoyed being needed. Like she said, Ricky could be a little bossy but he couldn't live without her or at least that's what he had told her. He explained that she was his whole world in a nutshell. Rushing to the fridge, she pulled out the pitcher of cherry flavored Kool Aid. She poured the red liquid into a tall tinted blue glass. He loved her Kool Aid because she made it with a ton of sugar like his mama had. He said she made it better than anyone else he had been with and was a test to see how long the relationship would last.

She smiled at that thought as she made her way to the living room. Ricky was stretched out on the couch with a pillow between his thick thighs, looking fine as ever. He was half black and half Puerto Rican and his exotic look was one of the things that attracted her to him. And since he worked out, he was muscular and taut.

He popped another chip in his mouth, his eyes glued to the large screen TV alive with the sport of the season. He was a diehard Washington Nationals' fan, which would be obvious even to a perfect stranger. Not only did he have on a cap but a T-shirt and socks. He had seen just about every game from day one when they came to town two years ago.

She handed him the glass and he flashed an electric smile that caused her heart to melt faster than the gallon of butter pecan ice cream she had softening on the kitchen countertop. She knew that he was all worth it even as he turned back to the game. "Thanks babe."

"Anything for you," she said plopping down beside him, sighing for a second, twirling the gold cross she always wore on the thick gold chain. She needed to hit the books and hard. Her finals were coming up soon and she had to make straight A's. She prayed about it earlier during church service that morning.

"Yeah!" Ricky jumped up raising his arms in the air. "Home run!"

She clapped. "I'm glad for you baby."

"That's what I'm talking about. Come here! I love a woman with some meat on her bones," he said, falling back on the couch grabbing Joy and pulling her close. There was just something so amazing, so irresistible about him. "You're my sugar."

"I know that," she said happily enjoying that secure feeling she got in his massive arms.

"Let me get a taste." He nuzzled her ear. "Um, tastes good. I want to get jiggie with it. You know after the game." He planted another soft kiss on her neck and then turned his face toward the screen.

"Um hum Ricky, you don't love me," she teased.

"Oh and that's where you're wrong," he paused rubbing her thigh. "I love you more than the Nationals."

"That's comforting." She rolled her eyes.

"You ain't never going nowhere girl. You tell that to Autumn too." He tweaked her left breast. "Autumn needs a man to mellow her out. And I mean a man, not a woman."

"Stop playing," she said checking the time. It was after six. Autumn should be getting back soon. She wanted to hear all about her trip. She always had some outrageous story to tell and Joy lived through Autumn vicariously. Almost made Joy jealous that Autumn had the freedom to just fly up and down the Coast at will. She had started doing it a few months ago as a way to get away. Joy had imagined Autumn partying back. And dabbling in some wild stuff that she would normally not engage in back home like a sex orgy. Maybe meeting some guys and just doing her thing. Joy could only imagine and she hoped on her travels, Autumn would meet a nice guy. A 'do right' brother. She had always kind of steered clear of men, claiming she didn't have the time and instead poured her heart and soul into her business. Joy figured, with the correct one, Autumn would make room for him. Joy knew that all women needed a man.

Almost as if on cue, Joy heard the key turn in the front door lock. She scooted and jumped up as Ricky asked her to bring back the big bag of sour dough pretzels.

Joy found Autumn as always, looking dead tired like she had been doing some serious partying over the weekend. Physically she was small and curvy, which was one thing among many that Joy envied about Autumn. Joy could not even get a foot into one of Autumn's pants. And girlfriend was sharp and together as ever, dressed in tight hip-hugging jeans that flared out at the bottom, leather sandals and a plain black T-shirt, her braided hair still tight as always. She plopped down her red duffel and satchel purse just as they heard the sound of shots ringing out from up the street.

"They are starting early up in Lincoln Heights tonight. You know how it is when the temp rises," Joy said shaking her head with disgust. "They need Jesus or the police."

Autumn glanced at her gold watch. "Yeah I guess so. The projects are way too close for comfort J. *Way* too close. It might be time to sell while I still can."

Joy did not say anything. She knew that Autumn would never sell. It was their home. She followed Autumn across the hardwood floor through the beautifully decorated dining room and into the recently remodeled kitchen.

"It smells good in here girl. You're cooking up a storm."

"Trying," Joy said, going back to the oven to check on the time left. "Ten more minutes on the lamb chops."

Autumn went to the sink, got a sponge, broke out the Lysol and wiped down the counters, refrigerator doors and knobs, which was something she always did subconsciously because again she was anal about germs and dirt.

"The cookie jars aren't lined up," Autumn said, going over and straightening. Then she went about checking the shelves to make sure all the plates and cups were in their right place. Joy knew the drill.

Autumn pried open the fridge door, burying her head deep inside searching her fridge shelves, doing the usual inventory. She stuck her behind out.

"Ricky's still here I see," Autumn called over her shoulder. "He's almost a resident. I should be collecting some rent or something from that brother."

"Oh come on he contributes," Joy said, grabbing the carton of Edy's butter pecan. She picked up the plastic scooper and dug out two scoops of ice cream.

"How?"

"Yeah…well…he fixed the light on the second floor."

"Cool but that just compensates for him using the electricity and water," Autumn said rolling her eyes and putting a hand on her hip.

"Stop playing. You and Ricky may be like family one day," Joy said. She put the ice cream carton back in the freezer.

"You're still interested in marrying that fool?"

"If he asks." Joy sat down with her bowl.

"Whatever." Autumn emerged with a covered dish of salmon cakes that Joy had made over the weekend. "I'm starved too J. I had a burger attack on the way back but figured I'd better eat at home. Gotta stay on this diet and I went buck wild this weekend too. Stopped at Cracker Barn on Saturday."

"Yeah I know you went crazy girl. The cheese biscuits are divine!" Joy fluttered her eyelids, imagining the mouthwatering buttery biscuits hitting her tongue.

"Thought about you girl as I was smacking my lips. Food make ya wanna slap somebody," Autumn said.

"Who are *you* telling?" Joy paused leaning against the counter, wishing she could drive down there tonight herself. "So besides the good vitals, how was it? The trip I mean? You get in any real trouble? Any scandalous scenes?" Joy watched Autumn carry the dish to the microwave and place the entire thing inside.

Autumn shrugged, closing the door and stabbing at the buttons as it beeped. She pushed the start button and it came alive, humming as the light came on. Her dish slowly spun around inside.

Autumn avoided Joy's eyes. "Do I ever? Same old same old. Tourists, sun, beach, and blue skies. Just like any other time in Virginia Beach." She shrugged.

"No interesting stories?" Joy wanted something to brighten an otherwise dull day. "That would be a first Autumn," she said. She studied Autumn trying to figure out why she was suddenly getting a strange vibe.

"Nope none, so believe it." Autumn still looked anywhere but at Joy. Joy crossed her arms over her chest. Seemed like her friend seemed to be hiding some stuff when she came back from these trips. It was like Autumn was doing something she shouldn't and wouldn't tell even Joy, maybe a dark secret worse than Joy's? And whatever it was, it had an element of mystery. Her mind went back to the orgies.

"You didn't meet *any* brothers?"

"No," Autumn said point blankly, setting her plate on the table. Joy was disappointed.

"How was the water?" Joy asked, really trying to get a conversation going. She didn't want to go back and watch a boring baseball game or crack open her books either, come to think of it.

"Girl you know I would not set foot near a wave. But I guess it was as it should be this time of year," Autumn said slowly, turning and locking eyes with Joy. She was irritated and Joy knew when to back off. "Let's change the subject. What's new with you?"

"Just another weekend here. The shop was busy as always." Joy blinked, not sure what else to say. She had been managing Autumn's shop for two years and covered on the weekends that Autumn went away. "Someone came in to apply for that vacant stylist position. But girl I don't know what to say other than I thought that it was a woman." Joy put hands on her wide hips, frowning. "I mean she, he or it had breasts and hips for days but then the voice was so deep, and the hands were as huge as baseball mitts."

"That's a telltale sign church lady," Autumn smirked.

"Then I saw the bulge in her, uh well, his pants girl." Joy shook her head in disgust. "I almost fell out right there. Took everything to keep a straight face."

Autumn cracked up. Once she got herself together, she asked the only thing she really needed to know. "Well could he do some hair J? Because that's my main concern. You still checked the references right?"

"Excellent, perfect, everyone loves him." She put another scrumptious bite of ice cream in her mouth.

"Hire him," Autumn demanded.

"Will do boss," Joy said. She knew better than to go against Autumn. She was in charge and if she wanted that kind of person, it was her business, no pun intended. She trusted Autumn's judgment. That's why she had been so successful. Taking it one step further, the sister was phenomenal actually and had started her own business at the tender age of twenty-two. It had paid off and she was well respected in her field. Staying afloat even when other places had closed. She was a diva. "I keep my eye out for talent. And you know men stylists sometimes work it better than women anyway." Autumn sipped on her glass of Kool Aid watching the seconds dwindle on the microwave display window.

Joy was not too surprised at Autumn's reaction. Her boss always wanted the best people in her shop and gender preference would never be an issue.

"What's his name?" Autumn opened the microwave and pulled out the dish with two potholders.

"Sasha," Joy said.

"Shut your mouth!" Autumn grinned.

Joy shook her head. "No I'm not playing."

Autumn snorted. "Hum, sounds like *he* will soon be a *she*? Another sex changer." She shrugged. "Okay no problem as long as he brings in the clients. Make it happen."

Joy nodded.

"Hey babe!" Ricky shouted. "Where's my sour dough? Ya need to get a move on!" Ricky shouted, causing Joy to giggle.

Autumn rolled her eyes. "Um, you would think this was his house. You need to check your man J. He is still ordering like this is a fast food restaurant."

"Hey Rick, come get it yourself! Get a move on man!" Autumn answered, going to the kitchen table.

"Shhh!" Joy jumped down from the counter and grabbed the unopened bag of pretzels. "He'll hear you."

"Good I want him to." Autumn frowned, eyeing the bag in Joy's hand. "Uh those aren't mine are they?"

"No, no I just bought these last night," Joy said quickly, not wanting to cause even more confusion.

"Okay then we're straight," Autumn said, dumping two salmon cakes on her plate and pouring yellow mustard over them. She always put mustard on just about everything. "But you need to stop waiting on that man hand and foot. He'll expect that crap for the rest of your life, Joy."

"Well he's my man," Joy said. "And I love him so what's the harm."

"Do you really want me to go there?" Autumn took a bite of the cakes and closed her eyes. "Lord these are heavenly. You put your foot or toe in this. Missed your calling girl. I know you love psychology but ya need to think about cooking. Being the next B. Smith's. "

"Thanks but I want to be the next Mo'nique. Big girl magic."

Autumn laughed, pointing the end of her fork at Joy. "I see that. I know, big girl's rock."

"In more ways than one," Joy said winking wickedly.

"TMI. But since you're on the subject, let's go there?" Autumn repeated. "About the opposite sex?"

"Try me?" Joy crossed her arms.

"No man is worth it baby." Autumn smacked her lips. "So stop dreaming about me being with one."

"Every brother can't be bad girl," Joy said softly, putting a hand on Autumn's cold one. "You just haven't met the right one."

"I *said* no man would be good enough for me," she growled her eyes flashing red.

"Let Uncle Harry go," Joy suggested. "You're taking what happened too far."

"Mind your business," she said in a hard voice and Joy knew to back off.

"Where are my chops?" Ricky shouted.

"See what I mean?" Autumn shot out. "They always want some-thing."

Joy sighed and got up. In silence she pulled out the chops and dumped potato salad on his plate. She ran out of the kitchen before Ricky screamed again.

"And for the record I have met all the right ones." Joy heard Autumn murmur in an almost unrecognizable cold voice. "Plenty of them."

# Chapter Seven

Autumn was always the first one in the shop, which was natural. After all Killer Do's was her baby, her life, her dream after modeling became a mute point. She spent ninety percent of her waking moments in what she called her haven, working to make it the top beauty salon in town by turning sisters into black angels with the stroke of a comb. And it was finally starting to pay off in a big way. A few weeks ago she had actually been written up in *The Washington Post* as one of the best around. She had been mentioned in a couple of black hairstyle magazines getting special praises for being open on Monday, which was unusual for a shop. It was all good because the accolades brought in the clients, which in turn brought in more cash for her. If things continued going like this, she would open another shop maybe in Prince George's county in another year or two. She had been blessed that she could make it in the one of two things that made a black person rich. The other was the ministry, but God had never called her for that so this was it…And to create beauty in the ugly world she lived made her feel good every day…and that was in her genes.

She blew a kiss at a blown up framed shot of Mama J picking out an Angela Davis size 'fro. It had hung in Mama J's shop years ago and now hung on Autumn's wall. She was just keeping the family legacy alive. To show that Mama J's life had mattered even if she had a brutal death.

After dusting everything down and making sure things were just so, she opened the Japanese horizontal blinds, allowing the sun rays to filter in and fill the inside of the shop. She remembered that the weatherman said it would be another scorcher. She peered out onto Georgia Avenue as cars flew up and down on that early commute track.

The Avenue was especially alive on the inbound traffic lane, with commuters pouring into the city from Silver Spring and other parts of the DC metro region. She caught sight of the green banners hanging from tall poles along the street. In bold white lettering it said, "Georgia Avenue: Good things are happening."

She had always loved this street especially as a kid. Her family had always had some type of business going there. Her parents had owned a soul food restaurant for years there and Mama J had had a beauty shop there too. That was where Autumn had learned about hair. And now she had the salon. Seemed almost like destiny.

*Little girl, you are my reason for living. Your parents gave me to you as a gift. Look how we fit together?*

Uncle Harry's voice invaded her mind. She shook her head from side to side and tried to shake it out.

"You're not spoiling my day Uncle Harry. Oh no, you have ruined too many already sir. It's a new day!" Autumn shouted, smoothing down her sundress nervously. He had been interrupting her thoughts more and more lately. Especially after the twentieth year anniversary month before last.

She went behind the receptionist desk, which still had the vase full of wilted daffodils and petunias that Vanessa's cheap boyfriend had bought. A half-deflated balloon and birthday cards were still on display from last week as well. She turned on the flat screen computer she had just purchased for the place. It had cost her a mint and a half but she had to be professional and progressive. Every decent salon had at least one including the shop with the Dominican Republicans up the street. They were her direct competition, snatching clients from all the area salons because they were hot, and the new mantra. Autumn planned to stay in style and keep up with the latest trends in black hair. Nobody would put her out of business or take away even one of her customers. She went out of her way too, offering her clients everything from facials to hair care.

She switched on the computer and it hummed softly, reminding her of the motel room air conditioners that would be making all kinds of noise. She rubbed her arms and sat down in the plush seat. It came in handy so she could keep a detailed database of each of her clients from hair type to birth date. It was that personal touch that her clients appreciated. It kept them coming back too and with the new professional black woman, who demanded quality, it worked out in her favor.

She crossed the new blonde hardwood floors that she had installed last year and went back to the small room where she kept her washer and dryer. There was a small kitchenette complete with microwave for her stylists. Turning on the back light, she screamed, losing all cool at the sight of a gigantic 'brown roach scurrying frantically over the side of the table to avoid being seen. Oh damn it was on and popping! She would not tolerate roaches or any other bugs! .

"Oh hell no! I ain't havin' it!" she said storming over to the counter with lightening speed and kneeling down, staring up underneath to see if she could spot it. Unfortunately it was nowhere to be found. But that was all right. It was time to call the exterminator. That was one thing she just could not deal with. She ran over to one of her cabinets and grabbed the can of Raid. Like a crazy woman, she sprayed the entire counter top and underneath, using half the can and coughing from the fumes.

Oh from now on her stylists would have to eat outside. She was not going to have anything upset the order in her shop. And bugs meant there were no order, no control.

She dialed the numbers to the exterminator from her cell phone and blasted Squash 'Em Dead out for not doing a good job the first time because the nasty critters were back. Unfortunately they were booked up for the day but promised to be out first thing in the morning. She hung up on them, pissed.

"Can't get any good help these days," she mumbled, picking up the can of Raid and spraying the entire back area. Then she went to the fridge and emptied it out. She went back and bleached the floors. Then she went to the bathroom and washed her hands until they turned pink but suddenly before her eyes blood was running from her hands. She jumped and screamed, shrinking back against the toilet, scared. What the hell? Her chest rose and fell for a second as she convinced herself that it was just an illusion. It couldn't be real. No way. She was just jittery from the roach episode. She leaned against the wall until her heartbeat returned to normal before she crept to the sink. With shaky hands, she switched off the spigots. Was she losing it?

Shaken, she left the bathroom just when she heard the sound of loud voices booming from out front. She had to get herself together. Her peeps were here and she was in charge and had to represent as the diva owner. She had to be in control. It was the one thing that she had.

Pushing aside what had just gone down, she smiled and went out to see two of her stylists, Gwen and Janet walking through the door talking a mile a minute. Gwen was lugging her bag filled to the brim with curling and flat irons, brushes and combs.

She never left her things behind at her station, swearing that the other stylists might use or steal her supplies. Of course that was ludicrous but Gwen was the best stylist in the shop. Once people overlooked her abrupt manner and loud voice, they enjoyed the miracle she managed to do on every single head her magical fingers touched. She smiled at Autumn, popping on a wad of gum.

"Whatsup boss lady?" Gwen set her heavy bag down on her counter and pulled on her smooth blonde ponytail that hung down her back like a horse mane. She was still trying to be sexy at forty, rocking jeweled stilettos, a bright orange midrift and blue jeans so tight they could have been painted on. And she didn't care that her hips were too wide and her stomach too pudgy for it. She was determined to look like a twenty year old, despite the fact that she had three kids at home.

"Making money and more money." Autumn put hands on her hips. "Oh by the way, no more eating in the back. I found an unwelcome visitor running around."

"Oh no damn, are you serious?" Gwen pulled up her jeans, which needed a belt. "What, a rat?"

"Not quite."

"A roach?" Janet asked.

"Yup."

Gwen turned up her lip in disgust. "Damn you got to be kidding. Are you really serious?"

"As a heart attack." Autumn picked up her remote control and turned on the MP3 player and selected radio. Tom Joyner's baritone voice bounced off the bright yellow walls. He was cracking a joke on people who have extramarital affairs.

"Sounds like he's talking about me ladies." Gwen laughed as she picked lint balls from her top. "I have no shame in my game though.

People can hee-haw all they want but Jamie takes care of business. In fact I'm giving him a promotion." She slapped hands with Janet. "Brother drops it like it's hot!"

Janet let out this old lady cackle. "All right Chiquita."

Autumn shook her head, bringing out a stack of fresh white towels. "You're right Gwen. Shame isn't part of your vocabulary but I say it shouldn't be. Life's too short to carry around a bunch of guilt. Do what you have to do period."

"Yeah my sentiments exactly. What his wife doesn't do, I *do*." Gwen smirked, setting a can of hair sheen on top of her counter. "And *do* it weeeellllllll ladies!"

"Tell it right or not at all now," Janet said, primping in front of the mirror. She looked even more like a Hispanic doll baby since she had just dyed her hair jet black. It lay in dark smoky coils around her heart-shaped, made up face. "See Jamie's wife never learned what I did a long time ago when my first husband left me. Handle your business in the bedroom and there will be no creeping, stepping out and all that nonsense. He'll run home to you every single night."

"Ain't that the truth." Gwen's phone chirped. She glanced at it, sucked her teeth and rolled her eyes. "Damn, it's DBD. He didn't pick up the kids the other night trying to be a big Willie. I need to blast him out for that," she muttered.

"What does DBD stand for?" Autumn frowned.

"That means deadbeat dad!" Janet screamed, pointing the end of her rat-tail comb. "Still not pulling his weight Gwen? That is too sad. But I bet those kids are his claim to fame. Bragging rights since his family jewels were working," she sighed. "Talk about a lack of conscience."

"That's right. You have him pegged down to his underwear." Gwen threw her hand in the air. "He's going to have a lack of life if he continues to dog his obligations." She stopped to sneeze. "I tell you, your cousins."

"*My* cousins. Those are your people. I'm Puerto Rican. Can't you tell?" Janet pointed to her hair.

"Janet you are only *half* Puerto Rican. The half I'm talking to can relate to what I'm saying, capiche?" Gwen said, narrowing her eyes.

Janet sucked her teeth and began speaking in Spanish.

"Oh naw baby. You need to speak English to me baby," Gwen said putting a hand on her hip. "I don't know what you're saying. Could be calling me a name or something right in my face, like they probably do down at that market. I'm tired of you immigrants coming over here not speaking standard American."

"Would you two tone it down," Autumn warned. She shook her head at the trifling tone of the conversation. She went back to the front area thinking about her own lack of conscience. It had been beat out of her a long time ago. And since then she had decided not to feel one bit of guilt over anything, especially what had happened to good old Uncle Harry.

She could still hear his screams in her dreams but he had deserved everything he had gotten, just like the others. As far as she was concerned, karma was a wronged dog and it had finally come back to bite him…Now he was six feet under. Buried with all her bad memories and tap dancing with the devil down in hell.

Autumn checked the schedules on the computer. "You have a full plate today Gwen?"

"Uh-huh, you know it boss lady," Gwen answered, sucking her teeth as she wiped down her countertop. "Mondays, Mondays," she said wiping down her station. "Worse day of the week for sure. Once I make it past a Monday I think I can make it through but it's tough. Whoever said that day was blue was right on point boss lady," she paused. "And why do you open on that day anyway? We're like the only black salon anywhere to do that."

"To stay ahead of the competition Gwen. Think about it, we offer what the other salons don't. Convenience. That is the word of the year," Autumn said.

"And I guess that's why you're a step above." Janet added, putting a hand on her hip. "One of those cutting edge sisters, progressive and innovative."

"I'd like to think so," Autumn said as the door opened bringing in a burst of heat. In walked the twins, Michelle and Mikelli fussing like rattlesnakes in a cage as Mama J used to say. They were identical but it was easy to tell them apart. One had shoulder length curly auburn hair and a mole on her right cheek and the other had a honey-brown colored bob and a mole on her left cheek. Their hair may have been different but they had the same sense of style, flamboyant with sequence, feathers and beads on everything they wore from foot to toe and this day was no exception. Almost like they were about to work the runway. And they were model tall too so they probably would have qualified. In fact Michelle had dabbled in it for a minute before getting that calling to do hair.

"I'm not going to lend you my ride again Mikelli. Remember the last time it came back with a bent fender and I couldn't roll up the back window." Michelle waved to Autumn and made a beeline to her station which had pictures of several made up clients stuck in the sleeve of the mirror.

"Oh God help us! It's too early in the morning for all this, but damn if there must be a show I need to get a good seat," Gwen muttered, still pulling packs of rollers and clips from out of her bag. "Break out the popcorn, extra butter and a box of Raisinets, ladies?" Her eyes remained trained on the sparks flying between the two sisters.

"Forget you!" Michelle said to Gwen and turned back to Mikelli.

"I'm your sister and you treat me like a damn step child!" Mikelli put her hand on her hips and rolled her neck in typical sister girl mode. "Blood is supposed to be thicker than water *sister*. Thicker than money or even property *sister*. Supposed to be able to count on you for everything *sister.*"

"Yeah well blood can't pay my repair bill," she paused, flipping her hair away from her face. "No, I treat you like a grown woman who needs to get her own ride. You make more than enough damn money up in here. Money is coming out of your behind."

Michelle shoved the flattened palm of her hand in Mikelli's face. "Talk to it."

Mikelli turned and bent over, slapping her right butt cheek. "You talk to that. Bootylicious."

"All right ladies." Autumn got up and stood between them. "Can you all take this up on your own time? This *is* a place of business and I *assume* you came here to work. Settle it later."

"Yeah *later*." Mikelli smacked her full lips and glowered at Michelle before storming off to her own station.

*Just another day at the shop*, Autumn thought, shaking her head.

# Chapter Eight

By noon Autumn was absolutely pissed. Vanessa still had not shown up and it was the second time in three weeks that she had pulled this. Autumn sat down in the chair, realizing that she would have to man the receptionist desk possibly all day. After awhile she starting hoping that Vanessa did show up just so she could fire her. She didn't take crap from any of her employees, especially those who had lax attitudes when it came to work. That was why she had been through more receptionists and stylists than anybody she knew but she expected perfection. She demanded it of other people because she expected it of herself. She had had this shop for over nine years now and had a good rep and the only way she could maintain that was to have people who had a strong work ethic. That was the only thing Uncle Harry had taught her was strong work ethics even though it never paid off for him. When he croaked, the only thing he had was that house she lived in and a few hundred bucks in the bank. She was determined to come out better than that.

*Who you been sleepin' wit? 'Cause that baby you carryin' ain't mine little girl. Who you been partin' your legs for?* Uncle Harry mumbled.

"Want some chicken wings?" Janet asked startling Autumn.

"No thanks." Autumn cleared the cards and flowers, dumping them into an empty cardboard box that had been used to store hair conditioner.

It didn't take long before the clients started streaming in one by one. They were all regulars, mostly the sixty-five and older crowd. They were retired women but still wanted to look great. The younger crowd didn't start pouring in until after work hours.

Autumn greeted each of them, asking how their family was doing. She had learned enough about each one for them to regard her almost like family.

"Yes, Naomi is doing just fine," Ms. Felis said proudly of her granddaughter. "She's graduating from Spelman College next year. Can you believe four years has gone by already?" She pushed up her steel-framed glasses.

"No it's hard to believe." Autumn smiled while Janet led Ms. Felis to her station. Seemed like yesterday when Naomi was coming in with Ms. Felis. Now she was finishing up in pre-med and on her way to med school. Time flies.

After things died down, Autumn went back to her financial books from the weekend. It was a week after July fourth so things had been a little slow. It was like that right after any holiday because everyone had her hair done from the week before. Only those with standing appointments would come in for at least the next few days. She cracked open the red book and suddenly saw Scott's face twisted in agony. She shook her head to clear her mind. She needed to get a grip.

She checked her gold watch realizing that Joy was also late. Joy never came to work this late. She was one of those straight-laced people, who always did as she should. There was probably not a devious bone in Joy's body. Maybe the result of her childhood. Both of her parents had been ministers. Now usually offspring of the clergy ended up being crazy and rebellious but she was the ideal preacher's daughter.

"Uh excuse me, miss?" A deep voice caused Autumn to look up. An extremely, oh so damn fine, gorgeous tall dude with a thick mustache stood on the other side of the counter grinning down at her. His skin was as smooth as melted chocolate, which was even more defined against the white Izod polo that clung to his muscular chest. Yeah, he was probably arrogant too but in her profession, she had to be nice to everybody, even men. It was all about money.

"May I help you?" She laid down her book; curious as hell to find out why he was even there though. Could be he needed directions to one of the other shops? Or wanted to buy a gift certificate for his girlfriend or wife? Something about him seemed familiar to her though, but she could not place it.

"I'd like to get a manicure," he said in a normal tone, not lowering it even an octave. Apparently he was not at all ashamed even though just about every woman's head had turned in his direction.

Autumn nodded, figuring he was probably one of those metro sexual brothers that liked to keep it tight. "Uh, no problem we can do that," she paused, glancing at the wall clock. "But our manicurist isn't coming in until ten. If you want to wait, it shouldn't be but another fifteen minutes or so?"

"Hey, I've got nothing but time." He winked.

Michelle appeared out of the blue scooping him up like he would be her next husband. "Do you need anything else until then? A trim, a facial, me possibly?" She twisted a thick lock of hair around her finger. Autumn rolled her eyes, knowing that if Michelle kept it up she was going to be standing on the unemployment line before the month was out.

"No," he chuckled. "Uh, I'm cool." He slipped his hands in his dark slacks. "I'll just wait over there." He pointed to the comfortable pale pink seats lined up against the wall.

Autumn had to give it to Michelle, she had good taste. He was definitely attractive. Even still she would never allow herself to get close or even imagine the possibilities. Men were all the same: bottom line. They used a woman up and spit them out just like Uncle Harry had done to her and other females. She refused to allow another man to do her like that.

She went back to her books, trying to focus even though she could feel his eyes on her. The door opened and in came Joy. She was dragging her feet and looking whipped. Besides the fact that her eyes were hooded, she had bags bigger than the one she carried over her shoulder.

"Are you okay?" Autumn raised an eyebrow.

"School, girl. Wore me out!" Joy yawned. "Sometimes I want to quit."

Autumn nodded as Tonya, the manicurist marched in wearing a pair of sunglasses that covered half of her face. Autumn wondered if her man had been beating on her again.

"You have someone waiting," Autumn said, studying Tonya who was still fly in a white summer dress and gold sandals. Her hair was in a tight chignon.

Tonya nodded without saying a word, going to her area and plopping down. When she did not remove the glasses, Autumn knew for sure that she must've gotten another black eye. That made Autumn's blood boil. If she had a chance, she would love to give that man a taste of his own damn medicine. Nothing would give Autumn more joy. The man was an animal just like Uncle Harry and the others. Monsters like that should be eliminated.

Autumn got up, went over to Tonya and leaned down, whispering in her ear. "Are you up for this? Seems like you had another run in. Want to talk about it?"

"No, there's nothing to talk about," Tonya said quietly. "I just ran into the door last night that's all." She gave a nervous laugh and shrugged her shoulders. "Trust me, I'm fine."

"Let me know if things become anything else," Autumn said. She patted Tonya on her shoulder and waved Mr. Hershey Bar over.

An hour later, Tonya finished with Mr. Hershey Bar and he seemed pleased. Autumn felt good about that. She aimed to have everyone smiling, even this man.

Instead of leaving he hung around the counter.

"I'd like to make another appointment now if possible," he paused, focusing on Autumn. She was picking up something from him. "I'm sorry that I didn't catch your name."

"Of course I'm glad that you were satisfied and it's Autumn."

"Um beautiful name for a lovely lady." He kept his eyes on her. "You're the owner right?"

"Yes, how'd you know?" Autumn looked up, keeping a straight face. She was not impressed with his feeble attempt at engaging her in conversation.

"Tonya told me," he said.

Autumn stared at the computer screen to escape his sexy as hell eyes. "What day is good for you, Mister uh?"

"Anders. Cole Anders. Next Monday at the same time?" he asked.

Autumn scanned across the date and time. "Looks like that will work." She typed it in and handed him a square index size card. "Now if you could fill out this little profile. We do it for all of our clients to keep track of their needs."

"Cool, no problem. Sounds like a great idea to me," he said, scooping the card as their fingers touched and it actually brought pleasant thoughts to mind for once. For one they were warm like Daddy D's had been. She thought back to when he used to take her down to the park and she would try to keep up with him. Three of her steps had equaled one of his. Losing patience, he would pick her up in his arms and swing her around. She would throw her head back and watch the sky and clouds blur together as she grew dizzy.

"You happen to have a pen?" he asked. She gave him one then watched him go back to the chairs and sit back down. He immediately started filling it out and she found herself not able to take her eyes off of him. He seemed so different from the others but she wasn't sure why.

She took her eyes away, figuring she was just fantasizing. She sat in front of the computer and confirmed that the slot was open. She found herself staring at Cole again.

Where had she seen him before? At a club, the gym, or a restaurant? He was the same color of her father and that was comforting. And the mustache reminded her of Daddy D's too.

"Cole, I'll give you an appointment card," Autumn called out. He nodded and came back, handing her the index card and she passed one of her pink cards. "Well, we'll see you next week." She blinked.

"You certainly will." He winked again and went out the door and into the sunlight.

"Um that was a fine mama-jama, sweet Jesus, Mary, Joseph and everybody else," Michelle said. "He would qualify as a candidate for my next man, know what I'm saying. I'd love him to chain me up or beat me with a night stick anytime," Michelle said, running a wide-toothed comb through her clients' tight curls to loosen them. "You feel me Gwen?"

Tonya made a little noise from the corner almost like a trapped animal.

"You have issues," Mikelli said shaking her head. "Hard to believe we're related."

"Put your eyes back in your head Michelle. This is not some meat market," Autumn replied. "Get back to it."

"I feel you Michelle. I really do," Gwen said. "He was fine even though I don't think he was feeling you to be honest boo," Gwen added, twisting her lips like she was really sympathetic. "Probably gay though. How many brothers do you know get their nails done? I suggest that you watch your back on that one. You know all these DC brothers are on the DL." Gwen put the last roller in her clients' hair and patted her on the shoulder, signaling it was time for the dryer."Did you know that black women are the fastest growing cases of AIDS? You can't play like you used to or at least not without him wrapping it up."

"I don't want to hear that Gwen! Don't be jealous because he spoke to me and *not* you," Michelle hissed as she went to the sink to wash out a comb.

"Uh Michelle, you threw yourself on that man. I guess you did exchange words but they were all about play and rejection." Mikelli stopped to get in a laugh and hand slap with Gwen, then continued running a flat iron through her girl's head, pressing it into bone-straight tresses.

"Bite me," Michelle said.

"I think he and Autumn would make a cute couple though." Gwen smiled. "He is fine and you are beautiful. He is tall and you are tall and guess what, he is even taller than you which you don't find every day."

"Whatever Gwen. Cole is my customer and that's it," Autumn replied even though Gwen was on target with the tall thing.

"I think he's a cop right?" Mikelli smoothed out her client's chestnut brown hair into a wrap.

*A cop*, Autumn wondered? She checked his profile card. First off he had very neat handwriting, which was highly unusual for a man. Most of them preferred chicken scratch. He lived over in Penn Branch, an upper middle class community across the Anacostia River. And he did list his profession as police officer in their precinct. That is where she had seen him. He had been patrolling the area.

Of course this new information made her uneasy. She figured it was probably irrational but she still wondered if he was actually coming to the shop to investigate her and his cover was getting a manicure? She swallowed and filed the card under the A's. When the next receptionist came on board, they could type the information in the computer.

Speaking of the devil, the bell to the front door chimed and Vanessa made her grand entrance in a loud yellow biker suit, slurping loudly through a straw to draw whatever the heck was in the corners of her plastic cup. She waved to Gwen like she was right as rain and then wiggled over to the desk and was about to say her standard "hey" before Autumn picked up the small box with Vanessa's stuff in it. She slammed it on the desk, causing Vanessa's eyes to zero in on it. Her orbs grew wide. She opened her mouth but Autumn put up a hand to silence her.

"Vanessa, you have real nerve stepping in here now." Autumn gripped the edges of the box and cocked her head to the side, barring further entrance to the desk. She wanted to erase the smug grin from this chic's face.

"I had a doctor's appointment." Vanessa frowned, tossing her cup in the trash and smacking her lips. "When was that a crime?"

"And did you call and let anyone know about this appointment?" Autumn blinked.

"Uh no, I didn't think I had to." She put a hand on her hip and rose up to her full height of six whatever. "And then the metro broke down again."

"Step." Autumn stood tall too. She was only five nine but she was bad enough to squash any bug that stood in her way.

"But—"

"Uh...bounce." Autumn blinked. "Good day to ya and take your mess with you." She passed Vanessa her box.

"What about my check?" Vanessa's bottom lip trembled as her eyes darted to Gwen, her cut buddy. But Gwen kept silent as she flat ironed her customer's long hair, not wanting to put her behind on the line.

"Look for it in the mail baby doll. It'll be next to your unemployment check," Autumn said.

Vanessa stood there for a minute debating on whether to fight Autumn or leave. She wisely chose the latter.

On her way out, she mumbled the "B" word but Autumn was not phased in the least. She had been called much worse.

# Chapter Nine

Autumn locked up around eleven thirty. Some people would say her days were way too long but they were not long enough actually. She scrubbed the place down, double-checked to make sure there were no crumbs anywhere. She was still mad about that roach.

Sighing, she made sure that the lights had been switched off in the back room and the computer as well. She saved money everywhere she could to keep overhead low.

She passed the station where the new stylist would be sitting come tomorrow. Over the phone, Sasha had been interesting just as Joy had said. He had come down from the Big Apple and all references had come back as mad stellar. Even better than that, he had been the top stylist at three salons where he had worked including the world famous Glass Hair Factory. That alone was enough to get him through the door. So needless to say, he would be a right nice addition. Might even give Gwen a run for her money and with her jealous streak, he would need to watch where he laid his drinks.

Autumn picked up her purse and sighed. Another day down and she needed to grab a bite and head on to the homestead. Funny how normal her life was ninety percent of the time. Just like the average Joe. Go to work, come home, eat a hot meal, go to bed and start the same thing all over again. But it was that ten percent that would shock the hell out of most people, even her sometimes. Honestly, she didn't start out to hurt anyone. Never thought that Caramel would be a part of her life. It just evolved into this need to feel vindicated. This need to release. To get rid of the rage within, even if for a little while.

*Baby girl, you got to spread all that lovin' around."*

Autumn paused, feeling paralyzed at Uncle Harry's voice invading her space. She whirled around but she was alone in the shop. Even still she smelled English Leather, making her want to gag. She closed her eyes, seeing Uncle Harry's friend, another trucker in a light blue uniform, standing beside Uncle Harry. Both had their arms crossed, inspecting her. She was crouched in the corner of the motel room, shaking and needing to go to the bathroom badly. Not sure what they planned to do with her.

*She's damaged goods,* Uncle Harry said in a flat voice

*Yeah but she's cute as a button,* his friend added, a smirk on his face.

She knew from just looking that he had already made up his mind. She started over, as her heart was going so fast that she thought it might stop. As he grew closer, she picked up this awful scent and wanted to throw up. It was armpits and unwashed behind, like he had not seen water in days. Maybe weeks.

*Enjoy her. I've had a lot of good times with her.* Uncle Harry chuckled. *I'd like to watch.*

*You are kinky,* the man said. He had lifted Autumn up and carried her to the sofa. She couldn't fight him off and he had done what he wanted with her...She wished that she could find him now. She had tried...If she had he would have paid for what he had done to her...She would have stuck the butt of a gun so far up his ass...

A light rap at the door caught her off guard and she jumped, dropping the pair of scissors on the floor. Well who the hell would be trying to get in this late? She went over and peered out the glass to see Cole, the cop standing there in uniform. She unlocked the door, wondering why he was here.

"Hey Autumn," he paused, his eyes searching behind her. "I saw a light on and since it's late, I was just checking to make sure that it wasn't an intruder or that you were all right."

She gave him a sweet smile. "No it's just me." She used her body to block the doorway. Cop or not, he could be crazy. Crazier than her. "And I'm fine."

"Okay." He nodded. "Just looking out since I was in the neighborhood."

"I appreciate that," she said.

He gave her a sideway glance. "I'm not trying to get in your business but are you planning to stay much longer?"

"No actually I was just leaving," she said.

"Good, I can at least walk you to your car," he said.

"Sure," she said.

She slung her purse over her shoulder and pulled out her car keys, not seeing anything wrong with that. If he wanted to do the Officer Friendly deal that was cool with her. No harm to that.

They stepped out into what felt like a wall of heat, which had no signs of letting up. They both turned at the sound of an ambulance siren wailing as it zoomed by, unsettling Autumn's nerves to the point where she gripped the handle of her bag.

She had parked a block away so they had a bit of a walk. Their walk was done in silence and she hoped it would stay that way. She had no interest in this man and she would be happy if the feeling was mutual.

Despite the late hour, Georgia Avenue was still buzzing with activity. They passed the barbershop next door where two barbers were still clipping away at heads. Then they came up on the jazz spot, the sounds of Coltrane drifting out onto the street. Most of them had been in existence for more than fifty years. And they were mostly black-owned businesses. In fact she remembered Daddy D bragging about it. So she was surrounded by relics and culture.

She saw Cole's unmarked cruiser parked directly behind hers. She quickly noticed that her meter had expired. She gave him a side-glance wondering if he had noticed. She needed to go on and acquire the land located directly behind the shop for a paved parking lot.

She turned to him. "Well thanks for walking me to my car." She hit the remote control button.

"No problem. Just be careful out here this late. Not trying to scare you but they had a rape nearby and a string of robberies over the past month." He licked his bottom lip. He was sexy, like one of those bachelors in *Essence* or *Ebony*.

"Good advice." She paused as an awkward silence settled between them. She reached for her car door. "And good night."

He stepped back and slipped his hands in his pockets. "All right Autumn."

She got behind the wheel of her car while he still stood looking in. *What the hell?*

She pushed down the automatic release button to see what he needed from her. She had a sudden urge for a cigarette.

He seemed to be a decent guy but still, he was also dangerous to have around. Like stepping in a minefield.

"I just wanted to say that you have a nice shop," he paused as the CB radio crackled and a voice asked for Caramel. She was shocked to hear it. Of all times now? She reached over and quickly switched it off.

"You were saying?" she asked giving an innocent smile.

"I've passed by it several times and I'm glad that I finally stopped in," he said.

"So I can impress a cop?" she asked.

"You did. I'm not just saying that either Autumn," he said.

*You can make this hard or easy.* She jerked her head to clear it. Uncle Harry wouldn't stop messing with her. Cole frowned.

"You okay?"

"Yeah…fine." She peeled her eyes away, and started her car. "I need to get home. I've got to get up early."

"Understood, I won't keep you. But if you need me for anything, let me know." He backed up. "You take care and I'll see you next week. For the appointment."

"See you then." She watched him walk off and go back to his car. As soon as he pulled off, her shoulders slumped. Why was he even in the area? Was he spying on her? She began to wonder if he was investigating her after all. Yeah, her imagination could get the best of her.

She maneuvered her car into the flow of traffic, telling herself to pull it together. There was no reason to be jumpy. Number one he had nothing on her and no reason to suspect her of anything. She was just a business owner. Harmless. And for two most of her activities were done outside of the city on her travels.

"It's just your nerves Autumn. You need to get a grip." She pulled out a cigarette and lit up, feeling calmer after the first puff. She felt in control again.

She drove by Chicken and Ribs Galore, the place her parents had co-owned before the incident. It had been right next door to Mama J's old hair shop.

Autumn had a sudden taste for fried chicken wings but she could never go into that restaurant. Too many memories…She made a right on Colesville Road ignoring the shops lining both sides of the street. Just then she heard a horn honking behind her. It was a familiar black Mercedes. The person behind the wheel was waving but she ignored him, stopping at the light. He pulled up right next to her and she turned to see that it was Ricky.

She looked off quickly and screeched off down the street, watching in the rear view mirror as he turned off in the direction of the City Place Mall.

"Bastard," she mumbled. She happened to look to her right and saw a guy trying to cross the street, holding the arm of some woman. The man seemed familiar. Jonas? She squinted. Damn, was that Jonas? Sloping forehead, beady eyes, crew cut. Oh hell yeah, it was him! She mashed her foot to the accelerator as he stepped off the curb. He suddenly turned in time to see her barreling towards him and his eyes widened as he jumped back on the sidewalk, grabbing the woman. He shouted something as she passed by and she smirked. Asshole deserved to die.

She had only allowed herself to get involved with two men her whole life and Jonas had been one of them. He had used and abused her. She had him in the hospital though. Cracked his skull open with a food processor. He deserved what he had gotten.

The other guy had been decent like Officer Cole until he left her. Told her she needed to seek a psychiatrist. Of course she didn't let him get away with that. Hell no, she had taken care of him like the rest of the losers. He had ended up being no different than the truckers on the road that she found and eliminated…She had lost count of all the ones unlucky enough to get caught in her snare over the years. She had enjoyed seeing them suffer. It gave her great joy when they drew that last breath. They were all like her Uncle Harry. Believing that they could have her and she took care of them swiftly.

"Go tell it on the mountain," she started singing in a low voice. She remembered when Uncle Harry took her to that doctor when she was knocked up with her babies. She had just turned fifteen and had no idea how she would handle having twins. She recalled how nervous he had been telling the nurse she was loose and he didn't know what to do with her. "That Jesus Christ is born…"

# Chapter Ten

J oy was finishing up her second corn beef sandwich when Autumn came in. She seemed in one of those distant moods. Without saying a word, she went upstairs to her bedroom. Joy took her final bite and reached for another bag of chips, still feeling ravenous. It was like she had a tapeworm or something. She always wanted to eat and eat some more and it showed on her hips, thighs and stomach. Thank goodness Ricky liked her thick but she knew once he popped the question, she would go on a serious diet. And once she got those pounds off, she would be sure to keep them off. Having all that weight was just protection from her past. What she had done. She shut her eyes to block out the memories. Would she ever be able to forget?

She opened her eyes, determined to move on. She had too many things going on to get caught up in what she couldn't change. She sighed, closing her psych book, tired of reading about psychopaths. John Gacy. Jeffrey Dahmer. It was usually interesting but she just was not in the mood. Some people thought that her fascination with all that criminal stuff was a bit warped but somebody had to study it. And yeah it was scary to think that people like that existed. People that lacked remorse, a conscience or any feelings whatsoever. And the worse part is they seemed so normal initially. Like the girl next door or the guy down the street that helped to start your car. She found it all disturbing yet fascinating; her confirmation that she had definitely selected the right profession.

She made sure that the kitchen was sparkling to the point where anybody could eat off the floor. Then she switched off the light and went back into the living room to relax, watch some TV.

She found a movie getting ready to start on the *LMN* channel and she debated on whether to check that out or one of her favorite taped episodes of *Oprah, American Idol,* or *CSI.* She went on and decided to check out an old *Oprah* episode, the one with the cast of *Dreamgirls* in it. The one before Jenifer Hudson won the Oscar. She pulled out the super size bag of barbecue chips as Boris hopped onto her lap and curled up.

He proceeded to lick his paws and then for some reason he hopped down and ran off somewhere. She settled back against the sofa cushions and checked her watch, hoping that Ricky showed up soon. He was late. Really late and it was going to be a booty call soon.

Just as Oprah came out, looking gorgeous as ever and the audience started going wild, Boris trotted back over gripping an object tightly between his jaws. He dropped it at Joy's feet.

"Whatcha got boy." She looked down and chills traveled up her spine. "What the—?"

It was a bloody knife! A carving knife with a wooden handle. Where in the world had Boris gotten it from? It looked kind of familiar though. Had it been in the kitchen? But she would have seen it.

She jumped up from the couch, crept past Boris and the knife and darted into the kitchen followed by Boris. She grabbed a paper towel and headed back for the living room. She went back over to the knife and Boris was sniffing at it.

"Scoot!" She pushed him away and bent down. She picked it up, totally repulsed. There was a short hair sticking out of the end of the blade by its handle and she felt waves of nausea. A million thoughts raced through her head. It just didn't seem as if it had been used in cooking and whatever had been cut had been slaughtered and the blood was so thick.

Boris meowed and licked at his fur before looking up at Joy for answers.

"I don't know about this one boy," Joy said wishing that she could go ask Autumn who was sound asleep by now. She debated on whether to just throw it out and made the decision to just chuck it. Who would want to use it again?

She wrapped it in towels and tossed it into the trash. The lid closed with a loud snap causing her to jump. She definitely would ask Autumn about it in the morning. She was sure there was a reasonable explanation.

She went back to the couch and tried put it out of her mind. A bloody knife just didn't fit in with their comfortable home environment. It was like a rectangle peg trying to go through a square hole. She picked up the bag of chips, not focusing on anything but what she had just seen. It had disturbed her. And she didn't know how to wrap her mind around it. But maybe she was making a big deal out of it for nothing. Could be a gag. Last Halloween, Autumn had been dressed as a serial killer. Yeah that's what it was, a gag. The only problem was the hairs hanging off the knife.

She watched Jennifer Hudson, grinning all over herself, still in shock over the attention she was getting. She was Joy's hero, a big girl that made it; but as much as she tried, she couldn't focus. She turned off *Oprah* figuring she needed to watch when she could focus because now wasn't the time.

Suddenly the doorbell rang and she squealed with pleasure and relief. There was her man, better late than never and she needed him. She lifted Boris from her lap and set him down. He meowed in protest, giving her a pitiful look.

"I'll be right back," she said even as he hopped to the floor and followed her.

Joy padded through the living room and across to the hall floor. She would love to give Ricky a key but Autumn would have a fit. She would see it more like he was trying to move in than just a gesture of love.

She answered the door and Ricky gave her a long passionate kiss, then whacked her on the behind.

"Whatcha got to eat for a brother?" He threw his sports coat at her, loosened his tie and went straight to the kitchen without breaking his stride.

"I wondered if you weren't coming," she said.

"Naw just got tied up. Work was off the hook today. They're trying to work me like a slave. They are getting every dime and more from me. And in being the only brother I am still trying to prove myself." He grabbed the package of Oreos from the counter and ripped it open, pulling two out while Joy watched with her mouth hanging open.

"Those are Autumn's. She's going to give me drama and grief over that," Joy said.

Joy shook her head knowing it would be on and popping. Autumn hated when anybody touched her stuff. He shoved another one in his mouth, dropping crumbs on the floor.

"Come on Rick." She went to get the broom.

"Sorry." He crunched loudly as he leaned against the counter. "I'll buy her crazy ass another bag. I saw her on the street earlier. I beeped and this heifer looked at me like I was some stranger or some shit." He shook his head. "J I'm telling you, she has issues. She needs to see somebody seriously. Like a head shrinker."

"She's just been stressed out lately." Joy swept the crumbs into the dustpan. "Trying to hold down the fort at work. She just let go another receptionist, and we found out there are bugs." Joy shrugged. "It's not easy owning a salon."

"Whatever." He brushed crumbs off the front of his shirt. "I told you what's up with her nasty disposition. She needs a stiff one." He munched on yet another cookie and then reached for another. "The woman hates my damn guts and I haven't done anything to her."

Joy didn't respond, not wanting to go there in Autumn's own house. "Change the subject."

"Yeah alright." He pulled a cartoon of milk from the fridge. "On to bigger and better, guess where I went today baby girl?" He started to put the cartoon to his lips and Joy yelled out for him to get a glass.

"Damn you're uptight."

"I have to live here." She went to the cabinet and pulled out a cup.

"Well ask me where I went today?"

"Where?" She handed it to him.

"The jewelry store," he said smirking.

A jewelry store? Oh for what? Was it finally what she had been praying for? Was he going to make an honest woman out of her?

"What's at the jewelry store?" she asked, trying to stay cool just in case it wasn't what she thought. Oooooohhhh please Lord!

"This!" He whipped out a small red velvet box from his pocket. "Bam!" He held it up.

Before she could scream, he was on his knees on the kitchen floor. "Joy will you?"

"Yes I will!" she said between quivering lips. Tears of joy surfaced at the corner of her eyes as she held out a trembling finger. She had wanted this for so long. She loved him more than any thing.

He slipped the diamond ring on her finger and it sparkled in the bright light. She looked at it and figured it had to be at least one carat. It looked like it had been made for her, just like Ricky had.

"It's absolutely beautiful," she gushed.

"Like you." He stood up and kissed her gently on the lips and she knew life could not get better than this. She started thinking about her own secret.

The thing that really would hold both of them back from reaching all of their dreams.

She rushed into his arms, closing her eyes and wondering if she could ever tell him the truth about herself. Only Autumn knew the real deal.

# Chapter Eleven

Autumn was not the envious type. Especially when it related to marriage. She never believed in it personally and based on her past observations it was a crock of shit, but she was happy if Joy was happy. Joy was definitely the homemaker type although why she would settle for someone like Ricky was a total and complete mystery. It wasn't that he was a bad guy. Just not what Autumn would have pictured or wanted for her friend. Ricky had come from the streets even if he pretended that his button-down image had always been a part of him. Ricky had been around the block a few times, coming from the rough projects over in Southeast; and she definitely had his number. He had hit on her too many times to count, particularly when they had first started dating. She also knew that he had cheated on Joy at least once. She had let it go because Joy seemed happy and from what Autumn heard, it had been a one-night stand at a bachelor party. But if she heard of anything else, he would have to be dealt with. Joy was like a sister to her and she didn't mind dropping him like a hot cake.

"So, you are going to be the maid of honor Autumn?" Joy asked sipping on her freshly squeezed glass of OJ.

"Whoa slow down superstar," Autumn said. She sat down at the kitchen table and poured mustard over her turkey sausage. "You guys just got engaged last night. What is the damn hurry?" She frowned. Joy was so impulsive, always trying to just do it.

"No hurry, just thinking ahead." Joy gazed at her ring again.

Autumn shook her head. Yup, Joy couldn't see the forest for the trees. She was definitely sprung. Autumn knew the next few months were going to be hell. Joy would go absolutely overboard and her mama, who had been waiting for her only daughter to get hitched, would go absolutely out of her fucking mind. Mrs. Henderson always had to outdo everybody else just to prove that she was part of the privileged few, that she had been blessed and lived right.

"You have a right to be happy now." Autumn spread margarine on her wheat bagel. "But you have time."

"A part of me wants to do it before he changes his mind," Joy admitted.

Autumn frowned. "Why would he do that?"

"He's a very successful brother and he can get anybody." Joy twirled a thick loc of hair around her finger.

Autumn put down her knife ready to give a lecture. "J, Ricky needs to be damn happy you are agreeing to marry him. You're worth more than his sorry behind and you need to start seeing yourself that way or he's going to run right over you girl. Remember he needs you, not the other way around."

Joy's eyes grew wide as she listened. Autumn continued getting geared up.

"And what about your past?" Autumn asked point blank. "You can't hide that mess

forever. Eventually he will find out. You told him right?" Autumn knew from Joy's expression that the secret was still just between them. "I can't believe you haven't told him," Autumn said blinking.

"No." Joy averted her eyes because she knew how it must look.

Autumn sighed heavily. "Joy, you are setting yourself up big time."

"I realize that," Joy said swallowing. "I just don't know how to tell him."

"You need to find a way before you marry the man. Because again he will find out later on and you'll be the one hurt."

"I know." Joy nodded.

"I'm just looking out for you," Autumn said. "I don't give a damn about him."

"You always have my back. We have each other's back."

"Sure 'nough J," Autumn said biting into her toast. She didn't have anyone else but Joy.

"By the way," Joy paused. "I found something really strange yesterday."

"What?" Autumn asked chewing away. Joy reached for her coffee mug, her ring sparkling.

"Actually Boris found it," she hesitated.

"Come with it J." Autumn met her gaze and didn't let down.

"He brought me a bloody knife." She laughed. "Girl, I almost had a heart attack."

Autumn snorted, crossing her arms. "A bloody knife?"

"Yeah I think it's from last year when we went to Gwen's Halloween party."

"Oh yeah." Autumn nodded. "I remember that."

Damn that stupid cat was tryin' to ruin her game. She had put that knife in the basement and he had gotten to it.

Joy relaxed. "I figured that.

"What did you do with it?"

"Threw it out. Hope you don't mind."

"Whatever," Autumn said waving. "Where?"

Joy jerked her head toward the trashcan. "Don't want Boris hurting himself."

"Not to change the subject but I need to check out the weather," Autumn said, pushing the green button on the remote, hoping to get some juicy updates on the morning news. She was in luck. A tearful woman wearing a T-shirt and flanked by two teenage kids was speaking. Autumn turned up the volume.

"And please if you see my husband, *please* call the police. We want him to come home. He is a good man. He's also diabetic." The woman broke down, her shoulders shaking as her young children clung to her legs.

The reporter came back into the picture. "Scott Benson was driving a truck and supposed to show up in Elizabeth City, North Carolina but he never made it. His truck was found in a hotel parking lot in Virginia Beach. The Columbia, Maryland man has been missing for several days now and the company is posting a reward. Once again if you have seen this man, please contact local police." They flashed a picture of Scott and Autumn drudged up an image of him being tied up on that bed. He had been a local, which was a complete shock to her.

"Again this seems to be the work of the East Coast slasher. This is Veronica Harper."

"Wow, how ironic that you were just down there," Joy said slowly rubbing her arms. "Too close for comfort."

"Yeah that's scary huh?"

"Yes you have to be careful on these roads." Joy bit her bottom lip and shook her head. "Gosh what a shame. Can you imagine if that was your man? What that woman must be going through God bless her. Hopefully he's okay and there was no foul play. I'll have to pray for her."

Autumn grunted. She suddenly felt irritated. If Joy only knew how this man tried to prey on her. Tried to use her, she might not think it was such a shame.

Scott had gotten what he fucking deserved, period. Autumn was not interested in hearing the pity. It was nauseating. She turned off the TV and stood, taking her half-eaten food to the counter.

"Too much bad news. Do they ever report on anything positive especially in the morning? I don't want to start my day on a sour note," Autumn said knowing that usually she enjoyed seeing her escapades on the screen or in the papers but for some reason it really irked her. Could be because of her Aunt Flo who was coming and bringing Cousin PMS with her.

"I know, I agree about all that bad news." Joy dug into her bowl of fruit. "It makes you wonder if anything wonderful is going on in the world. Guess people don't want to hear that though. They think it's boring."

"Uh, well I better get ready to go in to the shop." Autumn headed out then turned to face Joy. "Oh yeah by the way, can you call the supply guy Joy? I double-checked the order and he left off three bottles of shampoo."

"I'll get right on it. No worries," Joy said.

Autumn flew up the steps two at a time and went into her bedroom. Pity for Scott, Puh-leeze! Give her a break! His wife needed to go pick out a coffin because Scott would not be coming home. At least not alive. He would eventually show up in one of those black body bags. He had wanted to use her like the others. Have sex with her and discard her like she was nothing. She knew his game and she beat him to it.

After she had killed him, he was like dead weight. She pulled him onto the dark plastic tarp she had gotten from her trunk. It took some time but she was finally able to wrap his body in it. She requested one of those luggage carts from the lobby. It was the perfect thing to carry the body out in. It had sat in her trunk all night and she ended up dumping it in the bushes along Route 67 not far from the Witchduck Road exit. She wore gloves and was careful not to get blood on the sofa or carpet either. She learned a while back how to make a clean cut that didn't yield a huge mess. She was becoming something of a professional and the first of her kind. A black woman doing what she did was basically unheard of. Well, there was a first time for everything.

The thing that did worry her was Joy sticking her nose in where it did not belong. It was for her own good to stay out of the kitchen, so to speak. It would save her life not to know.

As much as Autumn loved Joy, she could not risk anyone messing with her or her projects. She'd cut people for less if it came down to her or them.

She went to the drawer and saw the knife, wrapped in a white silk cloth. She noticed it had been misplaced and moved it before breakfast.

Satisfied, she dropped her robe and headed for the shower.

# Chapter Twelve

The new hairstylist was finally starting. He had to have time to move out of New York so Autumn gave him two weeks to get himself situated. He was waiting for Autumn when she pulled up. He was a thin brother holding two large gray nylon bags and they were both stuffed to the brim with supplies. He grinned broadly and she nodded, checking out his get up. Yeah, he was definitely different in a wavy black wig, wearing a lime green dress and matching pumps, which frankly would have gone unnoticed if it weren't for the stubble on his legs and on his face. Other than that he was actually prettier than most women, almost like Boy George gone hairstylist. He had to have been a fine man but apparently that had not been enough. He needed to be a fine woman, which really was not her business.

Autumn pulled off her shades and hopped out from her car. She offered up a pleasant good morning and a smile. Seems like he was going to work out just fine. At least he seemed serious about his job.

"Miss Autumn, you are gorgeous! And lookin' fierce today in that skirt. Is that Isaac Mizrahi?" He raised an arched eyebrow and tossed the wig.

"No, actually Michael Kors," she said looking down at the black and white print wrapped around her curvy hips.

"Ooooh yeah, he is amazing! Well it is lovely. It's one hundred percent silk too. I know my fabrics." He reached out and let the edge of it flow through his bony fingers.

"No kidding."

"You're a diva. A fly Betty. Had to be with this shop." He gestured his head toward the salon. "Only *another* diva would recognize that."

Autumn laughed, tripping off his referral of himself in feminine terms. She unlocked the door and stepped inside as he followed close behind her.

"Ooooh chile, yes, yes, yes, yes, ooo la la Miss Claudy I looooove the *smell* of a salon!" He waved his hand like he was testifying. "Yes Miss Glory, the shampoo always turns me on honey. Somethin' about the citrus just inspires me. I can really work my artistic talents then. Work 'em like a perm." He flitted past her, switching harder than any of the women she knew. Autumn could see a drunk in a dark bar possibly mistaking Sasha. He went to his new station and put this ugly brown stuffed monkey on the edge of his counter. "Okay Mandingo we're home so just settle down chile," he said to the monkey and Autumn gawked with her mouth open, wondering if she had hired a true loony, great reference or not.

Once he noticed Autumn staring at him like he had lost his mind, he giggled and rushed over. "Oh I'm not psycho or anythin'. That's my good luck charm. I've had it since I first started out. He and I have been ridin' this wave of success together."

"Hey whatever floats your boat," Autumn said, thinking back to her conversation with Joy earlier and the fact that the stupid cat almost messed her up. She needed a smoke.

The door swung open and a tall model type woman with a blunt haircut and pink sundress walked in.

"Saaaaaasssssshhhhaaa!" The girl ran over to Sasha with her arms outstretched.

"They told me you had come to town and I just couldn't believe it!" She fell into his chair twirling around. "Can you hook a sister up now? I don't have an appointment."

"I got you Nikki." Sasha grinned, running his hands through Nikki's tangled clumps of shoulder-length black hair.

"See how it looks since you haven't put your magic fingers on it? All brittle and dry just like a bone." Nikki blinked.

"That's all right. You're still a diva," Sasha said putting a hand on his hip.

"And you're a queen." Nikki pointed at Sasha giggling.

"And *you're* the woman." Sasha pointed.

Damn okay already, Autumn thought, amused by the exchange.

"I see your sex change operation is going well. You even have boobies now!" The girl reached out and tweaked the right nipple.

"Yes chile." He rolled his eyes and put hands on hips. "I will be a triple threat by Christmas. You watch. I *will* be a major contender!"

"You already are," the girl said. She crossed her shapely legs and stared at him like he was God or something. "Now, hook me up. You know what I like." She ran a hand over the nape of her neck. "And start with the kitchen. It's about to be set on fire."

"Um hum I'll take care of that and it will be cooking in a few." He separated her hair into four sections. "You'll leave here bouncin' and behavin'."

Suddenly the phone rang and some woman asked to make an appointment with Sasha. Before Autumn could hang up and take two steps, the phone rang again with someone else wanting to get in that afternoon. She hung up the reservations she had just fifteen minutes ago. She had never had anything of this magnitude ever happen behind the four walls of Killer Do's. It was almost like the man was a celebrity. She had made a good investment. Her instincts were still sharp.

Joy walked in looking frustrated. "Hey girl."

"What's wrong?"

"Got a test in an hour. Can't stay long today."

"No problem," Autumn said as another call came in for Sasha. Damn that boy had brought them even more business.

But after another hour, she wondered if she would have to rename her salon Sasha's. Four women came in looking for him. He was definitely good for business and it made no difference that Michelle and Mikelli were in the corner snickering at the way he was dressed. Thing was he would be laughing all the way to the bank. And poor Gwen didn't know what to make of it. She kept giving him strange looks. By noon, she was up in Autumn's face.

"You hired this transvestite Autumn." She huffed, her tiny chest rising and falling. "He will bring all these weird artist types in here and your rep will go down the drain." She warned, flipping her bob wig.

"You need to worry about your own business Gwen. Don't be a player hater."

Gwen narrowed her eyes. "That's the way you see it huh? I'm *jealous?*"

"Looks that way," Autumn said raising an eyebrow. She had to call a spade a spade.

Gwen shrugged her shoulders. "Okay it's your salon boss lady. You're right. I have nothing to say about it." She walked off without another word.

"I ain't mad at him, her or whatever you want to categorize it as. Shoot I might be able to learn a thing or two," Janet added, twisting a lock of her hair. "I say bring it on. The more the merrier."

"That's the right attitude." Autumn patted Janet's shoulder.

Gwen snorted. "Good for you Janet but you'll never hear those words come outta my mouth." Gwen mumbled.

Gloria Gaynor's "I Will Survive" came on the sound system.

"Hey, can you turn that up?" Sasha asked raising her hands in the air. "That's my song chile! She and Chaka are the *original* black women powerhouses. I mean they can blow and tell the truth."

Autumn went over and increased the volume.

"Hey now, what about Diana, especially after seeing *Dreamgirls*," Janet said snipping around her client's head.

"That's not supposed to be about her life!" Gwen snapped.

"Where you been?" Sasha rolled her eyes.

"I wasn't talking to your trifling behind," Gwen hissed.

Sasha ignored Gwen, clapping wildly and hopping up and down on one foot with raised arms. "Woooo chile, oh yeah! I *will* survive!"

"Don't forget Aretha now." Janet massaged her client's sparse hair. Poor sister had lost her hair from a stressful job and crazy husband but it seemed to be growing in some now.

Autumn went to the back room to see that the supply guy still had not bought the shampoo yet. She was going to get on Joy's case when she got in tomorrow. This was totally unacceptable. She went back to the front and the new receptionist was on the phone talking to someone about some check she was supposed to receive. As soon as she was off, Autumn asked whether she had typed in the stack of customer profiles in the computer yet.

"Huh?" the girl asked squinting. Autumn repeated herself, hoping she was not going to have any problems with this chick too. The girl was Gwen's cousin and the only reason she hired her was because Gwen had begged her to give the girl a shot but if she didn't work out, she didn't work out.

Before she could say anything else, she heard loud shouting. What the heck was going on lately? It seemed like the heat had brought out the crazies in everybody.

She hightailed it back to the stylist area where Gwen was yapping up in Sasha's face. He was several inches taller than she was but Gwen couldn't have cared less. She figured she was bad enough to beat anyone's behind anyway, so size made no difference whatsoever. Sasha was looking down with her finger in Gwen's face.

"Hold up, hold up what is going on here?" Autumn asked.

"Miss Thing here used my combs. I don't let *anybody* use my stuff! I pay good money for my shit!" Gwen was almost shaking with anger. She turned towards Autumn. "Can you believe this shit?"

Sasha shrugged. "I needed it. I forgot my wide tooth. Besides, whatever Sasha wants, Sasha gets. I am the woman around here." She turned to the monkey. "Ain't that right Mandingo?"

"You got to be kidding me!" Gwen gave a sharp laugh. "He's talking to a damn monkey."

"Whatever." Sasha rolled his eyes. "You oughta be glad to be in my presence, you country ass bumpkin."

"Country?" Gwen twisted her face in a million knots and drew up to her entire five eight height. "Who're you calling country?"

"Hold on a sec!" Autumn stepped between them. "Let me restate the rules," she paused. "Sasha *everyone* here works as a team. There is no diva! Second, the rule in the shop is that if you want to use someone else's equipment, you ask. Is that perfectly clear?"

Sasha's eyes widened but he recovered by shrugging. "Fine." He tossed the comb back on Gwen's counter, deflated.

"Just stay away from me," Gwen mumbled, looking like she wanted to knock Sasha down. "Transvestite."

"What?" Sasha whipped around shaking.

"You heard me." Gwen smirked with hands on her hips.

"Enough or both of you are out. And that means *both*." Autumn looked from Sasha to Gwen. Sasha wasn't convinced folding his arms over his budding chest.

Gwen sucked her teeth and walked off. Autumn shook her head. She damn sure didn't want to get rid of her best stylists. Egos were on the top shelf because they were feeling each other out.

Autumn went back to the counter when the door opened and in came trouble with a loud mouth and Ricco Suave attitude. It was Darnell, the booster who came through every other day with his stolen goods. He bopped in like the brothers from back in the day.

"Yo what is up African Queens?" He threw out two arms loaded with hanging garments. He usually had a nice selection of things hotter than the 90-degree weather. Summer dresses, blouses, skirts and pant suits. "Got a new shipment in for you Nubian lovelies. Got something for everybody. If you Mo'nique curvy, gotcha. If you Tyra Banks tall and sexy, gotcha."

Autumn waved him in. "You have ten minutes Darnell."

"Oh it will take me less than that to unload this merchandise. All this stuff can be seen on the runways around the world ladies. Paris, Rome, Los Angeles." He went over to Ms. Felis who waved him away. "I got all the latest designers. Versace, Michael Kors, Vera Wang, you name it, I got it. I have everything you ladies like. Dresses, pants, handbags and even panties. Come get it while it's hot. Get it while it's in."

"Come over here chile!" Sasha gestured, setting his client's hair on large pink rollers. He shook his long hair giving him a serious diva hood. "I've been lookin' for somethin' to wear to the club tomorrow night. Need some new rags. I gotta represent now. Can't allow anybody to out do me because I am the one. I am the trendsetter in my group." Sasha eyed the things.

Gwen snorted.

"I hear you Ms. Sasha." He lifted up a low cut red wrap around dress. "Bam! Am I right? I *know* I'm right."

"You got a good idea. I'm feelin' you." She held out a mustard yellow low cut blouse. "Um I can work the room with this chile. Might give somebody a stroke. My partner would be too happy with me strutting in this."

Gwen smacked her lips but kept quiet.

Autumn was in the mood for jerk chicken and red beans and rice so she decided to take five for lunch. She asked if anyone wanted anything and Sasha asked for a bagel with cream cheese from the diner up the street. She threw on her shades and went out into the heat, immediately feeling the humidity. Even with the short walk to The Caribbean Hut, she expected to be soaking wet by the time she got there. She crossed the street passing the gas station when she heard the low whistle.

"Hey hold up!"

She kept walking.

"Hey baby in the black and white skirt with the badonka-dunk butt. Damn you are fine as wine! Can I get a taste? I could get intoxicated on you girl. I want to be drunk."

She turned around to see some slender dude pumping gas in a late model gold Toyota Corolla. He was grinning at her, which pissed her off even more. He had some nerve to think that he could talk to her any old way. Like she was some street woman or a whore. She would show him who she was if he insisted.

She stormed over. He seemed to get even more turned on, desire burning in his beady eyes. She was just a piece of meat to be ogled and felt up. He pulled on his white linen blazer and stuck out his chest like he was about something. She knew he wasn't shit.

"Were you referring to me?" Autumn asked blinking. She wanted to smash his face in with a tire wrench.

He looked her up and down like she was a snack. "Yeah baby you're turning a brother on like a light bulb. Can I get the digits *please Lord?*" His Adams apple jumped in his scrawny throat.

She watched him for a minute. Usually she didn't bother about losers like this but she was feeling extra bad because Aunt Flo had just dropped in about an hour ago. No he was not a trucker but he may as well have been. He was just like them.

"How about I get yours?" She smiled. He smelled like sweat, reminding her of Uncle Harry in more ways than one.

"Oh you are one of those women who like to take control. All right, all right I can respect that." He wiped his nose with his finger and gave a sinister laugh. He dug in his front pants pocket and pulled out a crumpled business card and pen. "Yeah, yeah *call* me baby. Name is Terrence with a T." He scribbled something on the back and gave it to Autumn. "Maybe we can get together tonight? I would be worth every minute."

"Um hum, I'm sure you will be." She would love to have fun. He was local but that was okay. He needed to be dealt with. He needed to be taught a lesson. She would enjoy being the teacher. That was her job, to rid the world of the Uncle Harry's of the world and the occasional non-trucker was all right.

# Chapter Thirteen

She met Terrence at his apartment making it easier, cleaner. Before she could get through the door, he was pawing her like some sex-starved animal. She pushed him off and he almost hit the wall. She wanted to kill him right there for putting his hands on her. "Can you wait until I get in please?" She blinked.

He nodded sheepishly. "Yeah sorry baby, couldn't help myself. You're just so sexy and beautiful Caramel and you changed up the hair. Real cute baby. Real cute. I like. Guess I need to wait on dessert but I'm a patient man." He gestured toward the sofa. "Why don't you take a seat and relax. Want something to wet your whistle?"

"What do you have?" She sat down on the cheap loveseat, feeling the hard underwire pinching her ass. She checked out two sleazy pictures side by side on the cracked wall. Both were of butt naked women in compromising positions. Oh yes the world could do without Terrence. Women would thank her. They would probably bless her. She might be considered the Mother Theresa of women.

"I have beer. Meant to pick up some wine but I just wanted to hurry home and straighten up especially in the bedroom baby. You don't mind if I call you that, do you? Baby?" He raised an eyebrow, his goatee making him resemble a devil. She figured that would make her like a dragon-slayer, getting rid of the beast.

"A beer will do actually." She laid her purse down beside her and turned her lip up in disgust at the very shabby surroundings in the efficiency unit. The room was sparsely decorated. Besides the broke-down sofa, there was a small TV and DVD on the floor, a cheap stereo and a stained mattress, which had been thrown in the corner. She found the entire place absolutely distasteful and realized he had not even thought enough of her to get a motel room.

On top of that he didn't even have the decency to take her out to dinner before trying to hit it. He could have at least pretended to woo her.

She crossed her legs, feeling the tigress inside awaken and she knew she would not be able to tame her. Realizing that he might be worse than most made it easy for her to do what she had to do. After all, he had it coming.

"Interesting place you have here," she called out, pulling out a tiny clear vial from her bag and slipping it into her pants pockets.

"It's not much, but I call it home. I just need to go on and get some decent furniture. Just too cheap, I guess. Besides that I'm so busy with my J-O-B that I just haven't had time to do anything else."

"What do you do anyway Terrence?" she asked knowing whatever it was didn't pay enough apparently.

"If I told you that I would have to kill you." He pointed and chuckled.

She smirked as he came back with two beer cans, which were a brand she didn't even recognize. He couldn't even spring for quality beer? He was beyond tight and it irked her that he apparently thought she was easy too.

He set one down in front of her and she blinked in utter shock. He expected her to drink out of the can? He couldn't even bring her a glass. But then on second thought would she want to drink out of it? Hell no. Probably too cheap to buy dish detergent either. She popped the top and he opened his, taking a huge swig then belched.

"I'm sorry," Terrence said.

"Uh, okay." Was all she could manage to say.

"How about a DVD?" he asked, sitting almost on top of her. "Or some music to set the mood?" He was so close the stench coming from between his teeth made her want to pass out. Couldn't brush his teeth either? Maybe he was too cheap to buy a toothbrush or had been using the same one for a year hoping it would cut down on cost. She moved away and was thankful for fresh air.

"How about a mint?" She reached in her bag and handed him one.

"Oh snap is my breath funky?" He cupped his hand to his mouth and huffed.

What a crazy bastard but she would play along for a minute. Like a spider bidding his time before he reached in the web and sucked the bug dry. "A DVD sounds good Terrence." She threw her head back and drank more of the beer, which frankly tasted like cold toilet water.

"DVD it is my dear." He got up and did some little dance over to the shelf. She could tell Terrence thought he was going to get lucky tonight. He was gearing up for the big romantic leap with a movie. His fingers ran over the dusty covers as he ticked off a few familiar titles. "Yeah I know these are ancient but hey, the best things in life are oldies but goodies right?" He turned to her and winked. She winked back thinking the best things in life are offing some jerk that didn't deserve to live.

"*Black Widow* looks like a winner." She took another sip of the beer then set the can on the floor.

He put his hands on his hips. "Oh snap I forgot that I still had that. Yeah an old girlfriend left that here. Think she was trying to tell me something. You're not trying to tell me anything, are you?" He leered at her.

"Course not Terrence. I thought it would just be, well, interesting." She watched him open the DVD cover.

"Hopefully it won't scare me." He laughed holding the DVD in his hand.

"Before you pop that in, why don't you get us some snacks Terrence."

"Umm I like the way you say my name. You'll be calling it all night long. I guarantee it." He pointed at her.

"Can't wait Terrence. Now hurry with those snacks," she said.

"Oh snap, sorry yeah I have some left over onion rings and dip," Terrence said.

"Sounds yummy." She felt in her pocket for the vial. She watched him go back into the kitchenette as she produced it. Pulling off the top she slipped the clear liquid into his open can. She was doing her civic duty, saving all the women who would have had to put up with his silly behind. She felt like superwoman. She was in control and her job was to rid the world of all the bad men in one fell swoop. It was like an exterminator working to eliminate roaches.

He came back with a one-serving size bag of onion rings and a half-eaten can of ranch dip. He dumped it all on the table, hurriedly put in the DVD and rushed over, plopping down beside her. He grabbed the bag and stuffed his big hands in it, pulling out a huge handful, not offering her one cruddy-ass ring. Not like she would have taken it anyway.

After munching for a minute, he passed the bag to her. She looked in to see three, maybe four left. She passed the bag back without even indulging in his crumbs.

"Come on baby."

"No you enjoy them," she said, studying him. He really was not that attractive, which made it even easier to do him in.

"These are my favorite," he said smacking his lips and pressing the remote. Then he slipped his arm over the back of the sofa inching it closer. It ended up on her shoulder. She didn't move, feeling irritated by the minute.

"You and me. Terrence and Caramel sitting in a tree. K-i-s-s-i-ng. Sounds kind of cute huh?" He picked up his beer and took a huge swallow as his hand caressed her shoulder. Then he grimaced. "Damn that has an after-taste."

She did not respond watching as the name of the production company flashed across the screen.

He looked over at her. "You enjoying yourself?"

"Sure Terrence," she said.

"Damn you smell so good baby. What is that? Bath and Body?" He leaned over and sniffed her arm like some dog. She wanted to break his damn neck right then but figured she would play it out a bit further. "Man, you are so delicious."

She kept her head straight ahead. "Thank you Terrence."

"I'd like to lick you," he moaned loudly, scooting over.

She still didn't look at him. "Is that right Terrence?"

"Baby you're wearing my name out but I like it. Turns me on." He reached out and grazed her cheek with his nasty ass finger. She pushed it off. "Damn baby, what's up?"

"Did I ask you to touch me Terrence?" she asked.

"How else are we gonna get busy? I mean you *are* going to let me hit that right?" Terrence asked.

"Of course." She turned toward him, her face flat. "That's why you asked me over to this dump Terrence?"

"Huh?" He started coughing then grabbed his throat. "What the—?"

"Seems like you are having some trouble Terrence. Why don't you wash it down with more of that two-dollar beer that you seem to love so much?" She stood up and backed away as he clutched his neck, white foam bubbling at the corners of his mouth.

"What did you do to me?" he gasped, falling off the sofa and writhing on the scratched up hardwood floor, obviously in a great deal of pain.

"Just doing a little cleaning up," she said.

"What?" Terrence gasped.

"Just taking care of a pesky problem," she said.

"What did you do to me bitch?" he repeated grabbing his throat.

"You wanted me to take care of you Harry," she said calmly, feeling so in control even though she was seething inside. She swore he was her uncle writhing around on that floor, his eyes bulging out of his head. Looking real sorry now. Wishing he had not invited her over.

"Who's Harry? You got the wrong dude," Terrence panted.

"No, I got the right one baby," Caramel said, smiling.

"Why?" He struggled to talk, blood dripping out the corners of his mouth.

"I needed to fix you *Terrence*. Because see you needed to be fixed *Terrence*," she spat.

As he started going through convulsions she slipped out, feeling good.

Avenged.

# Chapter Fourteen

Joy's head was bent over her heaping dinner plate, praying along with her parents as classical music played softly in the background. She loved the music; it had a way of soothing her.

"Amen," her dad said, lifting his gray head and immediately digging into his food. He loved to eat too and her mother had fixed all his favorites for his birthday, which happened to fall on Thursday night, the regular day that Joy went over for family dinner.

"Baby, have you given any thought to where you would like to get married? There's always the Country Club," her mother said, cutting into her Caesar salad. Her natural hairstyle surrounded her head like a halo. She looked graceful in a silk print dress that accentuated her thin figure. "We could get the grand ballroom."

"Haven't really thought about it yet mother." Joy lifted her fork and slipped a huge piece of braised lamb chops into her mouth.

Her mother looked stunned. "What do you mean? You can't wait now. We only have five months for a Christmas wedding. You need to book these places now."

"I know that." Truthfully, Joy had come up with a place or two on her own. But she needed to check them out for herself before she let her mother in on it. She wanted to control her own wedding.

"When is the young man coming over here?" Dad asked peering over his horn-rimmed glasses. "I had expected him to ask for your hand but he didn't do that. At least he could've stopped over so we can discuss this man to man."

"No one does that anymore daddy. But I'll bring him by. He had to work late." Joy knew her dad was old-fashioned. He liked everything done in the traditional way. A man of honor was worth a lot to him.

"You say he's Baptist?" Dad raised an eyebrow.

"Uh no he's—" Joy started.

"—A *heathen* John." Her mother cut in, turning her nose up in the air. "Can you believe *our* daughter would marry a man without religious standing? All those men at the church and she found this, this man."

"He's a good man mother, you haven't even given him half a chance." Joy sighed. She was tired of trying to convince her mother to be decent to her honey.

"Well, people can come to Jesus at any time," her father added. "That's really not an issue."

"Hmph." Her mother shoved a small piece of lamb between her pencil thin lips.

Joy was ready to dig in her heels, if she needed. She was going to do what she wanted and no one could stop her. She was no longer that little girl wanting to please them. As a kid and even young adult she had done everything they wanted. And even when she wanted to study dance, she had instead gone on and went to college, majoring in business because it would get her a good job. Frivolous things like dance were for people who had no direction, her mother had said.

"Well I'll be happy to have some grandbabies Joyful. So I could tell Nanny Wilson she isn't the only grandmother in our bible group."

Joy dropped her eyes not sure what to say in response to that. It was a touchy subject. She felt a sudden pain in her stomach.

"Everything all right dear?" her father asked.

"Uh yeah, yeah sure daddy." She forced a smile on her face.

"And have you thought about who would be your attendants?" Her mother prodded. "Your cousins Darlene and Laurel are a must. You were in their weddings. You know etiquette. We must follow *Emily Post*. Besides that your Aunt Cleo would be all over me. That could be World War III."

"Of course I'll do that. Darlene and Laurel are cool and Autumn will be the maid of honor. That's all I know right now."

Her mother let out a long sigh and rolled her eyes with disgust. "Autumn? We figured that but then I had a small hope that she wouldn't."

"She *is* my best friend mother." Joy felt herself tense up. Was she going to fight her mother over every single detail of her wedding? It would be easier to elope. "She'll always be my best friend."

"Unfortunately," her mother huffed.

Dad cleared his throat. "Joy, hey we don't want to cause problems for you." He shot her mother a warning. "Your mother is just being a fuddy-duddy. We knew that Autumn would be a part of your special day darling."

Her mother returned a nasty look to her father. "It's one thing to talk to her and be in her company in general but to announce to the world that you associate with her. I mean, she *killed* her uncle for goodness sake. And maybe even her parents. Everyone would recognize her as that girl with all that controversy. It would turn the event into a circus."

"Now Jocelyn, no one even remembers that far back and I don't think that Autumn was involved in any of the things you are accusing her of. We all felt sorry for the girl," her father said.

"Okay, remember that we had this conversation. It'll come out one day. He disappeared. He's probably buried out in the backyard of that house."

Joy was fed up. "Autumn has never been a suspect mother. No one knows what happened to him. He disappeared. Her parents were killed in a fire. It was no one's fault." Joy shot back.

Her mother clutched her pink pearls. "You expect me to believe that? I know that she killed him. I feel it in my bones. I worry about you over there living with her."

"Jocelyn, please. Let's talk about something else," her father gently suggested.

"I have prayed that you would cut your ties with that woman. I'm telling you, she's not right. There's something in that girl's spirit." Her mother shook her head. "Well maybe after you're married you'll leave her alone. You'll be so busy with your husband and starting a family."

"Everyone can be salvaged, Jocelyn. Remember that," her father said.

Joy lowered her head, wondering what her mother would think of her own daughter's secret?

"Harry was a good man. I don't believe it. Besides that she's such a negative influence. So, well, strange," her mother said.

"I am not ten years old Mother. I can make my own decisions," Joy snapped. "And we all need to move on. Autumn has."

"Hmph." Her mother cut her eyes.

Joy continued to push the food around on her plate, hoping that her mother would drop the whole thing.

"Someone with the kind of past she has can't possibly move on. She has been through so many traumas. It has to be acted out somehow. The devil never lies still forever. And she is not a Christian. If she doesn't come to God she will go to hell. Do you want to hang with someone like that? She might get to the point of no return. Where she can't be saved."

"Not true. I have seen even a murderer redeemed, not that I'm saying she is one." Her dad objected again.

Joy looked down, hating the fact that they were arguing over her relationship with Autumn. This wasn't the first time they had gotten into a debate over her friendship with Autumn, that's not what bothered her. What bothered her the most was that she wasn't completely convinced that her mother was wrong.

She had followed Autumn the other day and saw her go into that apartment building over in Mount Pleasant. She sat outside and watched her leave. She vowed to track Autumn's next trip. She just could not get the image of the bloody knife out of her mind. It haunted her and it was eating her up, not knowing what her closest friend was involved in. It was a mystery she just had to solve.

Joy reached for the bowl of au gratin potatoes.

"Now Joy, you have to watch your weight. You don't want to gain any more than you already have. Your wedding is coming," her mother said smugly. "And you are getting those locs or whatever they're called out too, right? It would be so nice to have it straightened for the wedding. Look like a lady."

"Mother, that's not going to happen," Joy shot back.

Just then her younger brother Jason rushed in loosening his silk tie and removing his jacket. "Sorry I tried to get here earlier. Happy birthday, dad. I got you something to improve your golf game."

"That's my boy, even though I didn't know my game needed improvement," her father said.

"There is always room for that right? Even good players like you," Jason said. He leaned over and kissed Joy on the cheek then he went and laid another smacker on their mother.

"Yeah son, I guess so."

"When you get some time, we have to try it out."

"I'm game. No pun intended."

He sat across from Joy.

"All right, let me see the rock…just to see if the brother did you right," Jason said to Joy.

Joy held out her left hand and Jason nodded with approval. "Yeah I knew he was a cool cat. And now it's been confirmed for him to come up with that. He'll be a good brother-in-law."

"You'll like him," Joy said.

"We better or you can't get married." Her mother laughed, though everyone knew that she wasn't joking.

"You can't stop love Jocelyn," her dad started. "Remember when we were that age?"

She sighed. "I know your mother hated me. She went to her grave cursing me. That didn't stop us, though did it?" Her mother reached across the table and grabbed his hand. He squeezed it.

"No it didn't sugar plum." Her dad had stars in his eyes and her mother blew a kiss at him.

"Aw shucks, now ain't that special." Jason reached for the bowl of potatoes.

Joy just wanted what her parents had. All that love going around, even after almost forty years of marriage. She prayed she and Ricky would make it.

"How are classes?" he asked.

"Great."

"You solve the East Coast slasher case yet? They think it might be a woman. What if it turns out to be a sister? The face of serial killers has been changing, so that's a possibility." Jason laughed.

"Can we change the subject?" her mother urged. "Not at the dinner table."

"Okay, on to a more interesting topic. How's that roomie of yours?" Jason asked. Joy knew that he had had a crazy crush on Autumn ever since they were kids.

"She's okay," Joy said, her stomach still grumbling.

"Ever ask about me?" he asked, dumping green beans on his plate.

"Every now and then," Joy said.

"She used to be my ideal woman. Now Beyoncè has replaced her. That's one fine redbone."

Joy shook her head. "Like your chances with her are any better."

"That's only because she's never met me. If she had, she wouldn't be hanging around with Jay-Z and would be hanging with *Jason*," he said arrogantly. She knew her brother almost believed in what he said too.

"And you better not bring home someone like that," her mother hissed.

"Mom please, don't start," Jason warned.

"What happened with the young lady we introduced you to, Jason?" her mother asked. "She was a lovely young lady. A member of the church and the women's auxiliary. She is perfect. And just beautiful."

"Sure was mom. Just not my type."

"You young people and your types. You need to be less discriminating with things that count and more with things that don't." Her mother bristled.

"I was," Jason replied, making a face at Joy that their mother didn't see.

Joy laughed. That was her little brother. He knew how to set it straight.

# Chapter Fifteen

"You don't have nobody but me little girl. I'm your everthin'." Uncle Harry had her pinned down and she couldn't get up. He wanted to pull off her pink dress. She wanted to kill him but she was only a kid. Only thirteen years old and having to fend for herself every day even though lately it had been harder because she was sick all the time. Throwing up and tired.

He lifted the hem of her dress and as she screamed the doorbell rang. He glared at her with red eyes. *"If you go off like that again, I'll kill you girl,"* he paused. *"All it would take is a snap of your neck. It would be like breakin' a twig in half."*

She rolled to the corner of the bed and cowered as he got up, pulling up his pants and zipping them.

*"Goddam, who is messing up my flow? Especially this time of night."* He turned back to her. *"Your ass betta keep quiet too. No shit from you girl."*

She heard his heavy shoes on the stairs, fading by the second. She heard the door creak open and him saying something incomprehensible. A woman could be heard shouting. Something about going to see his son. A son? He had a child?

Autumn crept out the room and stood at the top of the stairs, peering down. The woman was in the living room. She was large and round, like Mama J had been. She had large full black curls and smooth chocolate skin, wearing a red hooded jacket and black slacks. She was shaking her finger in his face, and he seemed helpless for once as he raised his hands.

*"Harry I'm not playing with you. Now I'm trying to raise your son! You had a bunch of fun making him but it ain't so enjoyable paying for him is*

it? I have him in that private school. The least you could do is help me pay
for it. Even half."

"Now I do what I can honey. They cut salaries and I'm barely makin'
it." He dropped his hands to his sides.

"What?" she screamed. "Puh-lease Harry! I got crumbs from you before
so I guess it'll be nothing now! You make all this money and you can't, excuse
me, don't give me money half the time," she paused, putting a hand to her
head like she was trying to get it together like Mama J used to do. "You
need to be a part of your son's life."

He put his hands on both sides of her arms like he was trying to still
her, like he did with Autumn. "You're right, I'll do better honey."

"I hope so Harry. He needs you. He's a black boy. Black boys need their
fathers Harry. They need someone to show them how to be a man. Someone to
show them the way. I can't do that alone Harry," she paused shaking her head.
"Now I know you damn sure ain't perfect but you're better than nothing."

With a flash he removed his hands from her side and pushed her
against the sofa. "Better than nothin'? What you talkin' 'bout bitch?"

"You hear me! That's right. Can't be decent to me, okay I can accept that
but my baby boy deserves better and I damn sure will make sure that he
gets it. I refuse to have my child fall by the wayside and end up in trouble
because no one was there for him. I won't be visiting him in jail Harry."
She wagged a finger in his face. "I will make sure that he gets what he
needs no matter what."

Uncle Harry balled up his fists and towered over her. "Is that some
kinda threat?"

"Take it any way you want." She slung her purse over her shoulder.
"I'm telling you what it is Harry. And if you don't come correct, I'll go to the
authorities with my suspicions about what you did with those people."

"What people?" he asked quietly.

"Your brother and his wife."

Why was she talking about Autumn's parents? She felt her heartbeat
speed up. What had he done to her mama and daddy? She had been
staying with a friend when the fire had broken out. Did he have something to do with it? But she didn't have time to think about it anymore
because Harry had the woman by the arm, shaking her like a rag doll.

"Look woman, you need to mind your own goddamn business you
hear?"

She yanked away. *"I'll mind what I want."* She pushed past him and headed for the front door. She turned suddenly. *"You got your women. I don't frankly care about all that now. That's your business but you need to take care of your responsibilities, Harry."*

He put his hands on his hips. *"What women are you talkin' about? Who told you that?"*

*"Don't worry about that."* She opened his door. *"I know and I ain't hurt. Whoever they or she is must be good because you haven't been sniffing around me for a while,"* she said in a matter of fact tone. *"Must be good. I'll pray for her though 'cause she's a fool to be with you."*

Autumn shivered. She wanted to run down the stairs and go with the nice lady but she was scared of what Uncle Harry would do to her. He was going to hurt her if she didn't do anything though. She took a step down but the woman had gone out, slamming the door behind her.

*"Bitch,"* he mumbled. *"Fuckin' black bitch gonna tell me what to do. I don't let no female get away with that."*

Autumn slumped against the stairs. He would be coming for her in a few minutes. Before she could blink, he was halfway up the stairs. She tried to get back upstairs but he moved too fast. Shock registered in his eyes when he saw her.

*"What the hell you doin' here girl?"* He snatched her up nearly taking her arm out of the socket. She yelped in pain but he would not release her. *"I asked you a question!"*

*"N-n-nothing,"* she pleaded.

*"Nothing huh? I'll show you somethin',"* he hissed, dragging Autumn down the hall. *"We're gonna finish what we started girl,"* he growled.

*"Noooooo!"* she whined trying to get away but he had a steel grip. *"Please stop Uncle! I'm sorry."*

*"It's bitches like you that make my life hard. Too damn hard."* He tossed her on the bed, yanked down her underwear and forcibly parted her legs before she could even fight back.

He hopped on top of her and rammed into her, causing pain to the point where she felt faint. Her screams did not stop him. He slapped her into silence and continued grinding into her. She hated him so much. She wanted him dead. She wanted to stick a knife in him and make him feel the pain that she felt. She managed to somehow get loose and punched him in the eye. Blood splattered and he grunted, his hand going to his face. She hit him again and he shrank away. She got him again and again, raining blows on him. She was winning. She was getting better but just then she fell off the side of the bed and felt a pain in her back.

Her eyes flew open and she was still punching the air and screaming, wrestling with him. Suddenly her light came on and Joy stood there warming the sides of her arm with her hand.

She blinked and squinted at Autumn who tried to detangle herself from the blanket bunched around her legs and get up from off the floor.

"Are you all right?" Joy asked quietly, her eyes wide in concern. She had a scarf wrapped around her head, auburn sprigs sticking out all over. "You scared me."

Autumn felt so damn stupid. Here she was on the floor, looking like a fool.

"I'm fine J," Autumn said casually, trying to play it off.

"You must've hit the floor hard."

"I'm not hurt," Autumn lied, feeling an ache in her side.

"Sure looks like it." Joy crossed her arms over her chest.

"Trust me." Autumn stood up and limped to the bed. "Just a little stiff."

"Well you know to holler if you need me." Joy stifled a yawn.

"Go back to bed girl. No worries."

Joy left and Autumn sat on the edge of her bed. Her dream had been so damn real. The sad part was that it was based on what had happened in her past. She had actually experienced that. She shivered, remembering the woman in the living room as clear as day. She wondered whatever happened to her or her little boy.

# Chapter Sixteen

Cole was the first customer of the day and Autumn was actually glad to see him for some reason. He looked positively scrumptious in a navy-blue polo, khaki shorts and sandals. And the man had nice feet too, which if she had been looking for a man would have been a major plus in her book.

"Good morning Autumn. You're glowing," he said, slowly passing by her on his way to Tonya. A smile played across Autumn's lips but she didn't respond, writing out her supplies; but all of a sudden it seemed less important than what was going on only a few feet away. She couldn't help but glance over as Tonya caressed Cole's thick hands in a soapy bowl of water. As she touched him and laughed about whatever they were talking about, Autumn felt something.

Was she jealous that Tonya was engaging in what appeared to be deep conversation with him? Maybe Tonya was trying to make a move especially since she had kicked that abusive fool out. But then, Cole was available so why shouldn't Tonya take a crack at him?

"I can't wait until the day is over," Gwen said breezing by.

Autumn smiled. There was a lot of energy in her shop. It was bouncing with activity because it was Friday, one of the busiest days of the week. Everybody was trying to get her do' hooked up for the weekend. Even Michelle and Mikelli didn't argue on that day because they were too busy pulling heads out of dryers, and curling and straightening. Gwen got in an occasional comment on how good she felt after her night with Jamie.

Autumn slipped in one of her favorite CDs, *Queen Latifah: The Dana Owens Album,* hoping to set a nice calm tone for her own mood. She was wired up from a week that had way too much going on. Between the wild tension and occasional flair ups between Gwen and Sasha and then the unexpected thing with Terrence, this week had taken a lot out of her.

Joy came over flipping the pages of a huge bridal book. She turned to a page marked with a paper clip and pointed to the picture of a tall willowy blonde in a stark white sequenced gown. "What do you think?"

"Umm." Autumn cocked her head to the side and put her hands on her hips. Frankly she couldn't have cared less, but she had to try and offer some opinion to her girl. "It's fine but keep looking."

"You think it's too tight for my body frame?" Joy asked.

"It's all right to me. I think you'll look beautiful in anything," Autumn assured.

"I agree. Well, what about this for you?" Joy turned to the next clipped page and there was a black woman in a red satin gown with a plunging neckline. "Since it will be in December, I thought about this."

Autumn eyed the festive piece. "It's, well, very uh Christmasy." She would not be caught dead in that get up. It was a hot mess. "Why don't we head over to the bridal shops in Rockville over the next few weeks and check it out. We can find some nice things there." Autumn watched Cole out the corner of her eye. He was getting up and coming towards them.

"Sounds like a good idea. I'll set something up." Joy nodded, walking off.

Autumn was already focusing on him as he stopped in front of her.

"Tonya handled her business," he said, grinning. He slipped his hands in his pockets.

"Good," Autumn said. She kept a neutral expression. He *was* a good-looking man. She definitely couldn't deny that.

"Hey can I ask you something?" he asked in a low tone. He grabbed her elbow and escorted her near the door, out of ear shot of the clients.

"What's up?" she asked moving her arm from his grip but keeping her cool. She smelled his cologne. It was spicy.

He tucked in his bottom lip, then spoke. "Some of my coworkers and friends are getting together tomorrow night at Ranchers in Bowie to celebrate my promotion and I wanted to know if you were interested in coming along?"

"Oh wow." She was shocked. Totally not expecting the invitation or his elevated status. "Well," she started. "Let me be the first to say *congrats*; but I'm going out of town for the weekend." She could never break her scheduled road trips. That's what drove her, made her feel like she was accomplishing her goals.

She watched the disappointment spread across his face. "Alright, cool." He slipped his hands in his pockets again. "How about getting together tonight then? If you're not busy, we could get a few drinks."

"That's doable." She smiled, surprising herself at the answer.

He broke into a wide grin. "All right, how about meeting over at Dominick's up the street say around nine?"

"I'll be there."

"Cool." He headed for the door and Autumn stared after him. He had a compact, tight behind, formed perfectly, like someone had sculpted it from marble. An Adonis. She still wondered if he had an angle though. Was he interested in her romantically or maybe he knew something? But he couldn't. No one could.

Someone tapped her on the shoulder and she turned to see Michelle up in her grill, eyes filled with hate.

"You're too lucky Autumn. I wish I had one crack at him. Can you make me a promise?" Michelle asked.

"What?" Autumn crossed her arms over her chest, waiting for the madness.

"If it doesn't work out, can you give him my number?"

"Michelle," Autumn started.

"What?"

"Get back to work," Autumn said abruptly.

"He has his eye on Autumn." Mikelli offered, winking at Autumn. Then she turned to her sister. "And your bony self is out of luck. He ain't thinking about you. Accept it, you can't get everybody."

"I hate you!" Michelle yelled from her station. "Sometimes I wish there was one of me."

"Strange but I feel the same way," Mikelli responded as the door flew open and banged against the wall. Everyone turned to the wild looking woman standing in the doorway with a reddish Afro that would have made Foxy Brown's do appear tame. She had on a gold print wrap dress, spiked heels and expensive jewelry including a chain around her neck and a huge diamond on her left hand. She seemed almost like a regular sister other than the off-look in her eyes. Autumn figured that maybe girlfriend just had had a bad day. Every sister was entitled to at least one a week.

"Uh, can I help you?" Joy asked pleasantly.

The woman wobbled over, unsteady on her feet and reeking of liquor. Autumn had to hold her nose and felt invaded.

"Where's the bitch? I know the home wrecker is in here," she shouted, tossing her small purse on the counter and squinting, putting her hands on her hip.

Autumn was truly taken aback. "Excuse me?"

The woman scanned the salon with her bloodshot eyes. "*Where* is Gwen Hudson? I want her."

*Oh damn.* Autumn glanced back at Gwen who had been putting in a perm. Her comb was poised over the head of her client and she was bug eyed. Or was scared a better word to use.

"Oh Lord," Joy murmured, touching my shoulder.

"Come on now bitch!!!! May as well get the ass whuppin' over with." The woman chuckled, pulling off her earrings.

"And who wants to know?" Gwen asked sashaying over.

The woman clopped over, jumping up in Gwen's face. "You been sleeping with my husband, huh? Can't find your own man?"

Gwen broke out into a devious smile. She put her hands on her own hips. "Don't get it twisted. Obviously somebody has been neglecting their *wifely* duties sweetheart."

The woman let out a bloodcurdling scream and lunged at Gwen. They tussled in the middle of the shop, sending everyone scattering like roaches. Some waiting clients rolled right out the front door as the two women tumbled to the floor with the crazy wife straddling Gwen.

Autumn tried to break it up but managed to get scratched in the process. She backed up and Joy put an arm around her.

"Oh I'm not getting messed up over this," Autumn said.

The woman cried out, "I'm gonna break off a shoe in you home-wrecker!" Her bony fist was wrapped tightly around Gwen's ponytail. She gave three yanks and it came right off.

Gwen jammed her elbow in the woman's tits and she bellowed loudly before tumbling off Gwen and holding tight to her chest. As Gwen tried to stand up, the woman grabbed her by the legs and they quickly became intertwined again. It seemed surreal to Autumn and she was not sure what to do. She didn't have her gun there.

Sasha came over and managed to pry them apart. They still swung at each other, swiping at the air as Michelle held onto the woman and Sasha kept a tight hold on Gwen.

"You better sleep with one eye open because I know where you live!" the woman said in a calm voice.

"Oh bring it on! I want you to come hunt me down so I can finish you off bitch! You will be baldhead and one-eyed by the time I'm done with you," Gwen huffed through a rapidly swelling lip and holding up a fistful of red hair.

"You two need to calm down. He's playing both of you," Sasha insisted. "Having his cake and eating it too. Is he worth it?"

"Yeah really, this is not good. I don't appreciate you bringing this nonsense into my shop. Get out. Beat it!" Autumn told the woman. "Before I call the police."

"Call them." The woman raised her hands, and made her way to the door. "Call the po-po. Don't make me any difference."

She reminded Autumn of Madea, Tyler Perry's popular character.

"I ain't done with him!" Gwen shouted. "He'll be at my place tonight, bitch! Yeah, that's right. *Tonight!*"

The door slammed shut behind her. They stood there for a second and Autumn hoped that the woman did not go to her car and come back with a weapon. She peered out the blinds relieved to see the woman drive away.

She turned back to Gwen. "Gwen, this mess has to stop now." Autumn touched the scratch on her chin. "You need to take some time out. Get yourself together. I can't believe you! Bringing this stuff to work!"

"My perm is burning!" The client screamed standing up. "You gotta take this out!"

Gwen rushed over and literally ran her client to the shampoo bowl. Autumn shook her head and hoped the woman's hair didn't fall out. She definitely didn't need a lawsuit on her hands.

She flew over, as Gwen seemed to be wrestling with the woman under the bowl.

"How does your scalp feel?" Autumn asked the client.

"It's still burning," she answered.

"Shit, I can't believe she would come up in here boss lady." Gwen poured half a bottle of shampoo over the woman's head. "I apologize. I don't even know how she even found out where I work. I can't believe that bitch!"

"Watch the language," Autumn said, totally embarrassed, eyeing the sharp client who was gripping the handrails. She happened to be the wife of a minister.

"I'm sorry," Gwen blurted out.

Autumn put a hand on her shoulder. "Hey, I'll finish this. Go get some air."

Without a word, Gwen stormed off and Sasha followed closely on her heels. Autumn took over the task of washing the woman's hair in hopes of bringing her some relief. After two bouts of neutralizer and three shampoos the water ran clear and thank God there was no hair in the sink. That was no consolation to Autumn because she knew that the poor woman's hair could still fall out. "I'll pray for you all."

"Let me put a deep conditioner in," Autumn said quietly.

"Thanks," the woman said feebly.

# Chapter Seventeen

Autumn changed into something a little more seductive for her meeting with Cole. She had chosen a black sheath dress that was low cut and stopped just above the knee. It definitely made a statement. She had to admit, it felt great to slide into something sexy and not have any other motive than to have a good time. She couldn't remember the last time she had had any fun.

She arrived right on time but he wasn't anywhere to be found so she took a seat at the long end of the bar. People milled around her as a man plucked on keys at a black grand piano. The tune reminded her of Daddy D who had loved jazz just like her. She could remember him sitting up late at night with a glass of merlot, listening. Sometimes she would crawl up in his lap and take in the soulful sound and the sultry voices moaning about things she had known nothing about back then. She would ask him and he would say it was grown folks business.

She eyeballed the crowd nervously, desperately wanting a cigarette. She had to laugh at herself for being on edge. That rarely happened when it came to her and the opposite sex. Mainly because she always worked from a point of power and hate, staying one step ahead of her prey at all times, but this one wasn't prey or maybe he would be. All it would take was one wrong move and he would be part of her game. For now she needed to feel him out, see what was in his head. For all she knew this one might be hunting her or maybe just simply trying to get to know her. Before the night was over she expected to have the correct answer.

Some white guy with an ill-fitted suit and a bad case of adult acne, possibly rosacea, pulled up, resting his elbow on the edge of the counter as he stood in her personal space. He tapped her glass with his raggedy nail. "Can I buy you another drink beautiful?"

"No thank you, I'm waiting for someone." She turned away looking toward the door. Cole was late. Maybe he wasn't coming.

"Is that a line just to get rid of me?" He asked, attitude registering on his face.

She didn't say a word. Just gave him her killer look and he backed up like a fish smelling danger in the waters. A shark would be closing in if he didn't leave right away.

He shrugged. "No problem miss. No problem at all. Have a good night."

She watched him hurry off towards a group of women glad that he had taken the sensible approach. He was about to get a beat down if he had not stepped. She thought back to Terrence who had not been so smart. She was really not interested in doing in anybody else outside of truckers. They were the ones she was really after. They were the ones who had hurt her. They were her target. Overall she had no beef with men in the general population. Terrence had just caught her on a bad day. He had been so damn obnoxious that she just had to off him. She wondered if they had found his body yet.

"Autumn." Cole appeared, laying a hand on her shoulder. She felt relieved that he had followed through. She rose and gave him a hug that actually felt great. He hopped up on the bar stool next to her, providing her comfort. He had on white linen shirt and slacks. "Been waiting long?" He signaled the bartender over.

"No not really," she said, running a hand over her hair.

"I got my first case that's why I was a bit late." He paused to stare at his cell phone screen and then snapped it closed and slipped it into his pocket.

"Wow, they already have you out there," Autumn said.

"Yup. So many cases and work to do in the District. *The Wire* could have been about DC just as much as it is about B-more." The bartender made his way over and Cole ordered a scotch on the rocks and sex on the beach for her. "Most people here would not want to hear that of course, but it's true."

"I hear that. I guess with police work, there's no simple way to ease you into it," she said.

"Nope, just jump feet first but I'm ready for the job. I've been waiting a while for this. My whole life actually." He gazed into Autumn's eyes and she understood.

"Sounds like your passion," Autumn said.

"It is," he said.

She nodded. "So what were you promoted to?" she asked as their knees touched ever so slightly.

"Homicide detective," he said proudly.

*Homicide detective?* She hoped her face didn't reveal what she was really thinking. Homicide detective? She was actually sitting here with someone who was trained to find murderers like her? It was unsettling but thrilling at the same time.

"That's uh, wonderful," she managed to say.

"I've always wanted it. Ever since I was a kid watching *Starsky and Hutch.* Then it went to *Miami Vice* except I wasn't down with those corny suits they wore." He let out a hearty laugh. "But what really convinced me was when someone close to me was, well," he paused, picking up his drink and taking a huge swallow, his Adams apple jumping in his throat.

"Killed?" She finished, watching pain take up residency on his face.

He nodded. "Yeah."

"Oh wow, I'm sorry to hear that. That must've hurt."

"It was my cousin. We were raised like brothers," he said staring down into the gold-colored liquor in his glass. He took a swig.

"Sorry to hear that," she repeated softly, understanding what it was like to lose a close family member. Losing her parents was something she would never get over. It would stay with her for the rest of her life.

"He and I were tight. But I went one way and he went the other. Drugs got him," he said.

"That's sad." Autumn shook her head.

"Yeah he was a big time drug dealer and was killed in a drive by." He took a sip of his drink. "He walked on the dark side like my father."

"Your father?" She took a sip of her drink. His was a sad but familiar story, especially in the black community.

"Never even saw the man in person. Only a picture once so not that much love lost," he paused. "He was trifling." He stared off in space.

"My moms said he was in prison, doing time for robbery. She wouldn't let me go to the prison to see him. So he was just a sperm donor."

"That's rough."

"Yeah well, it's life. But the case with my cousin really hurt. It went unsolved. But even if I can't crack that, at least I could try to help other people find closure and peace for their loved ones and in DC there's always plenty of work."

"Who're you telling?" She giggled nervously.

"So Autumn, tell me a little about yourself."

She tried not to fidget as he watched her intently. He seemed genuinely interested.

"Nothing much to tell. I was raised by my uncle over in Capitol Heights," she said.

"Your parents?" he asked.

Autumn gave him a fictitious story of how they were killed in a plane crash. He was as sympathetic as she had been with him.

"So you can relate to what I've been through?" he asked.

All she could do was offer a nod. Autumn could accept knowing who had murdered her parents. Good thing for her because she had exacted her own brand of judgment on that person. It was why Uncle Harry was not walking around anymore. He couldn't hurt anybody ever again.

"Cole reached out and touched her hair and she jumped back.

"You had something in your hair." He frowned.

"Oh," she said embarrassed. She took a deep breath. Now he probably thought she was a basket case.

"So what's your first case about?" she asked, anxious to switch topics.

"I can't give too many details except to say it involves an undercover cop who was murdered," he said.

"Really."

"He was off duty but we're not sure if it was related to the job or not." He sighed, finishing off his drink. "Anyway, I'm on it. I won't rest until it's solved."

"I believe you."

Just then a new reggae song came on. "Hey, you want to dance?"

"I'm not much on that. I have two left feet."

"Don't feel bad. I'm the same." He took her hand and pulled her up off the stool. "We'll struggle together."

They went out on the crowded floor and Autumn had to spend ten minutes just loosening up. It had been years since she had been out on the dance floor and even longer since she really let loose and just relaxed.

"You ain't so bad," he said moving in closer but not enough to cause her any problems. She closed her eyes wondering if this is what it was like to be with a man.

# Chapter Eighteen

"That was some good lovin'." Ricky kissed Joy gently at the nape of her neck. She turned over and lay staring up into his eyes. He planted a big smacker on her lips and then rubbed between her legs causing her to be aroused again. "I would go round two but I don't think I'll make it. Age baby. Might need Viagara to keep up with you Holy girl. I got a Bible toting sister on the street and a wild cat in the bed."

Joy giggled, running a hand over his black wavy hair. "I don't know about the Bible toting part and I'm fornicating."

"God will forgive you," he paused. "I know I'm blessed. Need to make sure I thank the good Reverend Henderson on my wedding day," Ricky said happily slurring his words. He was in the initial stages of falling off like most men after sex "Yeah just pat the good Reverend on the shoulder and let him know how happy you have made me."

"You're crazy." Joy smiled, imagining the look that would be on her father's face. Wedding or not, she would always be his little girl.

"You aren't going to change and start getting headaches on a brother once we jump that broom?" He opened one eye and focused it on her.

"No baby, I won't. Every night." She grinned, proud to be able to make her man feel totally satisfied.

"All right now." He lay back, checking her out. "Mind making me a roast beef sandwich while you're up?"

"Guess I could arrange that." She grabbed her robe, wrapping it around her body.

"You are the woman. My woman. I love you for life," he called out sleepily.

"You better," she said.

"I know that's right." He yawned, closing his eyes. He was out for the count but she still wanted a sandwich herself. That rabbit food she was trying out was not working for her.

She passed Autumn's room and it was empty. She went downstairs and crept into the kitchen looking for Boris. She started to make the sandwich and heard a crashing sound from the basement. She dropped the butter knife that had been in her hand and it clattered to the floor. She walked out and headed for the basement.

She switched on the lights at the top of the steps and peeked down into the blackness. It was late at night and she sure wasn't up for going down there but then she heard Boris meowing loudly. She took the steps down slowly, hating the creak of the steps. She felt a chill tap dance up her spine and jumped when she heard another crash.

"Boris!" She bumped past the washer and dryer calling for Boris but he didn't appear. She crossed towards the storage room and was surprised to find the door open. She never went in there because there was no need.

She slipped inside, immediately turned on the light and searched for Boris. She frowned at the stench of turpentine and paint.

"Boris?" She heard meowing but still didn't see him. Her eyes scanned the room cluttered with an old exercise bike, a few boxes of clothes that eventually would have to go to Goodwill and a computer monitor from the 80's with a screen the size of a large TV. Then she saw something move over near Autumn's old locker. She ran over and Boris jumped from out of the corner and hopped on top of the locker, his eyes glowing in the dimly lit room. His mouth hung open as he stared at Joy like she was a stranger.

"There you are," she said scooping him up. "Time to go."

He quickly leapt out of her arms and flew out the room. Before she could follow him she noticed a small yellow puddle moving across the top of the footlocker.

"Oh Lord, why did he do that?" She sucked her teeth. Great, now she had to clean up because the locker was Autumn's and she would definitely lose her mind. She grabbed a can of Lysol and a rag from the shelf and wiped it off quickly, going over the handwritten name 'fields' in muddy brown permanent marker. Joy knew she had to make sure there were no traces from Boris. The locker had sentimental value. It was the one thing Autumn had gotten from her mother.

Just as she finished cleaning, she noticed what looked like a bloody shoelace hanging out the side.

She felt a chill run through her as she bent down and tried to open up the lid but it was locked. She went over to the tall wooden bookcase and reached up on tipsy toes, feeling around until her fingers landed on the small dusty key. She knelt in front of the chest and stuck it in the lock. Turning the key slowly, she waited for the click and pulled open the top. The rusty hinges protested but eventually gave way, exposing stacks of neatly folded women's clothing. Gingerly she pushed them aside, exposing five or six shoes in the bottom. They were all mix-match and the shoe on top had what appeared to be fresh blood on the heel.

"Oh God, Autumn what is going on?" Joy whispered dropping to her knees. "What have you done?"

# Chapter Nineteen

*C*aramel was heading north for a change of scenery. She switched on her CB radio and it crackled, piercing the still morning air. She was feeling good after hanging with Cole last night. It had ended on a high note. She smiled to herself as she could still smell his cologne.

"If you want a good time, hit Caramel back. She is looking for somebody worth her time. Show me what you got." She waited but heard nothing but static. She hoped it wasn't going to be a slow morning. She slipped in her new Jill Scott CD and relaxed.

Suddenly she heard a deep voice break through the CB line and she quickly reached over to turn up the volume.

"BJ on the scene. I'm up for the challenge."

She smiled. "Are you now?"

"Makes life meaningful," he said.

The brother had a low-key sexiness brewing underneath all his calm. She smiled to herself as she picked up the receiver and pushed the talk button.

"I can respect that," she said.

"Caramel baby you sound wide awake for four in the mornin'. You're good."

"I take my vitamins BJ," she said, feeling the wind ruffle her wig. "And I *am* good."

He roared in laughter. "I bet you are. Where you headed Miss Caramel?"

"Approaching the Delaware Turnpike on I-95."

"Now that's some ironic shit. I just whizzed through the tolls myself 'bout five minutes ago. Damn now it must be destiny for us to be together."

"Must be BJ. Want to hook up?"

"Oh most definitely lady. You know the Dew Drop diner about ten miles up the road."

"Sure do." It was not far from the Sunspot motel so she knew it well.

"Can meet you in 'bout thirty tops?"

"Look for a tall sexy blonde," she said.

"I got you baby. Sounds real tasty. Real tasty. See you at the counter Caramel and be good 'til then."

"I'll try." She put the receiver back on the hook and grinned. She was ready to find out what BJ was all about. Typical trucker trash, she was sure. Just like Uncle Harry had been. Just like all of them.

*What a big girl. You're developin' some plump, juicy tits girl. Um, um, um can't wait to suck on them bad boys.*

She stopped at the tollbooth and smiled at a man with red eyes, thick glasses and thinning hair, probably enjoying the last years of work before his retirement. He was in the twilight of his life. She handed him a five-dollar bill and he gave her two dollars change back.

"Welcome to Delaware ma'am. Enjoy."

"Thanks. I plan to." She pulled off and joined the other cars fighting to get ahead of each other in three lanes of traffic. She was excited, realizing that she was getting ready to execute another project.

Joy was a safe distance from Autumn's car. She didn't want to be detected because she really had no excuse for following her. She was supposed to be back in DC, getting ready to go to work. Instead she was playing Nancy Drew maneuvering the shadows on Interstate 95. It was kind of crazy and it was probably nothing but she was curious as to what her girl was really up to. She pulled her cap lower over her face, thinking back to the shoes in the locker. Maybe it was some wild sex games or something minor and she had made a big deal out of it for nothing.

A part of Joy felt guilty about the fact that she was following her best friend. This broke their code of trust, didn't it? They had each other's back no matter what, right? She stifled a yawn, not happy that she had to get up at the crack of dawn. She sipped on a second can of Coke, thankful for the caffeine. She watched Autumn pull off the exit, turn left, go down a busy commercial strip and pull into a diner. Joy just needed to be able to put her mind at ease.

Caramel tossed her cigarette butt and ran a hand over her wig before adjusting her paisley mini skirt. The stilettos accentuated her model legs that could have easily worked the runway. She could hear the cheers from the audience as she passed the lot. It was a dream, she thought, knowing her real audience on this highway pit stop was a million crickets rubbing the hell out of their hind legs, almost serenading her as she made it to the door.

She threw open the door and let it bang shut behind her, startling the few people with her dramatic entrance. They were probably all drifters like her, passing through the dim days of life, going from one fix to another, searching for mama and daddy. She kept her head straight ahead, squinting against the contacts that were rapidly drying on her tired eyeballs.

Caramel's anticipation started building from knowing project eight was about to begin. She laid her bag on top of the white countertop and inhaled the heavenly smell of frying pork bacon, pancakes smothered in too much butter and syrup and hominy grits. The grease hung in the air so thick she had to wipe the film of grease that had already formed on her skin. She began imagining the artery clogging meal she could be throwing down on. Even still it probably wouldn't be as good as Cracker Barn. She drummed her manicured fingertips on the cracked countertop watching a pleasantly plump waitress with bouffant stiffened hair pouring steaming coffee for a hunched elderly man with a half-smoked cigar clamped between his sagging jaws. They seemed to know each other well though, having this easy manner and she imagined him as living up the road, and coming at the same time every morning, rehashing the old days.

The waitress finally caught sight of Caramel and threw a weary smile that said it all. She gazed out of cat green eyes full of quiet despair. "Be right wit'cha ya," she croaked in a northern accent, stifling a yawn. Her pink and white uniform, which visibly hadn't seen an iron in a long time, clung to all the unflattering lumps and bumps. Caramel felt her pain. Working in a place all these damn years just to get minimum wages and no health insurance. She was probably feeding five kids and living in a trailer or cramped apartment somewhere.

The waitress slowly made her way to Caramel, flipping her pad to the next page and pulling a ballpoint pen from her hair. She reminded Caramel of someone straight out of one of those fifties movies.

"What can I get 'cha miss?" She flashed stained teeth. Her nametag spelled out Molly in dull brown letters.

"Just coffee for now please." Caramel pulled out a pack of cigarettes.

"Oh you can't light up in here honey. See." She pointed to the white poster with a cigarette and thick red line drawn through it. Damn, back in the day there was none of this nonsense. And of course Caramel thought about the fact that the old man across from her was blowing a hole in his nostril but she couldn't even look at her cigarettes. She could have said something but decided not to fight that battle.

"No problem, can you make it decaf?" Caramel asked.

"Comin' right up." She placed a white cup and saucer in front of Caramel and went over to the pot with the orange handle and came back over yawning loudly. "Nice and hot for you miss."

Caramel took one sip then rubbed her hands together trying to generate warmth in the cool diner. The air conditioner was blasting and she couldn't understand why on such a cool morning. She pulled the pitcher of cream toward her and dumped the contents into her coffee cup. As she put the cup to her lips she suddenly got a weird feeling that someone was checking her out. She looked up to see the old man with the cigar cheesing at her. He kind of reminded her of Jack Nicholson portraying the Joker with his tightly drawn lips. The corners of his mouth stretched from one side of his flat face to the other. She met his gaze, challenging him until he backed down. That was one thing Uncle Harry had taught her....not to lose a fight, ever.

What was even more disturbing about the old man was that he was about the same age Uncle Harry would have been if he had lived or more specifically if she had allowed him to keep breathing. She hated thinking about him but it was like he was a part of her; imbedded in her every action was a memory of him. She wondered if that meant he still lived, still doing evil...yet through her.

*You'll never forget your Uncle Harry. He is your first, your last, your everything.*

"Bastard," she whispered, shaking her head to get his words out of her head. "Leave me the fuck alone."

"Are you okay?" Molly stood there studying her with a frown on her face. A set of freckles sprinkled across the bridge of her nose.

"Uh, I want one of those muffins." Caramel pointed to the glass-covered platter in front of her.

"You want that heated miss?" Molly grabbed a pair of steel tongs and lifted the lid.

"No."

"They just came out the oven. Made 'em myself." Molly beamed.

"I'm sure." Caramel blinked. Molly snapped up one on top of the pile and placed it on a platter. She set the plate down before Caramel and then placed both elbows on the counter, leaning forward. Caramel sliced the muffin in two with a butter knife while the woman watched. Caramel thought about how to tell this woman to beat it.

"You a model or somethin'?" Molly squinted.

"No," Caramel said, trying to suppress her feelings of regret.

"You favor that actress; you know the one who was Miss America, Vanessa Williams. Same color eyes. A real beauty."

"Please leave," Caramel said between gritted teeth and banged the butt of the knife on the counter. Molly backed up, face flushed.

Caramel felt good. Real good and she nibbled the crust of the muffin first. It was actually worth the calories. She glanced up to see the old man peeking at her over his copy of the *New York Times*. The motel, the Winter Leave in New York, was where she had been knocked up by Uncle Harry.

"Can't smoke in here Charlie," Molly finally called out to the old man.

Charlie waved her off and kept on reading.

"Caramel," a voice broke her out of her daydream and she faced BJ. Except for the fact that he was skinny, he was ruggedly handsome. Dimples set off his toffee-colored skin. Despite his good looks, she reminded herself that he was still a trucker. Just like Uncle Harry had been.

And truckers were bad people.

They hurt people. She smiled as he straddled the seat beside her.

"What does BJ stand for?" Caramel asked.

"Billy Jones." He reached out his hand for her to shake but she just stared down at it.

"I have a cold and wouldn't want to pass you my germs," she lied, sniffling.

"Yeah something's going around." He let his arm fall back on the table.

"So was my voice deceiving?" she asked.

"You look even better than I imagined." He flashed a white smile. So unsuspecting. So trusting. "And me?"

"You're cute," she said, studying him again.

He gave that loud laugh again, causing some people to turn around. "I'm glad I haven't disappointed you."

She smirked, taking another bite of her muffin. She wasn't falling for that nice boy routine. He was a pure through and through dog like the others. He was just playing like he was decent but none of these truckers were. They were just like Uncle Harry and his friends: Larry, Henry, George or Milton with the limp.

They ordered breakfast and ate slowly as they got acquainted. She found out he was a single father of two girls, had lived in Delaware all his life. He had been trucking for twelve years. What put the nail in his coffin was that he drove for the same trucking company as Uncle Harry. What a coincidence.

"So what brings you out on the road?" he asked.

"I have some business in Philly," she said, chasing the watery eggs on her plate and wondering if Molly put cyanide or something in them. She signaled the waitress over.

"You don't have a man? You're traveling by yourself on these dangerous roads? A single female?" His eyes took in all of her, apparently assuming that she was probably hot and liked to pick up strange men on the road, which was in actuality true, but the reason was totally off the mark.

"I can take care of myself BJ," she said.

"I'm sure of that sweetheart." He polished off his steak and eggs then sat back rubbing his stomach. "So Caramel, do you have an hour or so to kick back?" He put his hand on her thigh. The feel of his fingers were like daggers and she wanted to bash him over the head with the coffeepot that was only a few feet away. Instead, she moved her leg away from his reach. Yeah she knew that good brother act was simply that and the real person would come to the surface. She felt the tigress biting at the leash but she was restrained, at least temporarily.

"I'd love more time, but at least an hour?"

"We can work something out," she said between gritted teeth. "There's the Sun Spot Inn?"

"Sounds like a plan," he said.

That would be perfect. She had dreamed of returning to the scene from twenty years ago and now she was about to get her chance. This bastard would be the perfect sacrifice. Project number eight might be the best yet.

"I think it is a good one," Caramel grinned.

"Man, we're going to have some fun." His hand slid underneath her skirt and kept going north. She calmly took the last sip of her second cup of coffee, figuring she had justification for handling him. He would get the "special" treatment for that.

"I really wish that you wouldn't do that BJ," she warned.

"Do what?" he asked innocently, his fingers playing between her legs. She felt nothing but anger and the look she gave him said it all.

He reluctantly moved them and frowned. "I thought this was what you wanted Caramel? If not, what's this all about baby?"

"I'll show you what this is all about in a few minutes." She gave him a wink loaded with the unknown. "Pay the check so we can get out of here."

She slid off the stool, exposing her thigh and BJ's eyes almost popped out of his stupid head.

"Yes ma'am," he panted. "Bold, brazen and beautiful. Damn and an Amazon too! I'm buying whatever you're selling, baby."

He tossed two crumbled twenties on the counter and followed her out, panting, obviously in heat. When they got to the door, he held it open, letting her step through and she was reminded of what a toad he was. "Ladies first," he said with a hint of sarcasm that Caramel didn't appreciate.

The first yellow rays of sunlight peeked over the horizon as they made their way outside.

"Baby you got back and front. The total package. You're truly blessed sweetheart."

She was getting more disgusted by the minute and when he touched her ass that burned her up more than anything else he had done. She gripped her car keys. "You're so touchy feely BJ."

He seemed shocked. "That a problem for you?"

"Why don't I drive us over to the motel?" she suggested, feeling anxious to get started.

"Oh you are familiar with the place huh?" he asked smirking.

"Very familiar." She unlocked her doors and he slid into the passenger seat.

"Slick ride," he smiled, admiring her car.

"Thanks." She started her engine as Molly came out of the restaurant, apparently her shift had ended. She didn't see Caramel, or at least it didn't seem like it. She took out a cigarette and lit up.

"We are going to have one nice adventure." She patted his leg. "One you'll never forget." She put the car in gear suddenly and he slammed into the dashboard.

"Damn girl, slow your roll." He rubbed his chest.

She began to wonder if she should have grabbed a car seat for him.

"I didn't have a chance to buckle up."

"You should always be prepared for anything in life BJ," Caramel said to him as she picked up speed. The motel was only two blocks away and came to a screeching halt at the entrance.

*You and me gonna stay here tonight girl. Get your bags. I'm gonna show you what a man does to a woman. My buddies and I are going to show you.*

"Let me go get the room key," he said stepping out.

"You do that BJ. Oh and if they have room 777 available, take that one." Caramel watched him trot into the motel lobby before slipping on a pair of shades. She patted the inside of her purse and felt the hard weapon tucked in her pocket. Now that made her hot and she felt excited. Ready for an orgasm.

"Oooh yeah baby, hurry up. It's time to play," she said, licking her lips in pure anticipation. A small man, well, he had to be a midget, walked by and ogled her. She rolled her eyes and looked away. He didn't know who he was messing with.

Fifteen minutes later, Caramel was riding BJ like a bull and he was screaming like it was his first time.

"Oh Caramel, Caramel." He moaned his head thrashing back and forth on the pillow. "Put it on me!"

"You like it huh?" She squeezed her muscles down there.

"Yes baby!" he squealed.

"Whose is it?"

"Yours."

"Say it again," she demanded, gritting her teeth.

"Yours. Oh shit yeah. Damn!"

"It's good huh? The best you ever had. Say it." She moved frantically above him, making sure that he was really feeling it. Making sure he got it good since it was like a prisoner with his last meal and anything he wanted he should have.

His face twisted into something crazy. "Oh my God I'm coming for you baby."

She expected that from someone like him. That selfishness, just like Uncle Harry. Not even caring whether she was satisfied or not. Yeah it was just like a bastard not to consider her needs. Like all of them, not to think about her. He immediately went limp and she jumped up and eased her way off the bed, seeing shadows on the wall. There were other men in the room, their spirits lingered, taunting her.

"You have skills Caramel! Damn!" He closed his eyes, basking in his mediocre performance. "You have gold down there." He chuckled, pulling off the condom. "Damn, I'm worn out."

"You take a rest." She got up and went to pick up her skirt from the floor and threw it on. Then she went to her purse. She heard him snoring softly. She took out the knife and swiftly went back to the bed. She jumped on top and plunged the blade in his chest. His eyes flew open and he grabbed her by the throat, catching her off guard. She tried to pry his hands loose, struggling to breathe as he tightened his grip.

"You bitch! What the fuck is wrong with you?" he shouted, flipping her over as he continued to squeeze, blood dripping down on her. She felt herself loosing consciousness so the only thing she could do was scratch him. He yelped and jumped back and she kneed him in the groin. He groaned and fell back, holding his privates. She gasped for breath, lay on her side for a second, then quickly got up and tried to stab him again; but he grabbed her hand and bent it back. She dropped the knife and scrambled for it. As she got up, she saw him get up and limp to his clothes.

"I'm going to fix your ass bitch. I keep a piece on me." He scrambled, searching his pockets as she grabbed her purse and flew across the room.

"Yeah I got it right here." He turned, but she had already opened the door and ran out running right into the midget. She tossed him aside like a doll and made it to her car glancing over her shoulder…but no BJ.

# Chapter Twenty

Joy watched in horror as Autumn emerged from the hotel room covered in blood. It was all over her shirt and skirt. Joy scrambled to avoid being seen as Autumn stumbled towards her car holding the side of her face. She prayed that Autumn wouldn't see her because she didn't have a good excuse for being there. Why would Joy be out here all the way in Delaware when she was supposed to be back in DC getting ready to go in and manage the salon? Still she prayed even harder, sweat running down the inside of her armpits and her heart racing.

Autumn passed by without noticing Joy. She was cursing and muttering to herself. Joy sat up just as she heard a car engine and wheels on the gravel. She turned in time to see Autumn's car take off like a rocket. Joy watched the car go north, the red tail lights glowing like demon eyes.

"Oh God," she whispered, as the blue sky seemed to darken.

As the minutes ticked by she sat staring at the motel room door, debating on what to do. Should she get out and see what had gone down in the motel room or should she just forget what she had just seen, head back home and abandon her plan to follow Autumn for the rest of the weekend? She bit her nails, focusing on the open door of the motel room. It was still and silent. As a matter of fact it was eerily silent, like there was nothing living in it. She shivered against her runaway imagination. Her overactive mind came from watching too many re-runs of *Forensic Files* and *The New Detectives*. For all she knew, Autumn and the guy had some weird sex game or something and the guy had remained behind to take a nap.

She had to do something and the longer she sat the greater chance things could get worse, that is if things weren't already really bad. She thought back to the blood on Autumn's clothes. That alone was an indication that something had gone terribly wrong. Before she could change her mind, she pushed open her car door, and quickly crossed the small lot to the motel.

Ignoring the knot that was sitting in the pit of her stomach she knocked on the door but there was no answer. She tried again, her eyes darting between the door and her parked car. Maybe she needed to just leave enough alone. She swallowed the lump in her throat not knowing what to do. She tried the knob, expecting the door to be locked but it wasn't. She turned the knob, slowly pushed the door open and peeked inside.

"Hello?" She quickly searched the room. It appeared empty. The bed sheets were in a wild pile on the king size bed and the lights were off. She was just about to leave when she heard a noise. Her heart leapt into her throat as she tried to figure out what the sound was. She listened and realized that it was a groan. She stepped inside and saw a naked man lying on his back. His upper torso was covered in blood.

"Oh sweet Jesus!" she breathed.

She rushed inside the room and knelt down in front of him studying the dime size hole in his chest. Her heart pounded in her ears.

"Can you hear me?" she whispered.

He groaned but didn't move.

She stood up, her eyes darting wildly around the room looking for a phone. If she got him some help now, he might make it. "I'm going to call 9-1-1." She rushed to the door. Just as she was about to leave out, she heard a car door slam shut and then the sound of voices yelling. How had she gotten in the middle of this?

She peeked out and saw a couple staggering across the lot, apparently drunk. They were arguing about something and the man was waving his arms. The woman told him to stop running his trap and come on because she was tired. Joy waited for what seemed like forever before they went to their room. Relieved, she glanced back at the man who she prayed was still living.

"God be with you," she whispered, not interested in sticking around another minute. She darted out and closed the door behind her, wiping the handle with the sleeve of her shirt. She casually strolled back to her car, glancing over her shoulder to make sure the coast was clear. She slipped inside the confines of her car feeling some relief.

That relief was short lived as the realization set in that she was living with a killer.

"All those shoes," she whispered, pulling out of the lot and heading south back home. "They belong to dead men."

Twenty minutes later, she stopped over at the Chesapeake House rest stop. She went straight to the pay phone and dialed 9-1-1 with shaky fingers. They connected her to the state trooper and she told them that she thought someone was hurt over at the Dew Drop Diner. They agreed to send a trooper over there right away.

She hung up feeling that at least she had cleared her conscience.

# Chapter Twenty-One

Caramel was hurt but not badly. Her throat had gotten the worst of the whole ordeal. She touched the side of her neck and it was tender. She set the car on cruise control and tried to relax. That bastard had tried to kill her too. But he had deserved it all. Her only regret was she had not gotten a shoe. She always took that for her trophy but not this time. This time it was enough to get out with her life.

*Girl you got plenty of jelly with that roll. Your ass is getting nice and big.*

She decided to pull in a rest stop and get herself together. The CB radio was still buzzing loudly, almost having a life of its own. Now someone else might have to pay for what BJ had done to her. Her rage had been fueled, not extinguished.

She parked a good distance from the other cars near a gas station. She reached in her back seat, unzipped her overnight bag and pulled out a change of clothes. She leaned down and snatched off the top, and slipped on a T-shirt. Then she shimmied out of the skirt and wiggled her way into a pair of jeans. All without being seen. She had it down to an art form, a perfect science.

"Bastard, now I am going to have another project. I ain't satisfied."

Suddenly a Delaware State trooper car cruised by and she waited until it had turned out of the lot and jumped back on the highway.

"They'll never catch me. Because I'm Caramel. And I know what I'm doing."

She relaxed, got out and trudged to the dull brown pavilion. She pushed through the doors and immediately searched for the bathroom.

She only had to walk a few feet before she saw the grass green sign with the outline of a nondescript lady in a dress hanging over one of two doors.

She went inside and grabbed a handful of paper towels, wet half of them and stepped to a stall to clean up. When she emerged from the stall, the bathroom was packed with noisy, whiny kids and impatient parents unloading backpacks loaded with hand wipes. She ignored them, going to the sink and washing her hands. She could feel their foreign eyes on her neck. How was she supposed to conceal the purple handprints? It was too hot to wear a turtleneck, but if she had to she would.

One of the two women at the sink stared at her. "Are you all right ma'am?" the short blonde asked softly. There was a frizzed-headed kid hanging on to the bottom of her blouse. "You're hurt. Do you need me to call someone honey?"

"No thank you." Caramel shook her head and rushed out of the bathroom. She let out a sigh of relief as her stomach growled loudly. She had not eaten much with BJ, picking at her food.

She headed for the small cluster of fast food restaurants and decided to get some chicken from Roy Jays. She hurriedly paid her money and grabbed her greasy bag and went to the area where they had the condiments. Pulling napkins from the holder, she felt someone behind her, riding a bit too close to her. She glanced over and noticed a black Delaware state trooper, dressed in his blue shirt and black pants with the yellow stripe down the side. He was checking her out. He nodded at her, then paid for his food.

Lawd, what was that all about? He was probably just admiring her, she told herself. The thing was she damn sure wasn't going to stay and find out, though. She rushed out of the rest area and hightailed it to her car. As soon as she closed the door, she pulled off and back on 95 feeling jittery.

Once she had gotten at least ten miles away she relaxed. She checked the bruises on her neck again in the rear view mirror. She felt ugly for the first time in her life. That bastard. It would take a long time for the bruises on her neck to disappear. She could buy sleeveless cotton tunics and sport those for a while. What choice did she have?

Suddenly her CB radio crackled to life and she heard two guys talking about meeting up at some place called The Diamond Back. She knew it was a place located right outside Philly where truckers sometimes hung out. She had actually been a few times. It would be a good place to kick back, put down a few beers and meet some truckers. She would get settled in the hotel and then mosey on over to the Diamond Back.

She arrived at the Diamond Back by eight thirty. It was in Chester, but it was definitely a stop with all the trucks parked outside. She managed to pull her look together having found a few silk tunic tops at a nearby mall. She put on a sexy little black one with a tight black skirt and her black bob wig. She ordered a Philly cheese steak and a beer then found a little corner to fit into to watch for possible victims. A lot of the guys were hanging together, holding up the pinball machine or using the pool table. None of them stood out to her as she munched her sandwich. They were fat old guys dressed in jeans with plaid shirts, their bellies hanging over their belt buckles.

*Girl you give it to me good. I can't get enough of it.*

The cheese steak was excellent. She didn't realize how hungry she was until she actually started eating. She ordered another beer and watched the crowd in fascination. The overwatered, gruff-looking crowd was the type of people that Uncle Harry had hung out with. They would show up at the house to watch professional ball games or Friday night card games when he was in town. They always ended up drunk as skunks and smelling of body odor before the night was over. And then they ogled and touched her, not concerned that she was just a kid.

"Hey little lady," a brother with a medium build wearing a muscle shirt said, standing before her. She took another swig from her beer and crossed her legs so he could get a look-see. He smiled and sat down.

"You live around here?"

"No." She answered flatly.

"You seem like such a nice young lady. What are you doing in here?"

"It's not such a bad place is it?" She noticed a wedding ring on his hand. Were all truckers married?

He shrugged, looking around then back at her. "Can I buy you a beer?"

"Sure."

An hour later they were still talking. He revealed he had a kid and a wife in Camden, New Jersey.

"Oh I have pictures of my boy. Would you like to see?" He pulled out a plastic string of pictures before she could object.

She leaned over to see a baldheaded baby with a toothy grin. Nothing outstanding about it actually, but he kept going on and on. He slipped it back in his wallet and stood up.

"Well, I better get back on the road Caramel. I'm trying to get back to my family by tomorrow night. It's my kid's birthday."

"Aw how sweet." Caramel couldn't have cared less. "So you don't want a quick night cap?"

"Oh no but thanks," he hesitated. "Can I give you a bit of advice?"

She stared him down and didn't respond.

"A beautiful woman like you needs to be careful around these types. Some of them can be kind of rough. You need to watch your back."

Caramel nodded, still in shock on being turned down. Was she losing her touch? She watched her friend leave the bar, not looking back.

"Hey I'm glad he left."

Caramel looked up to see some old dude standing there. Was that the best that she could do?

# Chapter Twenty-Two

Autumn searched through her things again. What had she done with that wallet? Damn! She sat on the edge of the hotel bed and racked her brain. The last time she had had it was in the diner. Could she have left it? She definitely couldn't go back now. The scary part was that all her identification was in it including her driver's license. If the authorities go in and question the diner staff about BJ, the dead trucker, they would surely say he had been with a young lady and hand over her wallet. Damn, how could she be so stupid! She banged her fist on the wall.

Why did she carry the thing into the diner anyway? It's not like she expected to pay.

Sighing, she paced the floor. Okay, say all that did transpire and the waitress identified her as the last one with BJ and gave up her wallet, she could always say that they had said their good-byes outside the diner and she had taken off, leaving him alive. They didn't have any prints on her. She had been careful not to touch anything in the hotel room. They had nothing on her. So what if she had been seen with him. Was that a crime? No, the crime was in killing the man but her only witness was dead. She laughed out loud. No, she was cool. Everything was going to be okay.

Then there was always the chance that she had not left it in the Dew Drop diner after all. She could have dropped it at one of the rest stops. That was definitely a possibility. The good thing was there was no money in it. She had left her only credit card in the glove compartment having learned a while back to never put your whole life in a wallet. So it was really no big deal other than she was driving around without a license. She would have to be careful going back to DC.

She stared out the window, overlooking the Penn Building. She was not going to sit here and worry herself to death over it though. It was too late for all that. She did want to get out and see a bit of the city before she made the two-hour trip down 95 South.

She wanted to see the Penn Museum where Rocky had stood in his films. Then there was the famous South Street and Penn's Landing.

No, she was going to finish her weekend on a good note.

She tossed her cigarette butt in the ashtray and grabbed her bag along with her complimentary map of the city and headed out.

# Chapter Twenty-Three

It was ten o'clock Sunday night when Joy heard the front door open. She put down the psych book she had been reading and listened as the door slammed. Her heart hammered in her chest as she slid her feet into her slippers and slowly went downstairs wondering if Autumn would look different to her. She found Autumn in the kitchen, putting leftovers in the microwave, as always. She was wearing a sleeveless tunic that Joy didn't recognize.

"Hey there!" Joy called out in as normal a voice as she could muster.

She was living with a killer, what was she going to do?

"What's up Joy?" Autumn didn't turn around but instead kept staring at the microwave almost in a trance.

"See you went shopping, cute top," Joy said staying near the door.

"Oh, yeah, thanks." Autumn massaged her forehead and Joy grew concerned about her own safety. She wondered if she should have had Ricky come over earlier. She couldn't bring herself to tell him what was going on because she still wasn't totally sure herself. A small part of her still hoped that Autumn had hurt that man out of self-defense. The only problem was the shoes, especially the bloody one. How could she explain that away?

"You seem upset. Is anything wrong?" Joy ran her hands over her arms trying to calm the chills.

Autumn focused on her like she was seeing her for the first time. "My trip was just long. I am getting tired of taking them. That might be my last one."

"Where did you go?" Joy asked casually.

"Don't worry about that," she said harshly. She leaned against the counter. "Did Boston bring my supplies? If he didn't I am going to kill him so please tell me good news."

Joy nodded. "He came. And you just had a call from Cole. He just called half an hour ago."

Autumn brightened a bit.

"Did he try your cell?"

"No." Autumn glanced at her mobile. "So what did you do this weekend?" Autumn asked, making Joy nervous. What if she had seen her? No, she couldn't have, she had been careful.

Joy shrugged. "Just went to look at dresses. Ricky and I went to the movies. Very unexciting."

"Gwen and Sasha behaved?"

"Not really."

Autumn snorted loudly. "Guess that is the best we can hope for."

"Oh and uh Mikelli and Michelle quit."

"What?" Autumn laughed.

"They got jobs over at Sexy Scissors."

"Those heifers. I had a feeling they were going to bounce," Autumn said, shaking her head slowly.

"They left us a note," Joy said.

"Couldn't be woman enough to tell you face to face?" Autumn laughed. "Well good riddance. They were just mediocre anyway. We are trying to step up our game and now it's been made easy." Autumn gave her this creepy smile.

"Yup." Joy looked toward the floor. She needed to leave the kitchen, suddenly feeling uncomfortable. "Well I better get upstairs and clean up. Ricky is on his way over."

"Tell him to stay away from my stuff J," Autumn said.

"Oh don't worry about that. It won't happen again."

"Cool." Autumn stabbed the chicken on her plate. Joy felt a chill and stepped out of the room. She was going to find some way of telling Autumn she was moving out. She had a good reason. She was going to live with Ricky since they were getting married in just four months. It made sense to live with him; she just hoped Autumn understood.

Later that night Joy waited until she heard Autumn switch off her bedroom TV and all was silent before she left the bedroom, leaving Ricky snoring softly in her bed.

She slid down the steps, switched on the living room light and noticed Autumn's overnight bag sitting in the middle of the floor. Joy was tempted to go over and see what was hidden inside. Maybe that bloody dress was tucked away unless she threw it out somewhere.

Instead she went down the basement steps and into the storage room. It was quiet; too quiet, yet she kept on going. She needed to find out. She would not be able to sleep unless she did. She crept over to the locker and grabbed the key knowing there was a possibility that the truckers' shoe might still be in Autumn's bag upstairs. She unlocked it, lifted up the lid and peered inside. She noticed what looked like a new shoe lying on top of the pile. Just to be sure, she counted and sure enough there was an extra one but it was much larger than the others were. She sighed just as she heard a noise above her. She quickly closed the lid to the locker, replaced the key and snuck out of the room. What would be her excuse for being down there at this hour? Maybe she thought she left her pink blouse in the dryer. She got to the landing and saw Autumn heading straight for her with her bag slung over her arm. She froze in shock.

"What're you still doing up?" Autumn asked suspiciously.

Joy gave the excuse about the blouse, which Autumn seemed satisfied with. They exchanged good nights and she went on up to her bedroom feeling nothing but fear. She had come too close to the fire. Autumn didn't need to know that Joy was on to her.

Joy didn't want her own shoe to end up in the locker.

# Chapter Twenty-Four

Cole deducted that a woman had killed Terrence Hill. That was obvious by the long strands of red hair found on the couch. He flipped through the police report again even though it was late and he needed to get some sleep. He took off his reading glasses and rubbed his eyes. Some people considered him a workaholic and maybe he was, but investigations were his life. The only other thing that was important to him. He looked over at the framed picture on his desk. He picked it up, staring at the sweet little girl smiling back at him.

He had worked hard to get to where he was and eventually he wanted to make chief. It was obtainable because he had the ambition and drive to get there and make a name for himself. He wanted to make his mama proud even though he suspected she already was, gazing lovingly down on him from heaven nodding her head and giving that broad grin.

He got up and stretched his legs. He pretended to shoot a hoop in the air and then paced back and forth thinking. The victim was thirty-two, black and male. Terrence Hill would have had years to give to the department but instead his service had been cut short. To go out the way he had wasn't cool. It had been plain senseless, or had it?

Terrence had been an acquaintance of his. Not the kind of guy you would get close to. There had been something sleazy about the man; but then in his line of work he had to have a dark side or he wouldn't have lasted as long as he had. He had been working on busting up a drug ring over in Northeast; but again it looked like his murder had been totally unrelated to his work. He had been written up twice for sexual harassment. He had two ex-wives and one girlfriend who had a

131

restraining order against him. Yeah it could have been any number of females.

"A woman killed this brother. A woman," he said.

He went back to his leather recliner. He pulled out the filed reports and glanced at the sexual harassment records. One woman had been his ex-partner from when he had been walking the beat over in Northwest two years ago. The other was an assistant in his current office. Both had dropped the charges against him. Maybe one of the women wanted revenge and decided to go all the way. It had been premeditated but then these were policewomen and they wouldn't usually resort to poison. No, that just did not fit any more than a round peg would into a square opening. There was a certain profile of a woman that would poison a man like that. And in addition it had been a social call, not some confrontational situation. They had been chilling and watching *Black Widow* of all things. He closed his eyes recalling the lipstick on the can of cheap beer. That would give him the answer along with the hairs, which had been taken to the FBI Crime lab for DNA analysis. They would at least have that information but there would have to be a match in their files. This female may not have committed any other crimes.

He leaned back in the chair, staring at the framed picture on the wall. He had never understood men like Terrence but he had an obligation to get to the bottom of the case. Terrence reminded him of his own pops that he had heard had been a straight-up womanizer. Those types of men figured women were meant to satisfy their urges and that was it, period. Cole knew he could have turned out like that if wasn't for Miss Mable Anders, his mom. She had been one of those no nonsense black mothers. She didn't play, taking no mess and dishing out only the best. She expected the best and was determined that her son not grow up to mistreat people, especially women. *You are going to be a good black man if it is the last thing I do. I don't want any foolishness from you Cole. I want you to be top-notch. The kind of man that is dependable, strong and hard working. Someone a woman will be able to lean on one day.*

She had raised him alone, working herself into an early grave as a nurse. But he never forgot what she taught him. The lessons stuck to him like glue making him the man he was today. And one day he would find a woman to give his life to. He had been searching a long time for her. His thoughts went to Autumn. She was an interesting lady. He hadn't been able to figure her out yet though, but he was feeling her. Something about her was mysterious. Like she was hidden behind a veil. He wanted to pull it off and see what was underneath. Peel off the layers like he did cases. He sipped on his beer again. Yeah he'd like to find out more if she let him.

# Chapter Twenty-Five

Autumn was in the salon eating a salad as she watched the afternoon news on CNN. She listened intently as the anchorwoman reported on the Iraq war. She bit into her boiled egg and watched as Sasha wrapped his client's long hair. He and Gwen were trying to at least be cordial to each other since they were the only ones left for the time being. Janet had gone home to Puerto Rico for two weeks.

After the commercial break, a reporter came back with breaking news in the case of another trucker. Autumn put down her fork and turned up the volume on the TV. Sasha and Gwen turned their attentions to the screen and the reporter Veronica Harper.

"The decomposed body of another missing trucker was found early this morning on I-264. It has not been revealed how he died. A witness has come forward from a bar outside of Philadelphia. The witness saw the trucker talking to a young woman at a Pennsylvania watering hole this past weekend. Authorities believe that she is connected somehow," Veronica said.

Autumn tensed as the screen switched to a composite picture that looked nothing like her except for the wig. The witness had to have been blind.

A red-faced police officer came on squinting into the camera. "We would like to talk to this young woman. She is not a suspect at this time; we just have a few questions for her. She was the last one seen with Mr. Carter and she may have some information that would be helpful in the investigation."

"I'm not trying to be insensitive to the whole thing but that's a fierce cut that girl had." Sasha set his next client in the chair and opened a white jar of relaxer. He parted the girl's hair down the middle and put Vaseline around the edges of her hairline.

"Uh-huh." Autumn crunched on a piece of Iceberg lettuce, as the report continued. She wanted to tell Sasha where she had gotten the wig but why give someone a heart attack?

"Again police are making a possible connection between Mr. Carter's murder and a string of murders up and down the Eastern Seaboard. They are cautioning truckers not to pick up strange people. Right now they are not sure if the killer is a man or a woman."

"There are some crazy ass people out here chile," Sasha said straightening his lemon yellow skirt. "I mean we just got over the Lee Malvo thing and now this? Another Eileen Wuornos huh? I swear I think the world is goin' to hell in a handbasket. No one is safe. I'm gettin' me a gun for protection."

"Another serial killer on the loose. Just great. I was going to go down to see my aunt in Richmond but I'm scared to get on that road." Gwen had a pair of scissors moving quickly over her client's natural. "I'll never forget that Lee Malvo. I didn't come out for weeks."

"Makes you wanna move to the North Pole," Sasha added.

"Your behind can't even deal with air conditioning and you are talking about going somewhere cold?" Gwen snorted. "*Puh-lease.*"

"You all need to give your holiday schedule for Labor Day to Joy." Autumn desperately wanted to change the topic. To be compared to Lee Malvo was not making her day.

"No problem and what's up with the turtleneck boss lady?" Gwen asked.

"It is called a *tunic* Gwen," Sasha said lathering a huge handful of shampoo on the roots of his client.

"Whatever. Coming from someone who talks to stuffed monkeys," Gwen said holding a pair of scissors in mid-air above the head of her client. She grabbed a bunch of long hair. "Are you sure you want to cut this off, Loraine?"

"Yeah, I'm sure. Get rid of it. I want something snazzy and sophisticated." Loraine looked up from the magazine she had been flipping through. "I'm turning forty next week."

"I hear you." Gwen loped off a bit, cringing.

"Girl you could sell all that hair. Don't throw it out," Sasha said.

"Mind your own business," Gwen shot out.

"Talk about minding your *business,* you need to think about that when it comes to Autumn too." He paused and rolled his eyes. "A turtleneck."

"Look." Gwen pointed a comb at Sasha. "Miss, Mister or whatever you are, I frankly don't care but you are new in this camp so you have no say. You're a newbie. And whatever I want to say is my *own* business. Autumn and I go way back, okay?"

"Should I drop kick her Mandingo?" Sasha turned to the monkey.

"Y'all are killin' me. Chill out children." Autumn pulled on the tunic, which was itchy like heck. She had already heard the joke that she was covering up a hickey. If they only knew they would be running out of the salon screaming. She got up to throw away the rest of the salad. It had been a waste of five dollars. She needed to stop eating out.

As she headed out the door to smoke, she noticed Joy talking to the latest receptionist who had just started the other day. Autumn had to let the last one go too. There was something different about Joy over the last few days. Autumn could not put her finger on it but it was there.

Autumn's cell chirped. She looked at the number and it was Cole. She answered it, smiling.

"How was your trip?" he asked.

"Okay and your party?" Autumn watched Joy walk by. She could tell her friend was stressed about something.

"Cool. Hey, there's the Summer Jazz Fest this weekend. Would you like to check it out?"

"I'll let you know but it sounds like fun." Autumn fudged, knowing she was going to accept. She just had so many other things on her mind that she had to clear some things up first. "How is the job going?"

"It's going," he said sighing.

"Getting any closer to solving your first case?" she asked.

"Yeah even with the challenges," he said.

"Hey that's what keeps you going every day." She waved to a client.

"True dat, true dat."

"Trust me, I have my own drama over in the salon." She thought of Gwen and Sasha. "Keeps me on my toes dancing."

He laughed. "Sure 'nough I can relate," he paused. "I hope you decide to join a brother this weekend. Give me a little bit of your time."

"I think that can be arranged," she said.

"Cool, I'll catch up with you later."

After she hung up, she asked Joy if she could have a private word with her. Autumn followed her to the back office and shut the door.

"Are you going to tell me what's up?" Autumn sat behind her small desk and picked up a heavy glass paperweight. She tossed it from one hand to the other, studying Joy's face, which was red. Her eyes shifted from side to side. She was nervous, but why? What was she up to?

"Oh, just stress from the wedding." She waved, giving a fake laugh then looking away.

"It's too early for all that," Autumn said in a way that let Joy know she wasn't buying it. "Is it Ricky? Is he causing you drama?"

"No girl. He's always on point." Joy fidgeted with the sleeve of her long-sleeved silk blouse.

"Why haven't you selected a dress for me yet?" Autumn asked. She'd take the long route to get to her destination, but it was necessary.

"Just been swamped. Maybe we can go this coming weekend."

"I'll be around." Autumn paused. "Have you considered hiring a wedding coordinator to pull everything together?"

Joy nodded. "My mother is talking to a few people."

"Good, it would make your life a lot easier." Autumn blinked. She was going to find out before it was all said and done. Joy was as simple as picking a lock. "So what else is on your mind?"

"Nothing."

"What did you see Joy?" Autumn decided to be direct. Get to the point.

"Nothing."

"You can talk to me about anything. We're like family. We watch out for each other. Been through thick and thin. You would never hide anything from me, right?"

"Course not." Joy shook her head.

"Because I can keep a secret better than you." Autumn watched Joy's face. She knew what she was saying. "A long time secret."

"It's not anything. It's all that I have on my plate. The wedding, school, the job and then Aunt Flo came to visit this morning. I've been cramping."

"Yeah all that can get you down," Autumn responded dryly.

"I may need to take off a few days. Just to handle things."

Autumn crossed her arms. "Of course, Joy. You're my hardest working employee. My manager. Anything you need is no problem with me. When?"

"Next week. Monday, Tuesday and Wednesday?"

"That can be arranged." Autumn traced her forefinger on the desk. "If you ever need to talk about anything, you can come to me. We've got history. We've been friends a long, long, long time. What, some twenty years? That's longer than most marriages." Autumn laughed and Joy smiled for the first time.

Joy nodded. "Well I better go grab some lunch."

"Okay Joy. Oh and Joy!" Autumn stayed in her chair.

Joy came back, her hands clutching the edge of the doorway frame.

"You forgot to clean off the counters last night and there were some dishes left in the sink. I know that you have a lot on your mind but I like a tight kitchen."

"No problem Autumn. I'll clean up when I get in." Joy disappeared.

Autumn reached out for the faded picture of her parents. Why did they have to leave her? She could have turned out to be a different person. More caring and sensitive and definitely not a killer. Her father had been such a good man, from the old school, she thought staring into his dark eyes. Hardworking and dedicated to her mother. They don't make them like that anymore. Like appliances that break, men now were weak.

Except for Cole. Now, he was raised right.

# Chapter Twenty-Six

Joy stepped out into the afternoon sunshine feeling nauseous. Just being around Autumn made her sick to her stomach. She just couldn't get that guy out of her mind. It was like he was ingrained on her brain. Then, with the shoes in the locker and the knife. It was making her a bit edgy and thinking strange things. There was this East Coast slasher and people were saying it was a woman. Joy found it hard to imagine Autumn being capable of something like that. What happened was probably an isolated incident, just a coincidence. Still she was thinking about moving out next week, mainly for peace of mind, so that she could sleep at night. She dialed the number to the movers that Ricky had used last year. They gave her a decent quote but she and Ricky could handle it. She still had to talk to him. She had not told him the whole truth or what she saw as the truth. And she was not sure what she would say to Autumn. They had been together for what seemed like forever and Autumn probably wouldn't take it well.

She crossed the street and a patrol car rolled by. She glanced inside the car and saw Cole. He glanced over, smiled with recognition and then waved. She had a weird feeling that their destiny would be tied together somehow. He seemed to really dig Autumn though and it actually seemed like she might give him a chance though the mix was strange. Autumn may have killed someone and Cole was the law.

She picked up her pace, as the humidity level seemed to increase in the short two blocks to her food spot. She felt her hair drawing closer to her scalp as she got to the glass doors of Chicken and Ribs Galore.

She went inside and was immediately comforted by the smell of frying chicken.

This restaurant had belonged to Autumn's people on her mother's side and though they no longer owned it, it still had the best soul food around. And it still looked the same with the wood paneling and dark tables and chairs. She went to the counter, her stomach growling.

The owner, Ms. Betty smiled when she saw her. "Joy!" She gave Joy a hug filled with sunshine and made her feel that all would be right with the world. "Hi honey. Want some of my fried catfish? We just pulled it out the pan."

"Sure." Joy pulled out a twenty but Ms. Betty waved her off and looked over the rim of her gold glasses.

She put a hand on her wide hips. "Your money is no good here honey. Now how many times have I told you that? You're like family and I take care of my family," Ms. Betty said.

"Thanks." Joy slipped the money back in her pocket and watched as the worker put three thick golden brown pieces of fish in a Styrofoam container.

"Remember you get two sides. Macaroni and cheese, greens, turnip greens, string beans, or candied yams," the girl in the white uniform and plastic hair cap said holding the huge silver spoon over the yams.

"Candied yams and macaroni and cheese," Joy answered.

"How's Autumn?" Ms. Betty asked, her thin eyebrows knitting. It had been a long time since she had been in there. "She forgot all about me over here."

"No she hasn't. She's fine though," Joy lied, watching as the girl tossed in two corn muffins and closed the lid to the container.

"You tell her Ms. Betty asked about her and that I want to see her sometimes. She can pass through just to make sure I'm still breathing." She handed Joy the container.

"I'll do that," Joy said. "And thanks Ms. Betty."

Joy walked out and decided not to go back to the salon to eat. She needed time to think away from everything. She was going to have to think about a new job as part of her plans. She definitely couldn't stay at Autumn's. Not knowing what she knew.

She went and sat in her car, hoping no one spotted her. A car went by that looked like Ricky and she studied the license plates and it was him. He was too far to hear if she beeped her horn. It kind of hurt that he didn't stop by the shop. She figured he must be busy. She picked up the phone to call him but decided against it. She'd talk to him later.

Her mind went back to an incident when she and Autumn were in high school. They had been sophomores thinking they were too cute in snatch backs and Jordache jeans. They had been in the cafeteria standing in the deli line when some guy passed by, grabbing Autumn's behind.

She chased him down and beat him so badly he had to be out for a week with the injuries and she was suspended for a month.

Joy knew why her mother thought that Autumn was bad news. Autumn was the one who had introduced her to cigarette and pot smoking. Of course after two puffs of the cigarette Joy broke out in hives and took one drag on the joint and ended up almost coughing up a lung, so that was the end of her smoking career. Then there was the time Autumn convinced Joy to play hookey twice. They ended up being picked up by a truancy officer and Joy ended up being grounded for six months. She and Autumn had been through a lot together but this was too much. Autumn had always been scandalous but this was beyond that, this was not something either of them would be able to fix.

She plunged her fork into the mac and cheese and felt like she'd gotten a bit of heaven.

Ms. Betty could put it down.

# Chapter Twenty-Seven

Cole was exhausted. He had been on the job for over ten hours and it was time to call it a night. He was still waiting on the fingerprints found at the scene. Hopefully there would be a match, especially after the hairs came up zero. They had been synthetic, which meant the woman had been wearing a wig.

He clocked out and went out to his Navigator realizing he would have to finally wash the thing this weekend. The trucks white exterior was almost gray from the layer of dirt that had accumulated on the surface. Someone must've had the same idea, he noticed the words: *wash me* scrawled on the driver's side door with a greasy fingertip.

"You ain't never lied," he mumbled, slipping behind the wheel yawning. He knew this position wouldn't be easy and that it would take a lot out of him, mentally and physically. Mainly because he poured his heart and soul in everything he did. He rolled down his window.

"Night Cole!" One of the new young female cops waved. She wiggled away for his benefit but he was not interested, even if she had a shelf behind that would not quit. Maybe even five years ago he would have gone for it but he knew better now. To mess with someone on the job was not wise and besides that, she was immature and not his type. Now Autumn, she seemed to be his type.

He slipped in an old Bobby Womack CD and pulled out onto the busy street. He had other things to think about besides work right now. Other priorities.

He headed south on 95 toward Virginia. He hoped that Taylor would not be too upset with him. She had wanted him to spend the whole day with her but he couldn't of course. He hated to disappoint his daughter. She was his whole life. And he did whatever he could to protect her.

Keeping her from the rough streets and raising her in Northern Virginia was the best thing that her mother could have done. They were immersed in better schools, housing and all that good stuff. Too bad he just could not make a go of it with Lauren, Taylor's mom. They tried but things just didn't click. She wanted a bad boy type and told him that he was too nice of a guy for her. It hurt because he really loved her but she wasn't having it and he had to accept that. At least they got along for Taylor's sake. Their relationship was so unlike what went down with his mom and pops.

He checked the time on the digital clock again, it was seven o'clock. If he pushed it, he just might make it for cake and ice cream. He hadn't told anyone about Taylor. Not his co-workers and definitely not any of the women he had been involved with. If he ever got serious with anyone, and that meant engaged, then he would make the introductions. So far that had not happened, though he did dig Autumn. There was something mysterious and sexy about her and he just could not stop thinking about her. She had put some kind of spell on him and he wondered if she could be the one.

Of course he had been wrong before. At one point he thought a woman he was dating was right and she turned out to be totally off the mark, like Lauren. So he would take his time. Get to know her. Find out what she was really made of before making any real commitments.

His cell phone chirped and he knew who it was before even answering. Lauren.

"Are you still coming over here to celebrate your—"

"I'll be there in twenty minutes," he sighed, crossing the Woodrow Wilson Bridge.

Lauren breathed in relief. "Well good C. She's been talking about you all day."

"You know I wouldn't let her down," Cole said.

"We'll see you when you get here. Oh and can you pick up some Breyers chocolate ice cream?"

"You didn't take care of that earlier?"

"Oh, this is for me."

"Yeah okay, make that forty minutes then."

"We'll wait."

He hung up and shook his head from side to side. But what could he say? Lauren did right by his daughter so he didn't mind making small sacrifices.

When Cole finally made it to the house, Taylor ran up and grabbed his legs. "Daddy, daddy you made it!" She was only six but looked grown in a pink and white jumper and yellow sandals with daisies on them.

He lifted her up in his arms and swung her around.

"You like my hair daddy?" She twirled one of her thick wavy braids, a shy smile spreading across her chubby face. She would always be his little girl, no matter how old she got.

"Yes sweetie; it's beautiful just like you," he said.

She giggled and he tickled her, then put her down even as she lifted her hands. "Pick me back up again daddy?"

"Hold on sweetie."

He turned and handed Lauren the brown paper bag of ice cream and she took it barely looking his way. He checked her out and she was not in her usual jeans.

"You look good." He nodded as she whirled around in a slinky black dress that hugged her curves. Baby definitely had back. An image flashed through his mind of him running his hand over the small of her back and then over her round bottom as she lay face down on the bed. That had been a long time ago but he still couldn't forget.

She was glowing. "You like? Jay just called me. Do you mind staying here for about two hours while we go out to eat?"

Cole sighed, tossing his keys on the table. He had known about this Jay character for about six months now. He seemed to take up more of her time lately. And of all the nights, he couldn't believe she was hanging out on their daughter's birthday. He wondered deep down if it was jealousy, but then their daughter was a priority.

"Sounds serious!" He raised his eyebrow and met her eyes. She looked away, shrugged her shoulders, and picked up the black velvet handbag. "No, just having a good time. But the best part is that you and Taylor can spend some private time together. We left you some cake and there is vanilla ice cream in the fridge. If you could just leave this alone." She waved the bag as she walked to the kitchen.

"Daddy, daddy let me show you what mommy got me." Taylor grabbed his hand and pulled him to the living room where a giant sized doll, about Taylor's height, leaned against the wall. She ran over and dragged it towards him. He grinned.

"Wow, how niceeeeee! Mommy really hooked you up sweetie."

He went to the front door and picked up the black plastic bag he had left there. He pulled out a pink wrapped box with a white bow. She dropped the doll on the floor and ran over to him squealing.

"For meeeeeeee!!!" She grabbed the box from his outstretched hands.

"Taylor, you *don't* snatch." Lauren came over putting hands on her hips.

"Sorry daddy," Taylor said sadly, glancing up at her mother as she gripped the box.

"Let's open it together sweetie." Cole leaned down and he helped her pull off the bow and the paper that he had had wrapped at the department store. She pried the corners of the box and he gently peeled off the transparent tape and she peeked in to find a lilac purple princess dress.

She squealed, jumping up and down with her tiny fists on his knees. He pulled it out and held it up for her to see. Her eyes grew wide as she yanked the corners, looking back at her mother for a response.

Cole handed it to her and she hugged it to her chest. That made him too happy to see her overjoyed.

# Chapter Twenty-Eight

Joy sat watching her tape of *Young and the Restless*. She needed to focus on something mindless and take a break before figuring out what to do. She had to find a solution. The thing was Autumn had threatened her by bringing up the secret. But she had to at least get herself out of the situation.

The doorbell rang interrupting her thoughts. She set down her bowl of guacamole chips and turned back to Boris.

"Don't let me come back and these are on the floor." Boris rolled his eyes at her and turned his head. She padded to the front door and peeked out. A strange man wearing a baseball cap and dark sunglasses had his face almost pressed up to the glass. She backed up. This was not the safest neighborhood in the city. They had shootings up in Lincoln Heights and actually a few on their own street. Crack addicts and drug dealers were always a concern. She took another look at him. In a polo shirt and khaki shorts, he didn't seem like the type to bang someone over the head. She debated another second on whether to answer and decided to take her chances. She cracked the door a bit, glad that the storm door was latched.

"Can I help you?" she asked fingering her gold cross. Something about him seemed familiar.

"Uh, yeah." He dropped his head and held up what looked like Autumn's wallet. "I'm looking for Autumn Fields. She left this." He had an accent that reminded her of someone from up north. Maybe New Jersey or New York?

"Oh she's not here. I can give it to her." Joy unlatched the storm door.

"No uh I'd like to deliver it to her personally. We're old friends."

"Okay, well she's at her shop. It's over on Georgia Avenue. Killer Do's."

He nodded. "Bet. I'll just take it to her. She'll be happy to see me."

"Okay then." Joy nodded as he stood there for a minute staring. She started feeling uncomfortable and slowly closed and latched the door.

Without another word, he bounced down the front steps and headed for a fairly new Lexus. She felt another chill. Who was this brother? How did Autumn know him? He wasn't an old boyfriend because Joy would have known him. She contemplated calling and giving Autumn a heads up, but she didn't want to talk to her. Heck, she didn't even want to be in the same space.

And she definitely didn't want to share a house with her anymore either.

Autumn was sweeping up tufts of hair when Sasha finished with his last client. He must have had thirty heads roll through the door in one day! The man was amazing and Autumn was almost ready to call the man god.

"Your hair looks really nice," Autumn said as the sister got up from Sasha's chair, dressed to the nines.

"Thanks Autumn." She patted it. "Sasha is something else." He took her credit card and passed by Autumn, heading to the front.

"It's so wonderful to be loved," Sasha said.

Autumn laughed, throwing the pile of hair into the wastebasket. She was whipped and could not wait to get home and in the bed.

"Plastic is the best invention since electricity." Sasha hummed as he ran the card through the machine and waited, hands squarely on hips watching Autumn. Then he looked at the little authorization box for the approval code and furrowed his eyebrows.

"Uh-oh," he mumbled.

The client stiffened, visibly worried. "Wh-wh-what?"

"Declined honey." He handed it back to her, obviously embarrassed for her. "You have another one or how about cash? Check?"

The client shook her head and passed it back. "I paid the balance on that card. Maybe it's a technical problem. Can you try it again Sasha?"

Autumn wondered if the woman was a glutton for punishment. There would be no way she would go through that humiliation twice. There wasn't anything wrong with the authorization box.

"Sure can," Sasha said in a sing-song voice sliding the card again. He waited picking crud from underneath his nails. "I need to get Tonya to take care of these. They are some raggedy lookin' things."

The client pretended to be straightening out the straps on her expensive leather bag.

Sasha checked the machine, pursed his lips and shook his head. "Um um, Tasha, not today." He returned the card to the client. Tasha sucked her teeth and fished deep in her bag. She produced another plastic card, this one silver.

"This one should work," she said confidently.

Sasha gave Autumn a doubtful look as he ran the card through. The client shifted from one heeled foot to the other, trying not to appear anxious, praying she would not be humiliated a third time.

Sasha smiled. "Bingo." He passed the card back to her. "It happens to the best of us chile."

"I'll have to call them. *Must* be a misunderstanding." Tasha insisted as she put the card back into her wallet, which was loaded down with plastic.

"No worries." He looked her up and down with his hand on his hip. "You still comin' next week right?"

"Of course." She tied a silk scarf over her new do and rushed to the door apparently not wanting to deal with them another minute. "Night Autumn," she called out before flying through the door.

"Take care," Autumn said tossing tuffs of multi-colored hair in the trash.

As soon as the door closed Sasha was almost on the floor.

"That heifer knows she doesn't have the money! Spendin' it on all those fly rags pretendin' like she had it like that. *Puh-lease!*" He started stuffing his huge black curling and flat irons in one of two duffel bags. "These women trip me out! Then they want to put on airs."

Autumn shook her head. "I started to feel sorry for the girl."

Sasha rolled his eyes. "Don't feel sorry for these wenches. They all have these big time government jobs. They just need to pay their bills and stop rollin' up in Filene's Basement every single weekend. I see her every Saturday. I'm in there too, no lie, but at least I can take care of my responsibilities. You would never, ever catch Sasha being *declined.* And she knew it was going to happen too. Used to it. I could see her sweatin' and prayin' when she pulled it out." Sasha dug the end of his long pinky finger in his back tooth.

Autumn hollered so hard she had to wipe away a tear. Sasha could be downright crass but he was hilarious.

"But you know I'm tellin' the truth!" Sasha rolled her eyes.

"You're not right, that's what I know."

"You want me to stay and help you clean up? I know today was wild because people are getting ready for the Summer Jazz Fest. Guess tomorrow will be worse since it'll be Friday."

Autumn shook her head. "No go ahead. I'm just finishing up."

"Well Gwen jetted out of here early leavin' us," Sasha said nastily.

"She requested half a day."

"Um hum." Sasha put one bag on each shoulder. "All right then, be safe."

"I will." Autumn opened the front and let Sasha out. Before she could close it, a strange hand prevented her from closing it back. A tall figure appeared in the shadows.

"Uh, Miss Autumn," he said, moving into the light, shocking Autumn out of her mind…but she played it off.

Sasha stood there looking from Autumn to the stranger but Autumn waved casually. "I'll be all right."

"I'll make sure she's cool." He kept his eyes on her, burning holes in her forehead. BJ, the scrub she thought was dead by now. She wondered number one why he was still alive and two how he had found her. She didn't have to wait long for the answer. He held up her wallet between two of his fingers.

"You left this in the bed after you supposedly killed me." He gave her the coldest, most hateful look ever and she backed up. Damn he had been more difficult than she had ever imagined. He came in and shut the door still holding the wallet in his left hand.

"Wondered what happened to it huh?"

She calmly tried to think of a weapon as she continued backing up. He was going to try and hurt her, she was sure.

"You see." He stopped in his tracks. "I could've turned this into the authorities and let them handle this but I decided it'd be more enjoyable if I *handled* it myself." His eyes were ablaze with rage. Out of the side of her eyes, she saw Gwen's clipping shears. She could probably reach them; she just needed to make a run for it.

"Now what I want to know is, why? Can you tell me that? We don't know each other from Adam. Exchanged a few pleasantries and you do a brother in like that? As fine as you are, how could you be such a sick, twisted bitch? I tried to be nice to your ass and all the thanks I got was a knife to the chest. Damn." He shook his head, walking toward her.

"Give me my wallet and step," she said, knowing it wouldn't be that simple.

"Oh, I'll leave when I damn well feel like it *Autumn*. I knew you didn't look like no Caramel." He kept on coming.

Autumn dashed to Gwen's area and grabbed the clippers, holding them out in front of her. "I suggest that you drop my wallet right there and skedaddle."

He threw back his head and let out that awful laugh again. "Do you think I am scared of a pair of scissors? After what you did to me? Come on girl, you can do better than that."

"I ain't playing. Stay back." Autumn pointed them at him. "I can finish what I started."

"You are one sick puppy." He glanced around. "Sane enough to own a salon, but crazy enough to stab an innocent brother."

Autumn waved the scissors. "Look only one of us is walking out of here alive."

"Shit, you got that right." He snorted, taking another step forward, his eyes still on her as he reached in his pocket and pulled out a long rope. He held it out in front of him between his hands and pulled it tight. "And I will finish what *I* started."

She made a run for the back room but he caught up with her from behind, wrapping the rope around her neck. He pulled tight and she tried to grab ahold of it; but it was too tense and she felt it burning into her throat. She reached back and elbowed him, apparently in the groin because he let go and doubled over, groaning.

"Bastard!" She stood over him and stabbed him in the back hitting bone and gristle. He fell to the floor and she got him four or five more times until he stopped yelling. There was quiet and she crawled away and went to the corner. She saw a flashback of Uncle Harry's crumpled lifeless body. She had felt as she did now, happy. Relieved. Vindicated.

She saw blood snaking toward her on the hardwood floor. Oh this would not be easy to clean up. Might take all night. She reached up and massaged her neck. This was the second trauma to it.

She held out the knife again, waiting to see if he would get up again. He was like the guy who wouldn't die. Like the cat with nine lives. She laughed at that, using the edge of the counter to get to her feet. She went to the back and pulled a folded white towel from the laundry basket. Wiping the blade, she wondered how the hell she would get rid of this one. She searched and found some large black trash bags then she remembered Rock Creek Park. It was only a few miles away.

Yeah, that might work...

# Chapter Twenty-Nine

"What happened with all the towels?" Gwen asked, coming from the back room. "There were at least a half a dozen last week now we're down to three?"

"Don't worry, I'll buy more," Autumn said casually.

"And my shears are missing," Gwen hissed, shooting a nasty look towards Sasha who didn't stop plaiting his client's hair.

"Don't even think about it." Sasha suddenly pointed the tip of his rat tip comb at Gwen. "What would I want with your nasty scissors," Sasha said.

"Ladies, please. Be on your best behavior. We can talk about all this later." Autumn was expecting her first candidate for Michelle's slot in a few minutes. She was not ready for the bickering first thing in the morning. Especially this particular morning when she was exhausted after that clean up last night.

"Only for you Autumn," Gwen stuck her tongue out at Sasha. He in turn showed her his behind and smacked it. Those two would not grow up for anything. She shook her head as a woman came in with a bad burgundy-colored weave. She was wearing cut-up jeans and a rumpled T-shirt and Autumn was truly offended that anyone would come to an interview like that. The look definitely made for a very bad first impression. She had already lost points. A hairstylist should inspire her clients and be at her best, not look like she just came from a rummage sale.

"Can I speak to—" she paused and stared at a crumbled piece of paper obviously frustrated. "Kiwanese?"

"Autumn," she corrected in amusement. She knew right away that this was not going to work. This one could not even read basic English

152

but Autumn figured she would humor her. Hey, she had plenty of time until her next appointment, so she may as well be entertained.

"How long have you had your license?"

"For two years."

"You have any references?"

"Uh, well, no." The girl dropped her eyes. "I was…um…fired from the last job."

Autumn raised her eyebrow. "Reason?"

"I put the owner in the hospital but it was her fault. She should not have criticized me in front of other people. I mean I had warned her about that!" The girl sucked her teeth. "She would want to stay out of my way too."

"Thanks for coming in." Autumn gave a quick smile.

The girl looked confused. She remained standing where she was frowning. "That's all you're going to ask me?"

"For now, yes. Have a good day." Autumn walked away but she had the feeling that the girl was still there.

"Can you hear?" Sasha said.

Autumn turned to see the girl with her hands on her hips.

"You're not even going to give me a chance?"

Autumn walked back over and got close to the girl's face, making eye contact. "*If* we are interested, we will contact you, okay? Now good day." Autumn did not move but something in her eyes must have made an impact. The girl backed down, appearing suddenly nervous.

She backed out and rushed through the front door allowing it to close with a bang.

"We already have enough attitude in here, don't you think?" Sasha rolled his eyes at Gwen. "And that one was psycho for real."

"Bite me," Gwen said.

"I'd love to," Sasha replied.

Autumn went over and turned up the volume on the music to drown them out. She had a lot of thinking to do. Things were getting out of hand with the killing in her shop. That was way too close for comfort. She definitely had to get control. The main thing was that she had gotten the blood up.

However any CSI worth his weight and a bottle of luminal would find blood everywhere.

# Chapter Thirty

Autumn had another date with Cole. She thought she might have to push the time back but then Joy postponed their trip to the bridal shop so Autumn was able to leave her salon and meet him at the entrance of the Summer Jazz Fest, which was on the grounds of RFK Stadium that year.

"Thought maybe you might stand me up." He smiled looking gorgeous, as always. He had on a pair of dark shades, a fitted blue Nationals T-shirt, jean shorts and sandals.

"I am a woman of my word." She gave him a big hug, hoping he liked her outfit. A tie-dye sundress that showed off everything she had to offer. Deep down, she couldn't help but wonder if she was playing with fire by being with him. It was almost like she was taking a risk, but then why not? No one had anything on her. She always covered her tracks. Her extracurricular activities would stay with her. So why not have some fun for a change?

He grabbed her hand and she felt connected to him somehow. It had been a long time since she had felt safe with any man. Honestly she had not felt that way since Daddy D. He had made her feel that nothing in the world could harm her as long as he was around. He had been her protector and guardian.

They walked through the crowd, checking out the row of booths selling everything from jerk chicken, red beans and rice to gyros. Then they passed by the booths that held the standard black art prints or exotic silver jewelry from India. The sound of Melva Houston drifted in the air adding a pulse and energy. They checked out as much as they could in the jammed lot and she felt like a couple. It was like a fantasy. Something that could never really happen for someone like her but she could pretend for a minute.

Suddenly she heard her name being called. She turned around to see Ms. Betty rushing over in her standard white uniform, hair in wild gray dreds. Autumn was not in the mood for a lecture.

"Autumn, where've you been girl?" She embraced Autumn and pulled away ignoring Cole. "You've been on my mind a lot lately. Why don't you come over and get you a plate. You know I would never charge you a dime. You're family." She pushed up her glasses, finally noticing Cole.

Autumn made quick introductions and made up some excuse of being swamped as the reason why she had been scarce.

"I understand that, but now you're free so stop on over to Chicken and Ribs Galore. And bring your friend. Any friend of yours is a friend of mine."

Autumn agreed and as Ms. Betty sashayed off. Cole had to get the scoop.

"So you're a legacy on Georgia Avenue huh? You have roots?" he asked.

"I guess so," Autumn said, feeling so uncomfortable. She was really not interested in discussing anything related to her parents. It was a private thing with her but for some reason she kept talking. "I don't really like to go to Ms. Betty's. It reminds me of the past when my parents owned it. We had some good times in there."

"I feel you. The past can be painful and certain places, smells, sights and sounds can trigger things." He paused. "Like I can't stand the smell of Old English. My granddad told me that my pops would wear it when he came to see my mother."

Autumn could relate. She was reminded of Uncle Harry who used to put that mess on all the time. If she smelled it now she would get violently ill.

"It is nice when someone else understands," she said feeling free to express herself around him.

"Yeah it is." He squeezed her hand. "How about we try some of Ms. Betty's cooking though? Looks like she would make a mean pie. Like one of those old church ladies who can burn."

Autumn laughed. "Oh she can cook now. I guess there's no harm in dropping over to her booth."

"None at all." He took her hand again and it was so rare that she allowed any human contact.

They went over and sure enough Ms. Betty hooked them up with heaping plates. They took their plates over near the band and found a cool place to sit and eat. For once, Autumn felt like she was really and truly enjoying herself.

They ended up spending all afternoon and part of the early evening checking out the line up. Frankie Beverly. George Benson. Al Jarreau. They left around nine and decided to go get some drinks, but first Cole needed to stop by his house to pick up his cell phone. He had a nice single-family house. Almost seemed too much for a bachelor though. It was apparent that he planned to fill it with a family one day and she wasn't sure how she felt about that.

He gave her the grand tour of the two-level dwelling with four bedrooms and two baths. He had hired an interior decorator to give it the right touch and she was very impressed. It held a coziness and comfort with bold colors and warm furniture. There were several African art pieces that demonstrated his good taste. It had been some time since she had been around a cultured man.

Then he could not resist showing her his extensive jazz collection, which excited Autumn since she was a big fan. He had everything from Miles Davis and John Coltrane to Kenny J.

"Wow you have it all!" She stood near his collection. "I'm truly impressed."

"Yeah, I've been collecting for years."

"I have too."

"Get out of here!" He cocked his head to the side.

"Of course. Jazz and blues. Nina Simone, Grover Washington, and Lionel Hampton."

"I take it you've been to the Hampton Jazz Fest then too?"

"Every single year."

"Maybe we could roll down there together." He stepped closer to her fueling whatever there was brewing between them.

"We'll see." She smiled up at him. She hadn't missed that he was making long-term plans. He reached out his hand and plucked something from her hair.

"Looks like lint." He grinned at her and she wondered if he was about to kiss her. She stepped away and went toward a picture on the wall. It was an elderly frail woman in a yellow dress that resembled Cole.

"Your mom?" she asked.

"Yeah that was Miss Mable."

"You two look alike."

"That was my heart. The one woman in my life. I've been searching for someone who would remind me of her." He took her hands and held them between his. "I think I've found her."

"Let's take it slow Cole."

"Okay, but I need to tell you something first though. I was going to hold off but I don't think it's fair to hide it from you."

"What?" Autumn waited, wondering if he would tell her that he was married or separated or even divorced. She knew he was too good to be true.

"I have a daughter," he said quietly.

*A daughter?* That was it? Autumn nodded. He was over the age of thirty-five and most people by now had kids. Some had grown children. "That's not a big deal."

He closed his eyes and opened them, relieved. "Well I just wanted to share that."

"I appreciate your honesty. You have a picture?" she asked, curious to see a younger feminine version of him.

"Sure do."

He produced a framed picture of the most adorable little girl. She was about three or four years old with baby fat clinging to her frame. She had Cole's eyes and smile.

"Very, very cute," she said.

"Thanks." He replaced the picture on the desk just as Autumn's eyes landed on a pile of papers and a photo clipped to the top page. She felt her heart almost stop. She shifted to get a closer look. Oh my God it couldn't be. He noticed her staring.

"Oh that's the case I've been working on."

"H-how is it going?" Autumn asked casually even though she was shaking internally.

"We are just going through the forensics and asking the neighbors and friends kind of thing. Ruling out folk. All routine."

She nodded.

"Well, you ready to go?" he asked.

"Uh sure."

As they walked out, she turned to him.

"You know I'm not really feeling that well Cole. I better go home," she lied.

A look of concern crossed his face. "You think maybe it was the food?"

"I'm not sure," she said.

"Okay well uh, what do you want to do? I can take you to the hospital?"

"No. it's probably just Ms. Betty cooking with all that grease. I just need to lie down."

"Alright call me when you get in?" He looked disappointed, slipping his hands in his pockets.

"Will do." She touched his arm before he tried to kiss her good night.

She flew down his front steps, got in her car, and screeched off. She waited until she had gotten off his street before she cursed out loud. She just could not believe that of all the cases in the city, it would be the one she wanted no one to solve. And if she got too close to Cole, she would get burned. Even if she wanted to take a chance and enjoy Cole, she now had no choice but to stop seeing him. That damn Terrence…

It was shocking that Terrence had been Five-O. She would have never in a million years have figured him for the law. Not as goofy as he had been. Then his place had been jacked up.

"Terrence, you are coming back to bite me baby doll."

As if to answer, her purse fell off the passenger seat of her car.

# Chapter Thirty-One

"That dress is just what I pictured for you," Joy's mother said shaking her head slowly, tears in her eyes. The Victorian dress was so not Joy but she gave her mother a sweet smile and twirled from side to side.

"Do you really think it's me mother?" Joy felt like she should be on one of those old fashioned postcards with a fluffy umbrella in her hand. "Mother, I think that I need to find something else." Joy's eyes searched the rows and then landed on the other women posing in sexier gowns with splits up their thighs, showing more cleavage. That was more like it. Something with some pizzazz instead of the bathrobe she was wearing.

"Like what?" She cocked her head to the side. "You want to look like one of those sluts? You are the daughter of a preacher. A debutante."

"Mother I just want to wear what I want. I'm a grown woman, not some teenager," Joy said.

Her mother's face turned to stone and she pulled on her diamond earrings. "This will be the social event of the year."

"I'm not trying to be on everyone's *calendar* mother." Joy was tired of her mother telling her what to do. "I'm marrying the man that I love mother."

"Don't be so difficult," she paused. "I just want the best for you baby."

"I know," Joy said, wondering if she would still be her mother's baby if she knew the truth.

"We always wanted to give you the things my mother couldn't give me," her mother, said looking far off. "We were so poor growing up. I mean dirt poor. You know your Aunt Jordine still won't talk about it."

She seemed to go off into another place and time. "Five of us in one bedroom. And your father and I had no wedding. We went down to the courthouse and said our I do's and were back at work the next day. We struggled, Joy."

"I understand that mother." Joy shook her head, so familiar with her mother's speech that she could have recited it, word for word. "I'm not wearing this dress though." She glanced down at it. "Really it is not me."

Her mother sighed and rolled her eyes. Then she broke into a smile and crossed her arms across her chest. "You're right baby. I'm sorry. I love you. You have to wear what you want. My own dreams get in the way somehow. But it's all out of love. All because you are my daughter. My baby girl."

"I know that you have these expectations and I know that you wanted to see me one way, but I'm Joy. You don't approve of Ricky but he's going to be my husband mother."

Her mother nodded. "You were always more insightful than me. And I need to respect your wishes. After all, you're grown. No more baby in braids and little dresses."

"I would appreciate that." Joy felt relieved. "Now I need to get out of this." Joy could not wait to get out from the heavy material that was weighing her down by the second.

"Of course dear." Her mother gave a sweet smile filled with sincerity. She turned toward the saleswoman, a black woman with a long weave, and waved her over frantically. "My daughter needs some attention here." Her mother blinked, trying to be polite even if there was an edge in her voice.

Joy could tell the saleswoman wanted to give attitude but kept her mouth shut as she helped free her from the puffy contraption.

She already knew which dress she wanted. She had the girl bring what she had in mind, thinking about Autumn for the second time that morning. She had cancelled with Autumn and lied about her where-abouts for the day. True she had church choir practice and met Ricky for lunch like she had told Autumn, but after that she had run over to the bridal place to meet her mother.

She couldn't afford to have her mother and Autumn in the same environment for too long. Not to mention she was still disturbed over the weird things going on and she was still moving out. Her mind went back to the chest as the lady helped her into the dress.

Once she was zipped up she turned, staring in the mirror in awe.

"Wow, now that is you girlfriend," the saleswoman said, shaking her locks.

"I think so too."

"Oh baby," her mother gushed.

# Chapter Thirty-Two

Cole showed up at Lauren's house on time. He was taking Taylor for the night because Lauren had another date with that knucklehead. He wasn't pleased but what bothered him more was that he couldn't put his finger on why because it was really none of his business. He figured it had to be because this man was around his child.

Lauren answered the door barely looking at him. She was in tight blue jeans and a pink halter-top and for some reason that didn't sit right with him. It was like she really was more than a mother. She had developed a life. He closed the door behind him and watched her stand in the hall mirror, putting gold hoops in her ears. Her hair cascaded down her back in waves and he remembered running his fingers through it. It used to smell like cinnamon.

"Where're you going?" he asked casually chewing on a wad of gum and pulling off his baseball cap.

She shrugged. "Just to the movies. Why are you being so nosy?" A small smile crossed her pouty lips as she met his eyes through the reflection. "First time you cared."

"I don't, just curious." He looked away and slipped his hands in his pockets as she turned and grabbed her purse. Her hair shifted over her right shoulder and he caught a glimpse of the curve of her neck and remembered putting gentle kisses on it.

She straightened up. "Better get Taylor." She dashed up the steps as he watched her butt cheeks move like two grapefruits smooching.

Cole took a seat on the leather sofa and closed his eyes, breathing in the soothing scents coming from a burning candle. He was reminded again that she was a good mother.

He heard booming rap music outside. The bass made the walls vibrate. Cole looked out the window to see an old silver Thunderbird with rims parked outside reminding him of *Pimp My Ride*. Oh he knew this had to be her date. He would finally get to meet this clown and see what the fascination was all about.

"Your friend is outside!" Cole said feeling irritated. He crossed his arms over his chest and stared at a framed picture of Lauren and Taylor.

"Can you get the door!" she called down. "He's right on time."

Cole was kind of glad to do that. He wanted to check out this dude she had been seeing. And a part of him still felt this sense of ownership. Like this was his domain though he didn't pay the house note and his name wasn't on the mortgage. Still this was where his baby's mama and his little girl lived and he felt the need to protect them.

He opened the door and watched Jay or whatever the fool's name was emerge from the passenger side of the Thunderbird in a skullcap and big T-shirt. Oh hell no, Cole thought, raising his chin. This was the man? A dude from the hood? But then should he be surprised? After all she liked men that were totally opposite from him. Bad boys. She was not interested in a man who was about something. No that was too like right.

Jay bopped up the walk in black jeans hanging low. A thick gold chain hung around his neck. He had to be slinging. He met Cole's eyes and when he got to the stoop, Cole sized him up and made sure that he knew he was being sized up too, before opening the door. He wanted Jay to know that he knew his type. Had seen his kind thousands of times on the rough streets of DC. He was not intimidated.

Cole opened the door and let Jay slide past him, not escaping a critical eye.

"Whatsup cuz?" he asked, not even looking Cole in the eye like a man.

"Nothing, what's up?" Cole said folding his arms again and raising his chin.

"Where's Lauren?" He went into the living room and fell into a chair, leaning back and opening his legs.

"She'll be down." Cole remained standing. He wanted Jay to know that he was no punk. "So you need to just wait."

"I've seen you around." Jay flashed a gold tooth. What was Lauren doing? Did she need money? Was she making ends meet? Didn't he give her enough to cover child support? "You live 'round here?"

Cole blinked but kept his mouth shut. He didn't like this brother. He was going to talk to Lauren about him. He just wasn't right.

"I never forget a face." Jay continued, giving Cole a deadpan look.

"So what do you do Jay? For a living?" Cole asked.

"A little bit here, a little bit there." Jay massaged his chin. "You her man or something? Just let me know man. I don't want to move in on you."

"No I'm not her man," Cole said, looking him up and down. "She's a friend and I watch out for her. Make sure that she is taken care of."

Lauren appeared holding Taylor in her arms. Taylor looked like an angel in a pink jumper. She squirmed when she saw Cole and Lauren put her down. Taylor ran over and wrapped her arms around her father's legs.

"Daddy!" Taylor squealed.

"Daddy?" Jay sprung from the seat and turned his nose up, growing hostile. He squared his shoulders. Now he viewed Cole as a threat.

"Where'd you get this clown?" Cole started.

"Clown?" Jay looked him up and down, his nostrils flaring.

"You heard me."

Jay started walking like he was about to step to Cole. "Trust me, you don't want none of this, son. You better tell him to step off Lauren."

Jay kept coming and Lauren stepped between them.

"Everything is okay," Lauren said calmly looking from Cole to Jay. "Please chill."

"He's a clown daddy?" Taylor asked innocently, clutching her Dora.

"Be quiet Taylor," Cole said too harshly while Jay seemed like he was backing down.

"Naw everything is cool baby." Jay planted a kiss on Lauren's forehead, never removing his eyes from Cole. "I would never want to make my lady friend feel like she was in the middle."

Cole gave him a warning look. Jay looked away first. Chump.

"Daddy you like my Dora bag?" Taylor shoved the purple plastic up at Cole.

"I sure do." Cole took the bag with one hand and Taylor's little fingers with the other. "Y'all have a nice time."

"We plan to." Lauren grinned. What was up with her? She had no clue as to who she was dating. He'd definitely talk to her later.

Cole led Taylor to the door and they walked out.

"Daddy I want some candy!" Taylor whined.

"You mean *may* I have some candy." He put her bag in the car trunk then opened the back passenger side door. He set her in the booster chair buckling it, as he saw Jay emerge from the house followed by Lauren. He was going to keep his eye on this clown. See what he was really up to.

See what he wanted with Lauren.

# Chapter Thirty-Three

J oy paced the floor nervously. She knew tomorrow was her big day but she also knew that Autumn had suspicions that something wasn't right. And Joy still debated. She watched the time. Autumn was later than usual but maybe she was hanging out with Cole.

She sat on the edge of the bed and switched on the TV to try and calm her nerves. She reached for a glass of wine and sipped as the eleven o'clock news came on. She was feeling jittery as heck. Boris hopped into her lap and she petted his back as he purred. He seemed nervous too, sensing it. Then there was breaking news. A find in Rock Creek Park. The body of a man.

"Police have not identified him yet but when we get more information, we will bring it."

She got up and packed the rest of the things from her drawers into small boxes. She stored them in the back of her closet. Coward, she heard in her brain. Can't even face her. What would she do? Read the fear on Joy's face, but so what. She should never suspect that Joy knew. Still.

The phone rang and she ran to it.

"I found the perfect hall." Her mother sounded excited, like it was her wedding.

"Nice mother," Joy said softly not focusing on the wedding at the moment.

"Is something the matter?"

"Uh just tired. I'll call you back tomorrow."

"We can look at it this Saturday?"

"Sounds like a plan."

She still did not understand why Autumn was doing this. Even with a troubled childhood. She got up and decided to check on one other thing.

She went in Autumn's bedroom and over to her nightstand and saw what she wanted. Autumn kept a diary there. A thick one with a floral cover that she wrote in every day. Checking out the front window to make sure that Autumn was not pulling up, she was satisfied with the empty spot out front. She took the diary to her bedroom still looking over her shoulder. Sitting on her yellow comforter, she opened it trying to decide where to start. It went from the beginning of the year. Maybe she could check from the past few weekends and work her way back. She cracked it open and read three weeks ago.

*Did he really think I would have sex with him? Please! What did he think I was desperate or just plain ole easy? Did he think I was a plaything? He was just like Uncle Harry and deserved to be dealt with the same way too. I can admit that it was a relief to make that first stab too. It was always a relief. It felt like all the anger I had been carrying over the years came out in that knife. God, nothing could ever feel better. Those damn truckers. I hated them. I wanted to destroy all of them. Rid the world. I was up for the job.*

Joy felt little chills go through her body. She felt like she was in a mind so dark it was like she was lost in a fog. She put the book down on her lap, almost afraid to touch it, thinking it might infect her. She stared in space. God, Autumn had really done it. She had killed people and they were truckers. She had to be the East Coast slasher. The reality of that sunk in and it was frightening. She got up from the bed, hearing the creak and getting chills again. She was prepared to return the book but then something stopped her. She flipped the pages to the previous week.

*That ass had the nerve to try and get away. Did I have the opportunity to get away when Uncle Harry was enjoying himself at my expense? No one will get away. No one ever has in the past. But I got him anyway and then I went on to Philly. There was this bar and I ran into this straight-laced guy who wanted to lecture me on hanging out there. His wife was lucky that he escaped with his life. Then this fat dude came over. Old too. I was not feeling him but that never stopped me before. He invited me back to his motel room and I was happy to take him up on it. Ended up being one of my easier jobs. And it gave me back my confidence. That I could do what I wanted to them. Just like they wanted to do to me...*

The door downstairs slammed shut causing her to jump, dropping the diary to the floor. She got up and tiptoed back into Autumn's room, tripping over the footstool and stubbing her toe. She clamped a hand to her mouth feeling the hot white pain.

She quickly placed the diary back on the nightstand where she had found it and rushed out the room hearing Autumn clip clop into the kitchen. Joy went in her own room, slowly closing the door until there was a soft click. She locked it for the first time before getting in the bed. She pulled the covers up to her face and closed her eyes, trying to block out what she had read.

She ended up having nightmares until morning.

# Chapter Thirty-Four

Autumn knew that Joy had been in her room last night and had messed with her diary. How had she known? It was not where she had left it for one and it had been hanging on the edge of her night table and one page had been bent back.

"Joy, Joy, Joy!" Autumn thought slipping into a black tee and sleek pants. She had no need to do anything about it at least not immediately. What would Joy really do even if she did know? She had already been warned the other day. Joy would be loyal for no other reason than not having her own business in the street. But then if her conscience won out she could end up being a liability, something hanging out there like an annoying piece of meat jammed in Autumn's teeth.

Autumn switched on the TV and then crossed the plush carpet over to the bathroom. She was disappointed that they weren't talking about her favorite person, the East Coast slasher. *Meet the Press* was on and was truly less interesting. A bunch of white men going on and on about the 2008 elections and who was going to beat whom. Republicans against Democrats and yada yada yada. Obama against Hilary. Giulani. John Edwards…she had never been into politics so she didn't pay it any mind. She had no plans on voting anyway. What difference would it make, especially after Florida. Would anyone hear her voice?

Autumn ran a hand over her head. She needed to get Janet to take her braids out and redo them. Or maybe she could just throw a perm in it. Change things up.

She padded down to the first floor and decided to just chill for the day. It was Sunday and she never really did much anyway. Church was out.

169

She had finally accepted Uncle Harry's ideas on God. She didn't believe there was one. If there was, why would he have let those horrible things happen to her? No she figured she was the only one to control her own destiny.

She opened the front door and reached down for the Sunday edition of *The Washington Post* and carried it into her kitchen. Usually Joy went to early morning church service but it was quiet throughout the house and her car was still outside. She turned on her coffeepot and sat down. She needed to keep her mind on anything other than Cole. It was still amazing that he was working on Terrence's case.

There was a soft knock on her door. She got up and opened it to see Ms. Johnson, her next-door neighbor stooped over, leaning on her can. She was a retired schoolteacher who happened to know everything going on in the neighborhood. She had on a hair net and set her watery brown eyes on Autumn.

"Hi there Autumn my darling," Ms. Johnson started in her sweet voice. "Did you know that your car window has been smashed?"

"What?" Autumn gently pushed her aside and stared at her car, which sure enough was a wreck. Three of the windows had been smashed and to make matters worse, her CD player and CB radio were gone. Shit!

She ran out to the curb. She looked up and down the street like she would really see anyone. The thing was how it happened without her realizing it. She should have heard it but then she had been so tired last night. She turned and Ms. Johnson still stood there.

"Isn't that just terrible? People these days." She shook her head and hobbled down the steps, one hand on the railing.

"Thanks for looking out Ms. Johnson." Autumn patted her shoulder before running back in the house. She called her car insurance company to report it. Just as she hung up, Joy appeared in her church clothes, a silk green dress that made her look less chunky.

"What's going on?" She had heavy bags under her eyes.

"Somebody vandalized my car. Probably one of those damn kids again. I could kill them!" Autumn got out a sponge and wiped down the countertops, which she had just cleaned earlier. "They don't know who they are fucking with!" she paused to rinse the rag in the sink. "Now my insurance premiums are just going to jump sky high."

"I'm sorry Autumn." Joy croaked, sounding like a damn frog.

"What do you have to be sorry about?" Autumn went over the cabinets, scrubbing vigorously to make sure the germs were gone. Then she plopped into a chair. She picked up the phone to call a window replacement company. They agreed to be out within the hour. Autumn hung up as Joy headed for the door.

"While you're at that church, pray for me!" Autumn said sarcastically.

"I will," Joy turned wearing a serious look on her face. She left the room but Autumn wasn't done with her yet.

"Oh and Joy?" She played with the salt shaker.

Joy came back, her face tense. "Yes?"

"You think I need an exorcism?" Autumn gave a sadistic grin.

"W-what do you mean?" she asked quietly.

Autumn crossed her legs. "You know what I mean."

Joy looked like a deer caught in a headlight. "N-n-n-no I don't think that."

Autumn snorted. "I meant about the cursing girl. Relax. You're all tense like somebody with their hand caught in a cookie jar."

Joy gave a small laugh and forced a smile. "Oh yeah."

"Have a good service."

Joy nodded and closed the door behind her.

Autumn banged her fist on the table, knocking over her coffee cup and making a mess all over the floor.

What a crappy ass morning.

# Chapter Thirty-Five

Joy sat listening to the choir sing *Amazing Grace*, feeling somewhat inspired. She held tight to Ricky's hand for comfort. She was still shaken up by what Autumn had said earlier. Did Autumn know that Joy was on to her? Maybe she knew that Joy had discovered the diary or the shoes? But whatever or however she had found out, it was not a good thing for Joy. She knew there was no way she could go back to the house. She had already arranged to stay with Ricky because it was too dangerous and she had no idea what she would do about what she had learned yet either. She had not told Ricky the whole deal even now, but planned to later on tonight. He would know what to do. He was so level-headed.

All he thought right now was that she and Autumn had a slight falling out. It wasn't totally a lie. That conversation they'd had was very unsettling. Autumn was unstable. It was like she was unraveling right before Joy's eyes. The reason was unknown though. She had always been on the edge but it seemed to be out of control. Or had she always been like that and Joy hadn't realized it before.

Her mother stood in the front to give the announcements and Joy zoned out. She was worried about her safety. She was worried about those poor truckers on the road. Innocent men who just wanted to do their jobs. She had to do something to help before someone else lost their life. She looked down in her lap feeling surreal, like maybe she was in one of those crime movies or something. She wished she had not even been put in this position.

Joy watched her father take his place in the pulpit. "Church, the Lord God is really speaking to us today. He's directing our steps. Leading us down the right path. The path of righteousness."

Joy leaned up on the edge of her seat, all ears. She wanted God to speak to her. She needed Him to point the way. Give her a way out.

Suddenly a hand was on her shoulder. She turned to see Cole, Autumn's friend, standing there in a double-breasted suit and smiling down at her.

"I thought that was you Joy," he said. A beautiful little girl in a purple and pink dress sat beside him, swinging her legs.

"Hi Cole, nice to see you." She touched his hand as he sat directly behind them. She wondered if that was a sign from God. The fact that he was here, in church just when she was debating on what to do. He was an officer. Actually a homicide detective. He would be the one to talk to.

"Who's that?" Ricky asked. She detected a bit of jealousy in his tone. "Autumn's friend."

"A whacko case like her got some dude sniffing? Dog must not know the real deal about her," Ricky whispered.

"Sssh." Joy folded her hands in her lap, trying to pay attention. It had been obvious that everybody had known about Autumn but her. Well, she was aware of it now. She would talk to Cole after service. She had to.

After the final amen and service was over, Joy was immediately swamped by people including that annoying Betina Andrews who kept trying to get Joy to join the church woman's auxiliary. Joy had enough to do with the soup kitchen and then the charity work she was involved in. It was enough already and she was able to hold Betina off. So after a few seconds, Betina left and she had answered everybody's probing questions about the upcoming nuptials. She turned around to see that Cole was gone. Darn, her one opportunity had vanished in thin air. Ricky grabbed her by the arm and they went to join her father who was just talking to the last few parishioners.

"There is the happy couple!" her father called out, kissing Joy and embracing Ricky in a hug. "Life is good family and we are blessed. Let's go get some breakfast. That's after I find my wife."

"Sounds good to us Reverend Henderson." Ricky put an arm around Joy's shoulder. She wasn't hungry but knew she needed to at least pretend that everything was normal for now.

# Chapter Thirty-Six

Autumn drove up to the salon. She was not in the best mood. For one, Joy had not come home last night and she hadn't called. Autumn left two messages with no return call. It really made her nervous. She was more concerned with what Joy was thinking and what she planned to do. It was obvious that she knew. Was she growing some balls for once? Would she really turn Autumn in? They had been friends all these years and it seemed unlikely. Especially since Autumn had kept Joy's secret all this time. A favor for a favor was how she saw it.

Instead of going inside the salon, she smoked two cigarettes one after the other, watching the everyday traffic. It seemed like things were coming apart. Actually things were a hot mess. Just then her cell phone chirped and she pulled it out registering the name. Cole. Shit. She let it go to voicemail. He had left several messages asking if everything was all right. What could she say? Yeah, you're working on the case of the guy that I just killed? No eventually he would get the idea and move on.

She flicked the cigarette butt and pulled out the keys to her shop and opened up. She sighed, dumping her bag on the counter and checking the voicemails. Two cancellations and Boston the supply guy apologizing for not showing up last weekend. He had had a death in his family on last Friday. He couldn't get out until next week. That was it.

The front door flew open and as usual Sasha came in singing like everything was all right with the world.

He stopped in his tracks when he got a load of Autumn. "Damn what's wrong with you chile? Had a bad weekend? You look jacked up!"

That was an understatement. "Two people cancelled for you. Noreen and Latrice," Autumn said.

"My evening appointments. Good." He grinned. "I wanted to cut out early if you don't mind. A friend of mine is in a dance troupe and he asked me to come see him perform tonight."

"No problem." Autumn suddenly felt sick. She rushed to the bathroom and threw up. Must be nerves, she thought flushing the toilet. She remembered how sick she used to get when she had been pregnant with Uncle Harry's bastard babies. It had felt like she was dying. And then once they were gone it had passed like a storm. She felt tears coming. God knows the last time she had cried. It had been some time. She considered herself a tough cookie. Able to take anything that came her way.

Sasha knocked on the door. "Are you all right in there chile?"

"Yeah don't worry," Autumn gasped, leaning against the toilet bowl.

"Okay now. I have some Coca-Cola in the fridge. That's supposed to calm your stomach. You're welcome to it."

"I'm fine." Autumn felt irritated. She wished that Sasha had not come in early.

She tried to get herself together. It was everything starting to get to her. Take her soul. Take her spirit. She rinsed her mouth and washed her face before going back out and putting on a happy face.

"You want something from the diner?" Sasha asked, taking out his little pink change purse. "I'll treat you."

"I'll get something later." Autumn waved.

As Sasha walked out the door swung open again and Cole stood there. He removed his shades and approached. He had gotten a fresh haircut.

"Autumn?" He came over to where she stood. Why wouldn't he leave her alone? She didn't respond, feeling like maybe she was in the *Twilight Zone* or something.

"Are you going to tell me what's going on?" he asked cocking his head to the side.

"What are you talking about?" She avoided his eyes, deciding instead to focus on a small stain on the floor. She needed to mop that. Something she could control.

"You've been avoiding me. What have I done?" he asked.

"I just don't have time for a relationship Cole." What else could she say? Did he really want the truth?

"Is it because of my daughter? You don't want to be part of a ready made family?"

"No of course not." She blinked. "Cole please, I don't want to talk about it."

"Did I say something to offend you?"

She rolled her eyes. "You really want to know what it is?"

He waited, keeping his eyes on her.

"I'm just not into you Cole." She watched him raise an eyebrow. "I'm just not interested Cole. It's no big mystery," she said realizing she had probably hurt him. She really didn't want to do that. He had been so different from the rest but she had to protect herself. She had to make sure that she stayed away from trouble and he would definitely fall in that category.

He studied her for a minute with his hands on his hips. "Or are you just afraid?" he asked quietly.

"Of what?" She crossed her arms over her chest.

"Of getting involved. Because you can't tell me you weren't feeling me."

"I'm telling you that. You need to leave." She avoided his eyes. Of course she had been feeling him. He was a sweet guy and in another life they could have hooked up. But in her present situation, she couldn't involve anybody else. "I'm serious."

He blinked and stared at her one minute then threw his hands up into the air. "All right, if that is the way you feel, so be it. I can't beg you Autumn. I dig you but if it is not reciprocated, I'll move on."

"Good." She crossed her arms over her chest. "Take care."

"You too." He left out, leaving her feeling like she had been beat down. Why did he have to be a homicide detective? Why did she have to do the things she did? She was getting tired too. It was time to stop maybe. To let it rest.

The new girl waltzed in. "Sorry I'm late." She couldn't even remember her name. Jennifer. Janice. Jeanine. One of them.

Autumn could have cared less. "Look, I'm going to go home for a bit. Just tell Sasha please. I'll call you all this afternoon."

"Uh sure. I'll just set up. Is this area okay?" She walked over to Michelle's vacant area.

Autumn grabbed her crochet bag and threw her cap on her head. She went out feeling worse than she had in a long time. Her life was spinning out of control. And she was not sure how to get things back on track. "I'll be back in a few hours. You need any help, ask Gwen or Sasha."

She pulled up to her house and was shocked to see a moving van sitting at the curb. She parked behind it, bumper to bumper, feeling a headache coming quick and in a hurry. She sat with her mouth hanging open, stunned for a few minutes. What the hell was going on? Was Joy moving out on her? She got out the car and stormed up the walkway. Oh no she wasn't! And the bitch didn't say anything?

Ms. Johnson was sitting on her front porch in that old steel framed glider with the faded yellow flowers. She sipped on a tall glass of iced tea like it would be her last. She waved but Autumn ignored her, focusing on what was going on in her own house. She went through her open door and ran into Ricky who was carrying out a cardboard box. His eyes widened in shock.

"What the hell do you think you're doing?" she asked with hands on her hips. He was sweating like he had been working for a while, huge perspiration stains under the arms of his red T-shirt.

"Oh my favorite person is here." He set the box down on the floor. "What does it look like? I am moving my fiancée outta here."

"And why is that?" Autumn asked, knowing the answer to the question but feeling him out. How much did he really know? "She never said anything to me about moving."

"Because she was scared to say anything." Ricky got close to her face and she could smell the peppermint from the gum he had been chewing on. She could smell his sweat. "But I ain't afraid of ya. You're foul." He pointed a finger in her face. "Foul and I plan on exposing you for what you are."

"Excuse me?" She laughed, pushing his finger aside. "And you best watch where you stick that finger or you'll lose it. Might draw back a nub."

"You have some serious issues." He bent down to pick the box up, the top of his underwear peeking out from his jeans. They were red.

"Like what? Why don't you elaborate Ricky?"

"You know what issues you have. I don't want my girl involved in all that," he paused. "Because when you go down, it'll be by yourself."

"Is that right Ricky?"

He headed for the door. "Yup."

She went and sat down on her couch, feeling her head throbbing now. Had Joy told Ricky? She had committed the ultimate act of betrayal by telling this silly ass man?

Autumn was pissed but she wasn't sure what to do. She just could not believe that Joy, her only friend, the one who had been there for her through thick and thin, was walking away. Turning her back when Autumn needed her the most. She calmly opened her bag and lit a cigarette, hoping it would help her to think.

She was going to be here alone in this house with no one at least until the authorities came for her. She knew that Ricky would have them on her before dawn. Yeah he would call them up and say she was a murderer. That she was the East Coast slasher and her whole life would be over forever. She thought about Cole's face. The shock he would feel. The disgust too. That he had almost slept with the enemy.

Ricky stepped back into the house and went past her with a smug expression. She heard him climb the steps and knew he was going to get the rest of Joy's things. She wanted to hurt him. She didn't want him to walk out this house alive. How could she and take a chance? This was her life she was talking about. Her life, not his! With him around she would end up in a cell.

She got up and went into the kitchen and grabbed a carving knife. He had left her no choice. She had to do what she had to do. It was her or them. She went and locked the front door and went back to the entrance of the kitchen to wait until she heard his footsteps on the stairs. He crossed the floor and as he passed by the kitchen door, she leaped out and jumped on his back with the knife. She stabbed him twice before he threw her off yelping.

"You're one crazy bitch!" He rushed toward the door but she chased after him, hopping on him again and attacking. He held her arms and bent them causing pain but she wiggled away from him and stabbed him once more in the neck.

"You don't even know your girl has issues too. She just conceals them better than I do," Autumn spat.

He lay there unable to get up. She backed up as he moaned. She dropped the bloody knife. What the hell had she done now? She had attacked someone in her house? It was one thing to do it away from home but in her own place?

"Shit, now what should I do?"

She dropped onto the couch and watched him try to get up and fall twice. Then she heard a death rattle, which seemed to go on forever. Then there was nothing but silence. She sat there rocking for a minute. She lit a cigarette. She had to get rid of him before Joy missed him. And what about Joy? She had caused Autumn to do this.

She was not the Joy that Autumn had known. Joy had turned on her. She was as trifling as Uncle Harry had been. She would have to be dealt with too. If not, Autumn would spend her life in prison and she couldn't go out like that. Oh no, she wasn't going to. When it came right down to it, she had to defend herself. It was called the survival of the fittest.

She went and grabbed a pair of shears and started cutting out the carpet around Ricky's lifeless figure.

She had a lot of work to do.

# Chapter Thirty-Seven

Joy called Ricky but he didn't answer the phone. Where was he? She just had a bad feeling, which had started first thing that morning. And now it had been five hours since the move. He was supposed to call her when he was done but she hadn't heard a peep from him. She tried his cell phone again but it went directly to voice mail.

"Come on Ricky," she said, pulling onto their street. She pulled up to the house. The moving van was gone but should be anyway. But something felt wrong. She parked and got out. Autumn's car wasn't there either but she usually didn't get home until late anyway so that wasn't unusual.

She got out of the car and locked the door. She just needed to go in and check to make sure that he had gotten everything out of the house and then be on her way.

Walking up the stone path, she never thought that things would have come to this. Never. It went to show that life was full of surprises, sometimes-unpleasant ones too. She stepped inside and was shocked to see the carpet was all cut-up. A huge square was missing from the living room. She frowned, stepping further into the house as Boris came up to her, meowing up at her loudly. He seemed upset. Joy wanted to know why he had been left behind? Ricky forgot to take her baby with him? She picked Boris up in her arms and took the steps to the second floor as Boris still whined. He was fussing Joy out and she took it.

She went upstairs to the bedroom and noticed that half the boxes were still there. Maybe Ricky had gone to get something to eat and was coming back? That's what it is, she breathed in relief. Yeah she just needed to get it together. She sat on the edge of her bed, checking the number of stacked boxes in the middle of the floor. There were ten to go. Some of them were lightweight boxes too. She could carry those out herself. Then when he got back, he could quickly load the larger ones and they could be out. She'd leave Autumn a note, punking-out but she couldn't face her.

After resting for a sec, she got up and lifted a small box marked 'jewelry' and went to the door. Just then she heard the door open on the first floor. There he was.

She rushed out into the hallway with Boris on her heels, still meowing. "Ricky?"

There was no answer. She called again but nothing. Lord, she was really creeped out for some reason. She carefully made her way down the steps. The living room was empty. She went towards the front door.

"Joy."

Joy stopped in her tracks, almost ready to pee on herself at the sound of Autumn's voice. She glanced over her shoulder and saw Autumn standing near the coffee table, smiling. She almost peed on herself! Joy dropped the box on the floor and faced Autumn. She was busted.

"Oh hey girl. I didn't expect you to come home this early," Joy said.

"Obviously." Autumn gestured toward the box, holding one arm behind her back. "What you got there?"

"Oh yeah I was going to tell you before but didn't know how. I'm going to move in with Ricky for a while." Joy breathed, her heart thumping. Autumn had this crazed look on her face.

"So when were you going to tell me?" Autumn asked between gritted teeth. "I mean we're supposed to be tight Joy."

"I uh—"

"Don't worry about it." Autumn waved, stepping forward. "You've had this thing all planned out for some time. Then had your little boyfriend over here rolling through my house like he owned things."

"Autum-"

"'Cause I guess you couldn't deal, huh? Found out what I'd been up to on my trips, is that what it is Joy?"

"Uh no." Joy shook her head vigorously, suddenly terrified, sweat pouring down the side of her face and from her underarms. Where was Ricky? "I-I haven't—"

"Oh yes you did Joy." Autumn was inches away, her eyes on fire and her arm still behind her back. "Don't lie. It doesn't fit you very well. Ricky and I talked. You apparently gave him the skinny, the four-one-one." Autumn gave a devilish smile.

"Where is he?" Joy asked, trying to calm herself even though she knew. Something horrible had happened. The image of that guy in the hotel room flashed before her and she bit her lip to stop from crying. "Is he all right?"

"He's around." Autumn blinked. "But I don't want to talk about him."

"Where is he Autumn?" Joy whispered, searching the room. Did he need her help? That was the love of her life.

"Don't worry about him anymore, Joy. He was no good for you anyway. He wasn't worth the bottom of my shoe. He was slowing you down girl. Taking up too much of your time. These men, all they want to do is use you up. They want to take away your heart and soul, Joy. They want to destroy you. You have to get them before they get you." Autumn still had that weird look, rolling her neck. She was almost eye to eye with Joy, blowing peppermint-scented air.

Joy eased back toward the closed front door, watching as Autumn suddenly raised a knife. Joy started praying.

"Autumn please—" Joy pleaded, moving against the door.

"Please what? You let me down, Joy. I thought that you were different from Uncle Harry, Joy. I thought that you were my best friend and would never do me in, Joy. You disappointed me Joy. After all I've done for you. I kept your secret. I never told anybody. I loved you. I hated Uncle Harry but you were my heart. Now there are consequences." She poked the end of the knife into Joy's chest. "I could cut your heart out."

"Autumn you need help," Joy started. "We can get you to—"

"Shut the fuck up!" she barked, spraying spit in Joy's face. "I don't need your damn *help* Joy! Why, because there's nothing wrong with me! I'm perfectly sane. No, I'm not the one with the problem, Joy. No I'm fine, Joy. Maybe *you* have a problem, Joy. In fact you do with this knife in your face." Autumn had the end of the blade pointed at the tip of Joy's nose.

"Our father who art in heaven, hallowed be thy name," Joy whispered, touching the gold cross around her neck, praying it gave her power. She turned and tried the door but it was locked, which meant that it was over. There was nothing that Joy could do as Autumn grabbed her and dug the knife in her back.

All Joy felt was pain then darkness.

# Chapter Thirty-Eight

Cole took a huge bite of his crabcake sandwich as his office phone rang. Damn! He quickly wiped his hands on a napkin and picked up his office phone.

"Anders here."

"Yup, the prints came back," Judy said in that nasal voice.

"Okay and?" He cradled the phone between his shoulder and ear.

"They're not in the system. Whoever killed Terrence is not on file. A first time offender."

He closed his eyes and sat back in his chair. "Damn!" Was this another dead end? "Okay Judy, thanks."

He hung up and tapped the end of the pencil on the desk. He was not going to give up on this crime. Yeah, a lot of violent things in the city had gone unsolved but he wanted to come up with a victory. He went over the file again. He needed to go back out and double check with the neighbors. Make sure that they had not seen anyone. Every building and block had a nosy neighbor. Maybe someone was afraid to talk. Then the last time he went out the tenant across the hall had been out. He stood up, straightened his tie, and grabbed his jacket and cell, putting it in his pocket. Yeah, he had a feeling something would come up if he went back out there. He charged out of his office and went down to his cruiser. He always followed his hunches. Sometimes he got lucky. Though it seemed like he had been unlucky in love. He still didn't know what was up with Autumn. One moment she had been into him and the next totally turned off. He still wondered if it was because of his daughter. That really stung though. She didn't seem like the type to diss a brother because he had kids but some women were funny like that.

Taylor was part of his life and the woman who became a part of it would have to accept her without question. And he would not put any woman over his own child, no matter how they seemed to connect.

He pulled up in front of the five-story red brick apartment building and jumped out. He had to see if a Melody Shivers was in. She was the one directly across from Terrence's apartment. He took the elevator up to the third floor and walked down the dark hallway. The place was a dump and he had wondered for a long time why Terrence would have lived in a place like this. But then it recently came out that he owed some child support. Seems he had a couple of babies. Seven to be exact and he could not afford a better place.

He knocked on the door and waited but no one answered. He tried again, looking over at Terrence's door. Just as he started to walk away, he heard the lock disengage on the other side of the door and the door opened just an inch. An eye peered at him from between the rusty latch.

"Can I help you?" the woman asked.

"DC police. Homicide. I'm detective Cole Anders and I'd like to speak to you for a minute about Terrence Hill," he said holding up his badge.

"Can't see your badge, Mister police officer?" She squinted. "Bring that closer."

He held it up in front of her face. She closed the door and then slid the latch off, standing in front of him. She was much older than he had pictured. At least in her fifties with long wavy blonde hair with dark roots, a pale face with a red blotch on her forehead and gaunt cheekbones. She was wearing spandex leopard print pants and a black Lycra top and he thought about the eighties. She held a cigarette between blackened lips and puffed, half closing her sharp, sea blue eyes.

"What about Terrence? Damn shame how he ended up. He was a bit rough around the edges but that was no reason to kill him." She leaned on the doorframe, not willing to let him in. He smelled fried fish.

"Did you see anything the night that he was killed, ma'am?" Cole asked.

Melody nodded giving him a once over. "Yeah, I did."

Cole was pleasantly surprised and felt a glimmer of hope but he controlled himself. "Can you tell me about it, ma'am?"

"I suppose so but I ain't for gettin' on no stand or nothin'. Too many people get knocked off that way. I love life too much."

"Do you mind if I come in and we discuss it, ma'am?" He was not too keen on standing out in the middle of the hallway.

"Yeah, I guess so." She stepped back into her place and he followed. What shocked him was that she had at least six cats in there. They were all different colors; and cried loudly, moving around her feet as she went to an area that served as a living room. She pointed to a deep red velour couch, which had a leg missing.

"Have a seat, Mister police officer."

"I'll stand if you don't mind," Cole said blinking. The place smelled like cat too. It was dark inside, all the windows shut to keep out the light. A painting of a white cat perched on a throne hung crookedly on the wall. Okay now. He focused back on her. "I don't plan on staying long."

She shrugged her shoulders and studied him. "It's a free country."

"Ms. Shivers, what exactly did you see that night?" He put his hands on his hips, hoping she didn't tell him a Martian or space ship. She seemed like the type.

"Well mister police officer, first let me say that I've never seen a murderer in my entire life. Other than on the news and on crime shows. Columbo is my favorite. I would marry that man if I could." She pressed her thin lips together and then blew into her cheeks.

"Um hum." He leaned in, waiting for her to get to the point. "Interesting. So about that night."

"I was in here, just mindin' my business you know? I was sewin' a baby blanket for my grandbaby. She's turnin' two next month. Amber is my life," she paused. "Anyways, I was watchin' *CSI Miami* on TV, which was sort of ironic, don't you think?" She picked underneath her nails before leaning down to pick up two of the cats, placing one in each arm. She kissed the top of the head of the black one on her left. "This one is named Scatter. I found her outside in the cold last winter. She was a scrawny little thing but look at her now."

"Cute cats." Cole was used to massaging people into telling him what he needed.

"And I heard Terrence yellin' from his apartment. He was sayin', "you bitch! What did you do to me?" She twisted her face up and rocked her head from side to side.

"Uh huh." So she had not told him anything he didn't already know. The killer had been a woman.

"And then I heard the door to his apartment open and slam. I opened my door just a little bit like I did with you and saw a woman with red hair storm past me. She was a pretty black girl. Like a Vanessa Williams type."

"So you saw her face?" he paused. Now that would be progress.

"Just the side of her face." She set the cats down and scratched her scalp, frowning.

"All right good. Can you give me a physical description? Approximate height and weight?"

"She was real tall. 'Bout five nine or ten and shapely. Sharp features and I think a mole on her lip."

Cole took out his pad and wrote it down. "What was she wearing, do you remember?"

"A sexy-type black dress and sandals. Real classy look but then nothin' that would stand out."

"Anything else?" he asked, hoping to wrap this up.

"Well, her perfume was real nice. The expensive kind. It was like lemony or citrus," she paused. "That reminds me, do you want some lemonade? Or orange juice? I squeeze the oranges myself. Get 'em from my garden. Yup, I have one right out on my deck."

"Uh no thank you," he said, gazing at her closely, wondering if she was a reliable witness. "Okay well, thank you Ms. Shivers. You've been very helpful."

"I always cooperate with the law. Hey, do yall have any openings down there? My nephew is lookin' for somethin'," she asked, pressing her lips together again.

"Tell him to check online. There are always positions available, Ms. Shivers."

"I'll do that." She kissed the head of the black cat again and it meowed. She set both of them down.

"I can let myself out," he said heading for her door as the cats milled around.

"You take care, Mister police officer. And if you need anything else, come on back." She laid a finger on her right breast and rubbed the nipple, giving him a seductive look and he wanted to spill his beans right there. Damn, he might be able to keep it down for weeks after seeing that.

# Chapter Thirty-Nine

Autumn couldn't cry another tear. She lay in her bed, gazing at the TV screen, the volume turned up to drown out the silence. What had she done? She had killed her best friend. She clutched the covers, seeing Uncle Harry' face telling her that she was a whore. Then she saw Joy's shocked face. She had not meant to hurt Joy. She had just lost it…it was as if she just couldn't control the rage anymore.

She reached over and grabbed the bottle of Vodka and guzzled half the bottle. Truthfully she wanted to die. End it.

Tired of the pain.

Feeling bad.

Losing control.

Losing her mind.

She wanted to sleep forever. To meet up with Uncle Harry in hell. Or all the other bastards that she had killed.

"Police say they have another witness in the East Coast killings. A man at the DewDrop Diner in Delaware remembers a young lady with blonde hair who fit the description given by the first witness. This woman, who police believe may be the East Coast slasher, came in with BJ James who was found in Rock Creek Park a week ago."

Autumn knew it was the old man from the diner with the joker smile who had given up the juice. He had turned her in. Not that she was the least bit surprised. She pulled the covers over her head and marinated in the darkness. They'd be coming for her soon. It was only a matter of time. She was ready though. Tired of running. Tired of everything. She was all alone now. There was no one to talk to. No one to encourage her.

She thought she heard a creak and she stiffened. Sounded like the floorboards. Maybe Joy was coming back for her. Coming to drag her down into her shallow grave. Then the phone rang, causing her to shiver. Who was calling her?

She snatched off the covers and ran to the phone.

"Who is it?" Autumn asked, feeling a headache coming on.

"Uh hello Autumn, this is Mrs. Henderson, Joy's mother," a stiff voice said.

"Mrs. Henderson. Nice to hear from you," Autumn lied.

"Uh you too. Can I speak to Joy please?"

"She isn't here," she whispered.

"Oh," Mrs. Henderson paused sounding shocked. "It's so late. I've been calling her cell phone all day and I just can't seem to reach her."

"Do you want to leave a message? I'll make sure that she gets it."

"Yes, have her call me when she gets in."

"I'll make sure that she does."

"Thank you. Take care." She hung up.

Bitch!

"Never liked you either," Autumn hissed. Mrs. Henderson hated her guts. Always had. Only tolerated her because of Joy. Thought she was trash. Never good enough to hang with her daughter.

"Yeah, you think I ain't shit. That's all right though." Autumn nodded. "Um hum that is all right. You'll be waiting a long time before Joy calls. Like in the next world. Like after your own ass checks out."

Autumn went back to her bed, suddenly feeling like crying all over again. Damn she would miss Joy. She had loved that girl. She had been like a sister to Autumn. And now she was gone. Autumn had seen Joy's face. Her body had been cold and stiff. Like all the others. She was a nonexistent entity now. A nothing. Would she ever forgive Autumn?

# Chapter Forty

Cole watched his daughter sleeping soundly, cuddled up next to her pink teddy bear. She was growing up before his eyes. Before he knew it she would be asking to use the car. He would never be ready for those days. He got up and closed the door to her room. Lauren had gone out with that fool ass Jay and Cole had agreed to take Taylor. He even took off from work tomorrow so they could spend time together. Go to the zoo and check out the new kiddy flick over at the Silver Spring Majestic.

Man, he liked this pops thing but he wished he had a moms to go with it. He never wanted a baby's mama situation and his own moms wouldn't like it at all.

He walked into his study, figuring he could get in at least an hour of work before turning in. He was still frustrated about this case with Terrence Hill too and needed a day to think things through. Something just didn't sit well with him. It was like there was a missing piece right under his thumb. He went over to his papers. He picked up the picture. Terrence had this cocky grin, his arms wrapped around two fine sisters. Yeah, he had been a player. A baller.

"Who killed you man?" Cole asked.

He popped the top on his can of beer.

The phone rang. It was Lauren, sounding strange.

"Come get me Cole," she said quietly.

"Come get you? What's wrong?" He sat up in his seat, alarmed.

"Jay hit me," she moaned

"What! He did *what?*" Cole shouted, jumping out of his seat and knocking over the beer. That motherfucker had laid his hands on her!

"Yeah I'm at George Washington hospital. I had him arrested," she mumbled.

He felt his blood boiling. "I'm on my way."

He slammed the phone down. Shit! He would kill that fool!

He called his next-door neighbor, Ms. Harper, a sweet old lady who loved Taylor like she was her own. She agreed to come over and babysit and as soon as she walked in, he was out the door.

Autumn was locked up behind this steel cage in a dark room. There were whacked out paintings on the gray walls with trolls and witches, reminding her of the fairytales she used to read when she was a kid. Made her shiver. She had been scared of things that bumped in the night like everyone else. Now was no different.

Especially now because she knew there really were monsters.

She checked out her new home and saw that it was square shaped and only big enough for her to turn around in. She felt almost like a monkey in the zoo or maybe a lion, a lioness and someone was trying to contain her. Keep her prisoner so maybe she couldn't lash out again.

Problem was she started feeling claustrophobic and this intense desire to break out. To be set free. She felt too confined, like she was not able to breathe. She shook the bars and screamed, knowing she had to get out one way or the other. Of course the bars would not resist. They were ice-cold, almost burning her flesh. So she started screaming, and noticed a video camera hooked up to the ceiling and pointed right at her. What kind of sick bastard was watching her? He was probably mocking her. Laughing at her.

The hot lights were bearing down on her and she started sweating heavily as it came out of her pores and dampened the top she was wearing.

"Let me outta here! Let me out now!" she screamed, staring at a black door, which had materialized right before her eyes. It opened slowly and she cringed against the back of the cage, afraid of who was coming through that door. Shit, she knew this was a dream that was quickly turning into a nightmare.

She wanted to close her eyes but it was like they were forced open as she whimpered, knowing whoever was coming was not good. They were trying to harm her. Then they were at the bars, a dark figure without a face in a black suit and pimp daddy hat with a black feather sticking out of it. She stared hard and realized that it was Uncle Harry. He shook his head slowly from side to side, smiling as worms fell out the sides. He laughed, drowning out her screams. He put his hands on the bars and it was like steam was coming out from between his fingers.

She was starting to feel like she was going to pass out. She wanted to wake up.

"You been a bad girl Autumn. Very bad. You have to be punished," Uncle Harry said. He was suddenly inside the cage crawling toward her, his eyes now vacant holes. And then there was someone behind him. It was Joy and she was grinning hard, half her teeth gone and her hair hanging over her eyes, dirt in her nails like maybe she had tried to crawl out of that grave.

"We've been waiting for you," Joy said in a guttural voice.

Autumn knew it wasn't real and she told herself to wake up. Suddenly her eyes flew open. She lay breathing hard. Getting up, her legs felt like rubber and her throat like sandpaper. She made it into the bathroom and got up to get a glass of water. She gulped it down and filled her glass again with a shaky hand. Harry had seemed so real. Like he had really been there. And Joy.

There was another creak and she reached for the lamp switch, relieved when the room was filled with plenty of light.

# Chapter Forty-One

Cole's day off was not starting out as he had expected. He poured some Corn Flakes in a bowl for Taylor, yawning. He had only gotten three hours of zzz's last night. He and Lauren had not gotten back to his place until five in the morning. She had suffered a black eye, a swollen lip and minor head injuries. Then she had to talk with the police. Turns out Jay was a real knucklehead. Some small time drug dealer. Cole could kick himself. He had meant to check that fool out but hadn't had time. No, they were all excuses. He should have done a better job keeping up with it.

"Daddy?" Taylor asked sleepily, rubbing her eyes. One stiff ponytail was raised in the air.

He set the bowl in front of her. She dug her little purple spoon in.

"Where's mommy?"

"Sleeping," he said trying to keep attitude out of his tone. He still cared for Lauren no doubt but she had made some bad ass decisions. It made him question whether she was fit enough to raise their daughter to be a strong woman. Or at least whether she could do it alone without the other parent.

"You two are up early." Lauren stood in the doorway wrapped in his robe. Her left eye was purplish black and her lip was inflated like a tire but she was still beautiful to Cole. Taylor hopped down and ran to her mother.

"Mommy, mommy, mommy!" she screamed.

Lauren bent down and picked up her child. Taylor touched her mother's face and started crying, throwing her arms tightly around Lauren's neck.

"Don't worry baby. Mommy just had an accident."

"Accident?" Taylor said, her bottom lip trembling.

"Want something to eat?" Cole asked gruffly. He kept his back to her as he pulled out a package of bacon and a cartoon of eggs.

"Sure." She came into the room and sat down with Taylor facing her, straddling her hip. She was twirling a lock of Lauren's hair.

There was silence for a few minutes, and then Lauren spoke. "Thanks for picking me up last night Cole."

"Um hum." He kept his back to her.

"Trust me I didn't know he was into drugs. He told me he was in business for himself."

"And you expect me to believe that?" Cole whirled around, unleashing his pent up feelings. "You have a child Lauren! You need to use your brain."

"Yes," she said quietly, getting up and setting Taylor back in her chair. "Yes I do. You know I don't roll like that Cole. I am very careful of who I bring around. He owned two clubs and that's all I knew. And I definitely didn't think he was a woman beater. I would never let any man put his hands on me like that." She smoothed down fly-aways on her head and pushed back her bangs. They flopped back in her eyes. He used to love when they did that.

Cole turned away from her, breaking eggs into a bowl and using a fork to whip them. He was pissed too that she had allowed some man like that in her circle. What if he had killed her?

"Sit in your chair Taylor," Lauren said. Cole heard the high chair being pushed up to the table.

"Mommy and Daddy," Taylor sang, crunching on her cereal, her legs swinging.

"Cole." Lauren was now behind him. Then her arms were around his waist and her head rested on his back. "He was never as good a man as you. Never."

"Really? I thought he was the best thing since Swiss cheese," Cole said, turning so she could see his smirk.

"Um-um, well whatever," she murmured.

"Funny how you remember that now. That I'm such a good brother. Should be one of those Bachelors of the year in *Essence* then, huh. Maybe somebody will submit my pic."

He moved away from her and went to the other countertop, cracking two eggs in a bowl over the stove, not wanting her to see that he had been affected by her unexpected show of affection. He wanted to appear hard as a rock but damn she could still get to him.

She went back over near the table and rubbed the top of Taylor's head. "Guess Taylor and I will get out of your way then, Bachelor of the year."

He damn sure didn't want that.

"Who says I want you two to leave?" He turned and their eyes met and he felt something. He had to admit that it was cool. Okay, real cool to have them over, in his place like this. Almost seemed like they were a family. He had wanted a family. To feel like one.

She gave a little smile and lowered herself into the chair. "I'm glad to hear that, I really am."

# Chapter Forty-Two

Joy crawled among the leaves. She felt faint and wondered if she would make it. She had lost a lot of blood. She prayed to God to help her make it. She saw the main road. It was in front of her…and if she could just make it. She needed to make it. She had a life. Even one without Ricky. She forced herself not to cry. She couldn't waste any energy. She didn't have much left.

She heard a car pass by.

"Help me," she whispered, leaves clinging to the bottoms of her hands as she dragged along. She had to stop every few minutes because of the pain. The sun peeked between the thick green trees as she rested for a second. She was in shock too. Couldn't believe that this was real. She was fighting for her life. No one knew where she was. It looked like Rock Creek Park. But she had to keep moving. She had heard on TV that people in her situation should find super human strength and keep moving.

Autumn went to work as usual. She had to make it appear that everything was normal. Gwen and Sasha were at each other's throats like normal. Janet tried to mediate.

Autumn switched on the TV. There were the regular killings and then more stuff on the war. A reporter with strawberry blonde hair appeared on the side of 95 Interstate and Autumn perked up. Was this what she had been waiting for?

"The identity of the East Coast slasher is still unknown at this time. Another man has been found in Chester, Pennsylvania. The man, who was from Pensauken, New Jersey, worked for Merry Shoes Trucking

Company. That now brings the death toll to ten and then the unexplained death of another trucker in DC that is believed to possibly be the work of the killer too. Police believe that the killer is a young black woman who changes her appearance with wigs but they are still searching for her. They are pleading with truckers to not pick up anyone on their trips."

"Damn, well that could be a million people. Could they be a little more detailed?" Sasha put a hand on his hip. "Um um um. I tell you this world is going to hell, chile. Jesus is comin' soon y'all. Trust me on that. Can I get a witness?"

"Amen," the girl in his chair chimed in.

"I'm tired of seeing all that garbage on TV. Every time you turn on the news it's about some tragedy. That's why our kids are crazy now," Gwen said blowing drying a little girl's thick head of hair. The kid looked like she was about to burst in tears, her bottom lip trembling. "Autumn, where's Joy?"

"I don't know," Autumn said, trying to look worried. "She didn't come home last night."

"What about that man of hers?" Sasha asked.

"That's what I figured. She was probably at Ricky's," Autumn said casually. "I'm sure she'll just be in late. No biggie."

"They set a wedding date yet?" Gwen asked as the little girl whimpered.

"Nope," Autumn replied, irritated with the entire conversation. She didn't want to discuss Joy. She wanted to forget about her altogether.

"I'm sure it'll be a big one though," Gwen added.

"I think so." Autumn headed for the door. "I'm going to get some coffee. Anybody want anything?"

"I have a taste for a burrito," Janet said.

"For breakfast?" Autumn laughed.

"Chiquita, you can eat a burrito anytime, day or night." Janet was putting corn rows in a teenaged boy's head.

"I get you amigo," Autumn put on her shades. "Anybody else?"

"Yeah, I'll take a cup of regular black coffee chile," Sasha replied. "I was hangin' last night at a friends' birthday party and didn't get home until six this morning. I can barely keep my eyes open."

"Oh I'll get that right away. I wouldn't want you burning anybody's ear with that crazy iron. I can't afford for anyone to sue me, understand?" Autumn walked off.

"Can I get a witness?" Gwen added.

"Yes ma'am," Sasha started. "But I'm the ultimate professional. No matter how tired I get, I always handle my business properly now."

"I believe you." Autumn stepped outside. It looked like rain later, which would be a good thing. It had been so hot lately. She went into The Fried Egg diner and ordered two cups of coffee. She left and was on her way back when she heard someone call her name.

She turned to see Cole riding by in his cop car. Oh shit! She wanted to go in the other direction but it was too late. He spotted her. She put on a straight, emotionless face.

"Cole," she said, folding her arms over her chest.

"Hey Autumn, how've you been?" he asked stiffly, a distance there.

"Okay," she paused. "Sorry I didn't return your call. I've been busy."

"No problem." He studied the cups of coffee in her hand.

"Well, I better get back inside."

"Cool, take care," he said, pulling off. She stared after him. He had gotten over her just like that. Maybe the bastard hadn't been different after all. He had been like the rest.

She pushed open the shop door. It was better this way. They had no future together.

# Chapter Forty-Three

Cole was still pining away for Autumn, but he couldn't let her see it. Had to play like it was cool. In his rear view mirror he watched her disappear behind the dark doors of her shop. He wondered if he would ever see her again. But then he had been pondering on whether to get back with Lauren. She was a good woman and was the mother of his child. They were a family and might be able to get a good thing going. He loved Lauren, even if he was not in love. But then maybe that would happen later. And she wanted to give it a go, so they'd see.

He turned the corner, feeling hunger pangs hit him hard. He decided to stop in at Chicken and Ribs Galore to get some breakfast.

The place had several empty tables but he knew come lunchtime it would be packed. He heard they made a mean rib sandwich and he believed it after sampling her food at the Summer Jazz fest.

Ms. Betty was talking to one of her employees when he rolled up. She turned and smiled at him.

"Oh hi there. Your Autumn's friend, right?" She straightened her white apron. The employee batted her eyes at him.

He nodded. "Cole."

"Yes, Cole." She cocked her head and stared like she was deep in thought. "You're a police officer," she asked in wonderment.

"Yes ma'am." He grinned.

"Cole, you look so familiar. I mean even before Autumn. Are your people from here?" She cocked her head.

"Yes they are, ma'am."

"I swear you remind me of someone I used to know," she paused. "If you don't mind me asking, who're your parents?"

"Mable Anders was my mom," he said.

She shook her head slowly. "No, that doesn't sound familiar. Who was your daddy?"

"Harrius. I never even knew his last name. I didn't know much about him."

Her face lit up. "Oh Harrius! Yes I was an acquaintance of his."

Cole raised an eyebrow. "Really?"

"Yes, yes, he sold me this shop. He was some man." Ms. Betty smiled and Cole knew it had been more than that. They had probably been lovers. Papa was a rolling stone. "He mentioned he had a little boy. Yeah, Cole that's right."

"This is uh, some coincidence," he said lowering his head. This couldn't be happening.

"Matter of fact I have a picture of him." She disappeared and came back with a black and white of the man he had seen in the picture that his mom had shown him. He had his arm wrapped around a much younger Ms. Betty. He still didn't know what to feel. His pops had a life without him.

"Yeah, he was something. Involved in a lot of rumors and trouble. Wonder whatever happened to him?"

"What do you mean? He was in prison is what my mother told me."

"Oh he did some time, but that was way back when he was a teen. He actually went on to become a trucker. Then when his brother was killed in that fire, he inherited some businesses including this one. He gave me a good deal on it," she paused. "One day he just disappeared." She shook her head seeming stuck in the past. Then she turned to him smiling.

"I thought that Autumn was your girlfriend," she said.

He shot Ms. Betty a puzzled look. What did Autumn have to do with this?

"Autumn?" he said quietly.

"Yeah, she's your cousin! No wonder you two favor!" she squealed.

Cole was still confused. He wondered if this lady had completely lost her mind. "I don't know what you're saying Ms. Betty."

"Oh you didn't know." She felt bad. It was written all over her face.

"Honey, Harrius was Autumn's uncle."

"What?" He ran a hand over his face. He felt like things were reeling out of control. Autumn related to him? His cousin?

"Are you all right?" Ms. Betty seemed worried. "Sorry to break it to you like that."

"I've got to run," he breathed.

"Wait, lunch is on me!"

"I'll take a rain check." He headed out the door just as huge raindrops fell. He had almost slept with his cousin. He wondered if Autumn had been aware of it and just refused to tell him. He was going to find out. He reached for his mobile but before he could dial, the phone rang. It was Lauren sounding frantic.

"It's Taylor! She's been hurt!"

"Shit what?" he said.

"Meet us at Georgetown hospital."

Cole got there in record speed. His little girl meant everything to him. He couldn't imagine life without her. He tried to stay calm as he pulled into the emergency visitors' parking lot. But he felt an anxiety attack coming. He had them when under extreme stress. His chest tightened and he found it hard to breathe. He pulled open his tie as he stumbled through the door. A lady looked up from behind the desk and frowned.

"Sir, are you all right?"

"My daughter, Taylor Anders was admitted?"

The lady gave him a sympathetic nod and typed in the computer. "Oh she's still waiting. Apparently she sprained her ankle. You can find her in the waiting area. They are getting ready to call her."

Cole could barely let the lady finish before he flew towards the waiting area crowded with people. He spotted them sitting there. He ran over.

"Daddy!" Taylor called out weakly.

Cole embraced his daughter.

# Chapter Forty-Four

Joy made it to the road and found the inner strength, that super human kind, to stand on her feet. She saw a white car approaching and she waved. They pulled to the curb and she fell just as the car door opened and slammed and feet quickly approached. She felt herself being lifted by strong arms and carried to a car. She was laid on the passenger seat of the car. The handsome brother leaned over.

"I'll take you to the hospital okay?"

"Piece of paper," Joy whispered between parched lips. She needed to leave her statement in case she didn't make it to the hospital alive. He quickly reached in his front pocket and pulled out a crumbled piece of paper like a receipt and handed it to her with a pen. She scribbled a few words on the back and passed out.

Autumn was training the new receptionist on the phone system when the call came. She never expected it, but she had to play like she was actually happy that Joy had been found alive. Her mother had only been hours from reporting her missing. Damn, she couldn't have survived. But she had. Of course Janet, Sasha and Gwen wanted to go to Georgetown Hospital so they piled in Autumn's car. All Autumn could think about was if Joy would ever come out of that coma. She needed to stay there. She had to or else Autumn would be in big trouble. But her thoughts were constantly interrupted by Sasha who just could not seem to stop talking. Back in the day they called it diarrhea of the mouth.

"I can't believe poor Joy is laying up in some hospital. They found her in that park. Lord, the same one where that Levy girl was some years ago. What is wrong with people?" Sasha sighed.

"Who would hurt poor, sweet Joy?" Janet said quietly.

"Maybe that boyfriend of hers. You know domestic violence is on the rise," Gwen added.

Sasha smacked her lips. "I wouldn't put it past him. These men are so rough nowadays. And maybe Joy was pregnant and he found out. That seems to be the thing nowadays. Men killing their wives and girlfriends just because they're havin' a baby. Like that Lacie Peterson and that girl killed by that football player, Ray somethin'. Well, it is a real shame." He threw his silk scarf over his shoulder. "Autumn sweetie, do you mind if I open the windows and turn off the AC? It is dryin' out my sinuses?"

"No problem." Autumn let down the windows.

"Damn not too much!" Gwen held onto her hair. "My do' could blow away and I spent two hours under the dryer."

"Forget your hair. Joy is lyin' in some cold hospital bed fightin' for her life," Sasha snapped.

"And *forget* your sinuses," Gwen shot back.

"I need both of you to be quiet right now or I'll let you out on the street and you'll have to walk the rest of the way."

"Yeah, you hear that *Gwen.*"

"You can kiss my you know what *Sasha.*"

"Whatever." Sasha picked at her nails.

"Hey, should we all chip in and get some flowers?" Janet said.

"Sounds like a good idea," Autumn replied as she turned into the hospital parking lot. What the hell was she going to do? She really was not game for seeing Joy. What if she woke up?

"Maybe roses," Sasha suggested.

"You give those for romantic purposes," Gwen said unbuckling her seat and climbing out of the car.

"Well, what do you suggest brainiac?"

"Ladies, I'll take care of that later. Right now we need to worry about Joy," Autumn said as they made their way into the emergency room. Autumn pulled off her shades and went up to the lady with the short natural. She obtained the room number and they walked through the waiting area to get to the elevators. She happened to glance over and was surprised to see Cole sitting next to a pretty young woman. The little girl from his picture was on his lap. He was busy talking and she was thankful for that as they rushed by. She didn't have time to focus on anything but the patient on the third floor.

They rode in the elevator without talking and made it down the long hallway. Autumn hated everything about hospitals. The smell and the quiet. And she always worried about catching something. She remembered when Daddy D had been in the hospital. It was horrible. And seeing him had been worse than anything else had. He had been hooked up to all these tubes. She shivered. It was something she would never, ever forget.

And she was reminded when she got a look-see at Joy. She was all wired up. Her head was bandaged and she was very still. Her eyes were closed like she had already checked out. Autumn, in the back of her mind, hoped she might just expire on her own. Yeah, a part of her felt bad for thinking all this but if Joy had just minded her business.

Mrs. Henderson rose from her seat next to Joy and rushed over, giving Autumn a hug, which was unexpected. The Reverend Henderson patted Autumn's shoulder. Jason gave her a tight hug.

"God is so good," Reverend Henderson murmured then gazed over at his daughter. He had tears in his eyes. "She's alive. My little girl is still with us!"

"What happened?" Autumn asked going over to Joy's bedside.

"We don't know yet. She was discovered by the side of the road, in Rock Creek Park," Mrs. Henderson whispered.

"Unconscious," Jason added; his eyes red and swollen.

"Oh my goodness." Autumn put a hand to her mouth. She could come back later and finish it off.

"Who would want to hurt my baby?" Mrs. Henderson sobbed.

"Joy." Autumn grabbed her friend's cold hand. "Joy, it's going to be all right." She may as well have been talking to a stone or wall. There was no response.

"What are her chances?" Autumn asked innocently.

"Pretty good. She's lost a lot of blood and sustained some serious injuries but Joy always was a fighter." Reverend Henderson rubbed his wife's back. "That's my sugar plum."

"That's my baby," Mrs. Henderson whispered.

"We all love your daughter," Sasha offered quietly, folding his hands in front of him.

"Thank you," Mrs. Henderson sobbed before burying her face in her husband's chest.

"Yes, anything we can do," Gwen added.

"Anything," Janet chimed in.

"We didn't want to stay too long," Autumn started. "Just wanted to see her and let her know we are thinking about her."

"Of course." Mrs. Henderson had been transformed into a decent human being. Humble.

"I'll drop by tomorrow to check on her." Autumn tried to put on her sorrowful face. "Do you all need me to do anything?"

"We're fine." Mrs. Henderson managed a smile. "So glad that you came by."

"God is in control but we have faith that He'll pull us through," Reverend Henderson said shaking his head. "The devil thought he had her but he failed. He failed."

"He did." Autumn nodded, hating the sermon but agreeing with him. What he failed to understand was that the devil wasn't done just yet.

"Glad that you came by," Jason said, laying a hand on her shoulder. Then he wrapped his broad arms around her and sobbed. She pulled away, embarrassed for him.

As they walked out, she noticed a tall, nice looking brother in a suit talking with the police. She nodded to them and kept rolling.

She had to work out her plan.

# Chapter Forty-Five

Dexter gave the crumbled paper to the police officer. He had stayed at the hospital to make sure the lady would be fine. Well it turned out that she wasn't. She had gone into a coma, but he felt obligated for some reason. Then he wanted to make sure that the lady's message had been delivered.

The police officer seemed stunned by it.

"Do you mind staying a bit longer? We need to ask you a few more questions?"

"No problem officer. I kind of want to see how she's doing anyway."

"Well we appreciate guys like you. You're a hero."

"Naw." He shook his head. "Just helping someone in need. Anyone else would have done the same thing."

"Oh you would be surprised. Not necessarily." The officer pushed back his short blonde hair and rose from the seat, going over to talk with another officer.

Dexter got up and went to the entrance of Joy's room. Her father nodded to him again. They had exchanged a few words. He was a minister and kept going on and on, expressing his gratitude. Dexter understood. It was the relief of a father. Even though he had no kids, he could imagine how bad it would be to have one of them hurt.

He saw how banged up the lady was and he was really pulling for her. She had just come out of nowhere and he was just glad to have been there to help.

He thought back to what she had written. It still sent chills up his spine. *Autumn Fields did this. East Coast slasher.* He had heard of the East Coast slasher. Who hadn't over the last few weeks? It had been all anyone talked about. But had this killer really attacked Joy? It was hard to believe, but anything was possible.

He thought back to his own sister, killed by a serial murderer twelve years ago. It had taken a long time for him to accept that a perfect stranger could harm his innocent kid sister. She had been in college and just a random selection of this maniac. The man was still sitting on death row but if Dexter had his chance, he would have offed him quick and in a hurry. It had killed his parents. They had both died of a broken heart even if the autopsies said something different. Even being a doctor, he knew the power of extreme stress on the body. They had given up after Dara's death.

"Uh Dr. Barnes, we need to get your contact information." The blonde-haired officer asked.

Dexter gave his cell phone number, home number and address.

"And one last question. You're positive that Ms. Henderson didn't say anything else?"

"Yes," he said.

"Did she mention a Ricky Ferguson?"

"No," Dexter said.

"All right thanks a lot for your time. You're free to go for now. We'll be in touch."

Dexter nodded but he was not going anywhere.

Autumn paced back and forth over her hardwood floors, her heels clicking loudly as that dumb cat meowed. Joy had actually made it. She didn't think she would, frankly. And her father said she was a fighter. Had Autumn missed that side of Joy's personality?

"Damn, damn, damn!" She punched the air. Joy had to die. No question. But how and when? She was not going to let that girl take her down. Nobody could take Autumn down. She still had so much work to do. She had to keep cleansing the world. She had a mission. She had been sent to take care of the trash of the world.

The doorbell rang. She went to the side window and noticed her neighbor Ms. Johnson standing on the stoop. Damn what does she want? Autumn opened the door.

"Hi my darling." She was dressed in all white like an angel or something. Her silver hair was in a tight bun.

"Yes Ms. Johnson," Autumn sighed. She didn't have time for bullshit.

"I heard about Joy and wanted to express my sympathy."

"She would appreciate that." Autumn barred the door and hoped Ms. Johnson would be on her merry way in a minute or less.

"Where is she staying?" Ms. Johnson asked, leaning on her cane.

Autumn quickly gave her the information and got rid of her, making some excuse of bath water running. It burned her up that people were so concerned about that traitor. Autumn wondered if they'd feel that way if something happened to her. No one ever cared what she thought or felt.

The doorbell rang again. She was sick to death of people bothering her. Why wouldn't they just leave her alone? She yanked the door open and was shocked to see two officers standing there.

"Ms. Fields?" the Hispanic one asked.

"Yes." She put a hand on her hip, trying to stay cool as a cucumber.

He held up a piece of paper. "We have a search warrant for your property."

She felt panicky on the inside but still remained unflustered. "A search warrant? For my house?"

"Yes ma'am." The blonde-haired officer wore a serious expression.

She stepped aside. "Search away. I don't know what this is all about."

They came inside and she grabbed her purse for a cigarette. She felt out of control as she slumped on the sofa. They didn't ask where anything was, just went through the first floor quickly and headed upstairs. She crossed her legs. What was this all about? She had been careful. They had nothing on her. And even if they searched, they would come up empty. That is when she remembered the diary but it was way too late.

The blonde-haired officer came back holding it. "Ms. Fields, we need to take you down to our office and ask you a few questions."

"I'll get dressed."

# Chapter Forty-Six

They grilled Autumn and asked that she not leave town. They had even taken her fingerprints. She left out by three in the morning so she was still feeling tired even though she got up the next day as usual to go into the shop. She had a busy day and needed to make sure that Sasha and Gwen didn't tear each other apart. She got in and it was so quiet on the street. The sun had come up and seemed to be punishing her early. The dog days of August…she was determined to act like everything was normal…she had a lawyer. He was meeting her that evening after she took care of Joy.

She still went to the salon to take her mind off of things. She wasn't sure when she might see it again.

Since it was stuffy, she immediately switched on the air. She opened the blinds, hoping that letting in sunshine would make things seem brighter. Like everything in the world was still okay.

Sasha called just as Autumn pulled out the pretty new towels she had just bought. He was down with a bad cold and not able to make it in but could Autumn call all his clients? Of course Autumn didn't mind calling to cancel for her most popular stylist. She hummed to herself, popping in a Miles Davis CD. Maybe everything was going to be okay especially after she took care of Joy.

Gwen bounced in all smiles. "Hey girl, hot enough for you?" She had on a pair of jeans so tight they had to be painted on.

"You never lied. You see the air is on," Autumn responded.

"I don't think a lot of people will be coming in today. What would be the use? Their hair would just fall. It would be senseless." She plopped down in her chair and studied Autumn intently.

"Where is the transvestite?" Gwen spun around in the chair, searching the shop.

"Stop calling him that." Autumn went to the computer to pull up Sasha's client list. "You two should try and get along."

Gwen snorted. "Never. She, excuse me, *he,*" she paused with a smirk playing at her lips. "And I will never mix. Like oil and water. Besides that he's a Leo and I'm a Scorpio. It will never happen." Gwen squinted. "What's up with you? You look stressed out."

"Had a rough night, baby doll," Autumn said.

"I can dig. One of my old boyfriends came over and we tried to rekindle the flames. I need somebody since kicking Jamie to the curb."

Autumn laughed for the first time in days. She looked up from the list. "And did the flames glow?"

"Hell yeah." She broke into a grin. "They say the second time is always better."

"Hey Gwen," Autumn started. "I want to ask you something?"

Gwen got up and inspected herself in the mirror. She started fluffing up the front of her hair. "Ask away boss lady."

"I want you to take over the shop."

"What?" Gwen whirled around frowning. "You have to take a vacation?"

"No Gwen I'm serious. I want you to buy the shop."

"What? Why?" Gwen asked louder, confusion registering on her face.

"I'm going away so I need somebody to take it over."

"Where are you going?" Gwen came over and studied Autumn.

"We'll talk about it later."

The door swung open and Gwen's first client of the day arrived. That meant that Autumn could devote her time to making those calls for Sasha. But something still hung over her head like a dark cloud. She wasn't going to be able to shake it either.

At noon, they turned on the TV to check the news. Autumn was not so thrilled about hearing it but sat down with her chicken salad. The first thing was breaking news that there seemed to be a break in the trucker killings but they would elaborate after the commercial break. Autumn's heartbeat sped up and she gripped her fork.

"About time," Gwen said, working her fingers quickly to plait her thin client's shoulder length hair.

Autumn nodded her head, feeling in a trance. Maybe she should have run. To Canada or anywhere. She could have rolled out with her clothes on her back, she thought.

The door opened and she turned in slow motion. Two officers stood there with grim expressions. They zeroed in on her.

"What the devil is going on?" Gwen asked as she stopped plaiting, her mouth open wide enough to catch a whole gang of flies.

They marched over as Autumn started trembling. This was it.

"Autumn Ann Fields?"

"Yes," she whispered, getting up, her salad dropping to the floor. Salad dressing splashed against her legs.

"You're under arrest for the attempted murder of Joy Henderson and the deaths of Scott Be—"

"Just cuff me and take me," Autumn mumbled, holding out her hands while everyone looked on.

"You are being arrested on a warrant charging you with Murder One for Edwin Brown, Henderson-"

"Just take me. I know, I did it okay. Just take me away." Autumn was tired of the game and kind of relieved. She was ready.

"What is going on here?" Gwen demanded, storming over and grabbing Autumn's shoulders. "Girl what is he saying? He's wrong. They have a mistaken identity. You would never hurt anybody and especially Joy."

"Ma'am, I am going to ask that you step back," the officer warned.

"But this doesn't make sense." Gwen kept on going. Not getting it.

"Back off Gwen," Autumn said through clenched teeth as they turned her around and slapped silver cuffs on her wrists. "Just call my lawyer. Find it in the Rolodex under Harmon. Joseph Harmon."

Gwen had tears and confusion in her eyes. "Autumn," she whispered behind Autumn. The handcuffs were cutting in her wrist but she kept her head high like her mama had taught her.

"I'll call your lawyer! Don't worry girl! Stay strong! Whatever it is, we'll work it out!" Gwen called. Autumn didn't say anything. As they moved towards the unmarked police cruiser, she saw cameras flashing in her face and she lowered her eyes. Damn it was some media spectacle.

It was funny but she felt relieved though. Like it was finally over. She didn't have to feel pressure and kill anybody else. She knew she was not getting out either. No she was going down. They had several witnesses including Joy.

Her mind went to the man in the diner. The waitress. The state trooper in the Delaware rest stop. The nice guy she had met in Pennsylvania. Even Cole might be a witness. They would all point a finger at her.

# Chapter Forty-Seven

Cole was sitting behind his desk going over the facts of Terrence's case and a new case assigned to him of a woman who had supposedly fallen out of an apartment window when Roderick, one of the other officers came to the door.

"Hey man, did you hear they caught the East Coast slasher?" He raised a bushy eyebrow.

"Are you serious?"

"Yeah man. It's all over the news."

"Who was it?" Cole continued looking at the file. Then the picture of the woman's remains splattered on the sidewalk.

"Some black chick. Local girl. Name is Autumn something or other."

"What?" Cole dropped the papers and glared at Leon like he had grown two heads. "Autumn?"

"Yeah, gorgeous too."

"Where is she?" He felt his chest tightening and his breathing become different.

"At CCB." Leon frowned and then a light went on behind his eyes. "You know this lady?"

Cole got up and grabbed his cell. "I'll be back shortly."

Cole sat across from Autumn. He really didn't know what to say. He examined his fingers then he looked up and into her red, swollen eyes. Her hair, which had always hung in loose braids, was in a ponytail.

"Autumn, why are you here?" he asked.

"I refuse to talk to anyone but a lawyer," she said, avoiding his eyes.

He sighed and rubbed the stubble on his face. "Autumn, they pinned some serious charges on you."

She gave him a blank stare.

"I'm here because I care Autumn. We're family."

Her expression didn't change. He went ahead anyway. "Harrius Fields was your uncle right?"

For the first time she reacted. She blinked and swallowed. "So what?"

He realized that she really had no idea. So that wasn't why she had stopped seeing him.

"Autumn," he paused, leaning over the desk. "This may come as a bit of a shock." He stopped again. "He was my father."

Autumn's brows knitted in confusion. "I don't understand what you're saying."

"I ran into Ms. Betty and she mentioned that I seemed to look familiar. She had known Harrius. Had his picture, the same one that I had at home. I went home and found old papers of my mother's to see if his last name really was Fields. It was. I made the connection."

"You're my cousin?" Autumn shook her head.

"Seems so. I thought maybe you had learned that and had stopped hanging out for that reason."

"You're Harrius' kid?" she whispered, her eyes growing soft. She stared off. "I remember this woman came to the house back then..." she trailed off.

"Autumn it appears I'm his kid," he said it to remind himself.

She suddenly lunged forward but the rig holding her in place forced her to stay seated. Her hands were in handcuffs and attached to the rig around her waist. "You bastard! You know what he did to me!" she started screaming, throwing him off guard. The officer who had been outside the door rushed in and grabbed Autumn by the shoulders.

"Everything is all right." Cole said. The officer backed up and Autumn released her grip. Cole sat back, watching as Autumn broke down before his eyes. She dropped her head sobbing so hard it was scary. He got up and knelt before her, touching her back.

"Autumn," he started gently.

She raised her head. "That bastard raped me!" She started rocking and moaning.

"Oh my God I-I-I'm sorry that he hurt you Autumn."

"He did it for years," she cried. "I hate him. And he killed my parents!"

Cole felt like someone had dumped a bucket of cold water over his head. His father had been a pedophile? And maybe a murderer? It was too much to wrap his mind around but he took her in his arms.

"We're going to get you some help Autumn."

"He raped me over and over and over," she whispered. "All of them did. And my babies are dead."

"Sssh, everything is going to be all right," he mumbled.

# Chapter Forty-Eight

Cole thought the news couldn't have gotten any worse. But then the prints in Terrence's apartment came back as a match with Autumn's. He just couldn't believe it. And then Terrence's crazy neighbor from across the hall called to confirm that Autumn had been the lady she'd seen on TV.

He gurgled down his second beer as Lauren appeared in the doorway, her arms crossed, leaning on the entrance. She had on a short peach colored negligee that was enough to make even a gay man give in. She had been staying over on a trial basis. It had been working out better than he had expected and old feelings had flooded back. He wondered if his dream woman had been there all along. He had home-cooked meals and the house was spotless. He did his part too especially since her job was almost as demanding as his was…He had told her about Autumn.

"When are you coming up to bed?" She came into the room, her long legs turning him on.

"Won't be too much longer with you wearing that," he sighed, an image of Autumn flashing in his mind. "Damn!"

"You can't beat yourself up about what happened with Autumn? It wasn't your fault," she said.

"It was my blood that caused her so much pain."

"That was your daddy. Not you Cole. You're a good man."

He took another swig. Lauren put her arm around his shoulders. It was comforting to have someone around to tell him it was okay. Even a man needed that every now and then.

Joy opened her eyes, feeling pain from every inch of her being. She was lying in a bed and couldn't move. The first person she saw was the strange man who had helped her get up from his chair. He was wearing a white coat. He yelled out and ran out the room. She was scared not knowing where she was or what had happened. Last thing she could recall was crawling through the leaves. They had crackled underneath her. There were several footsteps and her mother and father were there clutching hands. They rushed to her.

"Thank you God!" her father whispered.

"My baby!" her mother screamed.

"Joy, you're awake!" Jason croaked.

"Hey there you are. Finally decided to join us?" A handsome man with red hair and green eyes was dressed in a white coat like the other strange man. He flashed a light into her eyes. "Good to meet you Joy."

She couldn't speak. Her mouth felt like it had been stuffed with cotton. She wanted to tell them that she wasn't dead although she was close. She had gone to that light and it had been so bright. And Ricky had been standing on the other side. And her grandmother and grandfather had been there smiling at her. They had all told her to go back. That she had a lot more living to do.

The strange man who had helped her was standing behind her parents grinning. He had been her savior.

Autumn was not going to allow anybody to make a spectacle of her. Oh no, she wasn't. She was in a cell. The kind that reminded her of the one in that dream she had had with Uncle Harry. That bastard had destroyed her life and they had her in some ugly blue uniform. She wasn't going to let them take her out like that. Oh hell no! No way was she going to let them put her on death row. She was going to have the last fucking word, something Uncle Harry had never allowed her to do. No she was going to have control over her own life.

She heard her bedmate below, snoring up a storm. She pulled off the bed sheet and crept off the top bunk and down to the cold floor. She was not going to let them take her out. She found a way to tie the bed sheet around the top post of the bed. She wrapped the other end around her neck and climbed back up to the top bunk and closed her eyes thinking about her mama and daddy. She might be with them soon. But then they would be in heaven.

"Go tell it on the mountain," she sang softly. "That Jesus Christ was born."

There was no time for prayer. Not that it would work anyway. She pushed off.

# Epilogue

Cole stood in the cold. A strong wind blew over him but he knelt and placed the flowers on the grave. She had deserved so much better. So much more than what she had gotten. Yeah those people had died and it had been a shame because they had been innocent. They just happened to be at the end of the wrath of a very damaged and troubled woman. He wished things had been different so they could have gotten to know one another.

"So much has gone on since you passed Autumn. I can't believe that it has been a year since you've been gone," he paused looking down at his left hand. "I got married. To my daughter's mother." He gave a short laugh. "Yeah, it's actually great. Your girl Joy got with the guy who saved her. Dexter. She forgives you too. Knows you didn't mean it. You just needed help Autumn. And I wish that you had gotten it. We all love you still. And I'm going to find out what happened to you and Harrius. Get the real story." He set the roses in the holder next to her headstone and stood up, slipping his hands in his pockets as a stronger breeze blew.

He knew that was her, giving him a sign. He smiled, nodded and walked down the hill.

The answers to all your burning
questions will be revealed
in the sequel, BROKEN IN TWO
coming soon!

# About the Author

Robin Ayele is the author of *Chocolate City Chronicles*, as well as the President and Founder of Chocolate Angel Publications. She holds a Bachelor of Arts degree in Criminal Justice from Temple University and a Master of Arts degree in Urban Planning from Morgan State University.

Robin is happily married to her husband Yidnkachew and divides her time between Hebron, Maryland and Addis Ababa, Ethiopia.

# ORDER FORM

Please Mail Checks or Money Orders to:

ROBIN AYELE
Chocolate Angel Publications
7871 Bitler Way, Hebron, MD 21830
broken@robbieayele.org
202. 615. 5257 (office)
702. 368.1298 (fax)

Please send ___ copy(ies) of *BROKEN*

Name: _____

Address: _____

City: _____ State: _____ Zip: _____

Telephone: ( )_____/ ( )_____

Email: _____

I have enclosed $14.95, plus $5.00 shipping per book for a total of $_____.

Sales Tax: Add 6% to total cost of books for orders shipped to MD addresses.

For Bulk or Wholesale Rates, Call: 1-202-615-5257
**Or email: *broken@robbieayele.org***

Please visit:
WWW. CHOCOLATE ANGEL PUBLICATIONS.COM

LaVergne, TN USA
18 September 2009
158361LV00008B/29/P